"YOU DO WANT ME, DON'T YOU?"

Donna nodded mutely, knowing she was falling under Hugh's spell but having no wish to resist him.

"I think we've both been stalling ever since the day we met," he said softly, "for our own reasons, but I don't think the reasons hold anymore, Donna. There's something very special between us. You do know that, don't you?"

Yes, she knew that. Whatever might happen between the two of them, this was their time. It might be their only time, but she was willing to take the chance.

She moved closer to him, cupping her hands behind his head, letting her fingers plunge deeply into his thick hair as she pulled his head down until his lips met hers. Her kiss was an affirmation, and he drank hungrily of what she had to offer.

ABOUT THE AUTHOR

When the freighter *Eldia* beached on the shore at
Cape Cod not far from her home, author Meg
Hudson knew she'd found the perfect background
for her next Superromance. Like the heroine in
A Gift from the Sea, Meg felt an affinity for the
distressed ship, and that particular stretch of shore
will always have a special significance for her.

Books by Meg Hudson

These books may be available at your local bookseller.

Don't miss any of our special offers. Write to us at the
following address for information on our newest releases.

Harlequin Reader Service
P.O. Box 52040, Phoenix, AZ 85072-2040
Canadian address: P.O. Box 2800, Postal Station A,
5170 Yonge St., Willowdale, Ont. M2N 6J3

Meg Hudson

A GIFT FROM THE SEA

Harlequin Books

TORONTO • NEW YORK • LONDON
AMSTERDAM • PARIS • SYDNEY • HAMBURG
STOCKHOLM • ATHENS • TOKYO • MILAN

Published August 1985

First printing June 1985

ISBN 0-373-70174-8

Printed in Canada

For Cima Estrella...partly because she's Cima
and partly because she loves the Cape the way I do.

PROLOGUE

THE TELEPHONE in the Hyannis condo rang at exactly ten minutes after six on a cold, dark Wednesday morning in late March.

Lifting the receiver, Hugh MacDonough mumbled a groggy, "Hello?"

"Hugh?"

"Charlie?" Hugh groaned. Charlie Evans was sometimes given to playing practical jokes, and he wasn't in the mood for that kind of humor. "Where are you calling from?"

"Key West."

"At *this* hour?"

"We're going out after marlin," Charlie explained. "We have a boat chartered for seven. Listen, Hugh, I happened to catch the six o'clock news...."

Half asleep, half awake, Hugh shifted himself upward in bed, propping his tousled head against the badly mussed pillows. Charlie, a college classmate from years back, was probably his best friend, but at times he could be trying. "I'm not sure I'm ready for this," Hugh said cautiously.

"You will be," Charlie promised. "There's a freighter going aground on Massasoit Beach."

"The hell you say!"

"Looks like a big one, and if what they're saying is right, she doesn't have a chance. I thought you'd be interested."

"Damned right I'm interested!" Hugh sat bolt upright, his mind meshing into gear. He was already planning a course of action as he muttered absently, "Thanks, Charlie."

He was about to hang up the receiver when Charlie protested, "Hey! If you're going to move out, ask the blonde next door to take care of Marmalade until I get back, okay?"

Hugh was occupying his friend's apartment, and Marmalade was Charlie's cat. He grinned as he surveyed the mass of orange fur on the foot of the bed, and two curious emerald eyes peered back at him suspiciously.

"Don't you think the blonde might object to my waking her up?"

"Not when you offer to let her have Marmalade," Charlie replied smugly. "Her name's Angela, incidentally, and she's a cat fanatic."

Hugh was still smiling as he got up, stretched, then ambled to the back window that looked out over a jumbled assortment of rooftops. It was a miserable day. Sleet splashed across the grimy glass panes and the wind howled around the ells and angles formed by the buildings. It was a hell of a day for a shipwreck.

As he headed for the shower, Hugh suspected that once again he was going to have his work cut out for him.

IT WAS A QUARTER PAST SIX when Donna Madison flipped off the switch controlling the fleecy pink electric blanket that had been keeping her so warm. As she listened to the rain pelting down on the roof she told herself that the perfect addition to her life just now would be an agreeable robot who would bring her a cup of steaming hot coffee at the push of a button.

Reluctantly she threw back the bedclothes, then, shivering, pattered barefoot across the rug to close the window.

The vista wasn't very promising. Cape Cod was in the throes of a severe northeaster, and Donna found herself facing a watery gray world, the rain beating a staccato rhythm along with the howling gale.

The Windcrest Motor Inn stood atop a knoll overlooking the far edge of Massasoit Beach. The apartment in which Donna was staying was located in an ell, separated from the motel proper by a small, covered breezeway. Her bedroom windows faced both south and east, with the ocean perhaps three hundred feet away. She'd gotten up in the middle of the night to shut one of the windows, leaving the other open only a slit to let fresh air in. Now, even with both windows closed, she could hear the heavy thud of the surf as it pounded the beach, and she knew the waves must be mountainous.

She pressed closer to the windowpane, but it was like looking through wet gray wool. Then she saw something—something vast and dark—looming against the oyster-colored sky.

She couldn't believe what she was seeing. She must be hallucinating. But the shape was unmistakable. She was looking at a ship, big—very big—and much too close to shore. It appeared to be practically on the beach.

Donna drew a long, shuddery breath, then raced to the closet. She yanked on her blue wool running suit, tugged on her thermal boots, pulled an extra sweater over her head and topped the helter-skelter outfit with a bright orange hooded slicker.

Although not a Cape Codder, she had spent summer vacations and holidays with her aunt and uncle in Devon over a period of years, so she knew that Massasoit Beach was miles away from any shipping lanes. Occasionally a freighter could be spotted far out at sea, making for Boston or another New England port. But most ships used the Cape Cod Canal, avoiding the treacherous, offshore shoals and currents. Even those ships that found it more expedient to take the open ocean on their way to port never came anywhere near this stretch of shore. It was far too dangerous. Years ago this area of the North Atlantic had been nicknamed "The Mariner's Graveyard."

Donna was only too aware that the ship outside her window was in serious trouble. She tucked the keys to her apartment in her slicker pocket and raced out the door, tearing across the public parking lot then hurrying down the path that led to the beach.

She was not alone. People were coming from all directions, undaunted by the weather, drawn, as Donna was, to the giant ship clutched in a death grip by the pounding waves. It was as if they felt that by being close to her and sharing her ordeal, there might be a chance of saving her.

THE PORTIA, a 526-foot, 10,200-ton Liberian freighter had unloaded her cargo of Brazilian coffee in Portland, Maine, on Monday afternoon. The ship stayed in port overnight and was scheduled to set sail for Wilmington, Delaware, early Tuesday morning. Another cargo, a load of machine parts, awaited the *Portia* in Wilmington.

Her captain, Alexander Bruce, planned to sail south via Cape Cod Bay and the Cape Cod Canal. Weather reports gave him no indication that leaving port might be dangerous, yet within twenty-four hours Bruce and his crew had been plunged into the middle of a nightmare.

The *Portia* was steaming down the North Atlantic shipping lane when she hit high seas off Boston. Soon the freighter was riding in the middle of a raging northeaster, spawned off Provincetown, and a short time later went out of control and totally off course.

Bruce tried desperately to swing his ship around and head for shelter, but she kept turning in circles as she pitched and yawed. He ordered both anchors dropped to try to stop the ship, but the *Portia* dragged the anchors with her as she veered crazily toward Massasoit Beach.

By this time, the point of no return had been passed for the ship and her crew.

CHAPTER ONE

DOZENS OF PEOPLE were gathered on the sand, shivering from the icy cold. As they stared out to sea, they felt an overwhelming helplessness. The listing ship had dragged herself off the sandbar she had first hit and was back in deeper water. Then she was caught again by the wind and boiling surf and forced directly toward the beach.

Donna lowered her head, as everyone was doing at intervals. The combination of raging wind, stinging sand and salt spray made it impossible to watch the ship constantly.

She heard a man nearby mumble, "It's like a great whale about to be beached and trying to fight for its life."

Suddenly she had the crazy feeling that she was watching a movie being made. She squinted, as if by doing so she could convince herself the scene really was in miniature. She imagined a giant fan somewhere off the set, whirring the waves into action so that the ship tossed like a cork.

Donna lost track of time, mesmerized by the struggling ship. Then she heard a familiar voice say, "I don't believe this," and turned to see Althea Nickerson staring at the stricken freighter, her lovely brown eyes glazed with horror.

"Mark's opening up the Snack Shack," Althea reported after a moment. "We figure people are going to need hot coffee."

Althea and her brother Mark had the concession from the town of Devon to operate the Seashell Snack Shack, but they usually didn't open until the Memorial Day weekend, and that was two months into the future.

"Funny," Althea mused. "Mark had the power turned on a couple of days ago because he wanted to do some work on the place before the season starts. Otherwise we wouldn't even have been able to make coffee."

Donna shivered. She wished she had a cup of the hot coffee Althea was talking about right now.

"Do you suppose Mark could use some help?" she asked.

Althea nodded. "Probably. I had to come down to see this close to. Mark can have his turn later. From the looks of it, the ship's going to be here for a while...unless she gets pounded to pieces."

"I'll go help Mark," Donna volunteered. She was chilled to the bone despite the warm clothes she'd put on, and although her slicker was waterproof, the rain had edged under the hood and her hair felt dank. But it wasn't her physical discomfort that was compelling her to seek a change of scene. It was the need to do something. Anything.

Standing there buffeted by the wind and pelted by the freezing rain, Donna felt totally useless.

As she turned back she saw men staggering along the sand, loaded down with both still cameras and portable TV equipment. The press, she thought wryly, was coming on the scene. Later that day the news of

Cape Cod's recent shipwreck would be featured on coast-to-coast telecasts and would make a banner headline in the next edition of the *Boston Globe*.

But what would have happened to the ship by then? Would she go aground? Or would she keel over under the force of the wind and the surf and be smashed to pieces?

As she edged away from the shelter of the dunes and turned onto the path to the Snack Shack, Donna was praying that the men aboard the ship were alive and safe and somehow could be rescued. She couldn't fathom how such a rescue could be attempted under these conditions, but it was scary to think of waiting till the weather cleared. That could be a matter of days.

Thinking about this prospect, she felt the on-slaught of a powerful gust of wind, so strong that it rocked her with a force too great to resist, and she felt herself falling. As she struggled to keep from going down flat on her face into the cold, swirling sand, arms reached out to grab her. Steadying herself, Donna looked up into the arresting face of a total stranger.

He was a tall man, tall and broad, and his thick, quilted parka made him seem even broader. The parka was a drab tan, the same sort of garb a lot of the people on the beach were wearing, yet this man was distinctly different. The difference puzzled Donna for a moment, then she pinpointed it. Most of the people around Devon at this time of the year were relatively pale or else sported temporary Florida tans. This man was deeply and evenly bronzed, and there was a weather-beaten quality to his skin that indicated he spent a lot of his time outdoors.

"Are you all right?" he asked, his voice low and pleasant.

Donna started to reply, then realized the man was no longer paying any attention to her. He was focusing entirely on the ship, and there was a strange agony in his deep-set gray eyes.

It was as if he'd lived through this experience many, many times before.

THE SNACK SHACK became the center of activity once word was passed that Mark Nickerson would be serving hot coffee, and before the morning was over it had also become Devon's central gossip mill.

"The Coast Guard's going to try to send out a forty-four footer to get the crew off her," Donna heard as she poured coffee into countless paper cups, then passed the cups into eagerly grasping hands.

Rumors sprang up quickly.

"There's no way they're going to do anything in this kind of weather."

"The radio must be out on her...or there's no one alive on board. Anyhow, they can't raise anyone."

"It'd be too dangerous to launch a boat in a sea like this. It'd get smashed into her hull. They're planning to use a helicopter instead. The Coast Guard's going to try for an airlift."

This latest prediction proved to be true.

Althea had taken over at the Snack Shack with a couple of townspeople she'd pressed into service, and Donna went back down on the beach with Mark Nickerson. Mark had done a stint in the Coast Guard when he was just out of high school, and his face was tense and knowing as they plowed their way to the high-water mark, then walked along where the sand was hard packed, making the going considerably easier.

Mark was in his late thirties, tall, blond, a skinny New England type with an almost homely face and a grin that could be infectious—on those rare occasions when he smiled. He'd come back from his time in the Coast Guard to find that the high-school sweetheart he'd been engaged to had married someone else. According to his sister Althea, Mark had retreated into his whelk shell, and so far no one had been able to pry him out.

Mark and Donna got along together. They had a certain empathy, perhaps because Donna understood the way he felt, having been through the same sort of experience herself. In her case she'd married her high-school sweetheart. Later, much later, he'd chosen someone else. She'd been the woman rejected, and sometimes she still smarted from the memory.

Mark guided Donna close to the shelter of the dunes and she peered through the rain, which seemed determined to keep on falling forever and ever. The *Portia* appeared to have swung around. Previously the bow had been facing straight toward the beach, yet now the ship was almost broadside and seemed to be swinging even as they watched.

"My God," Donna heard Mark say tersely, "they've actually sent a chopper out."

Then she heard a deeper voice add, "If you ask me, piloting that chopper takes a rare kind of guts."

The darkly tanned man wearing the parka was standing next to Mark, their faces tilted upward at the same angle. But the contrast in the two faces was such a marked one that Donna was more than ever aware of the stranger's ruggedness. Mark looked frail and pallid by comparison, even though he was just as tall as the other man.

For a moment Donna forgot about the stranger as she watched the Coast Guard helicopter approaching the ship, its course remarkably steady against the wind.

She heard someone say, "They got Devon's rescue squad and extra ones from Orleans and Eastham and Brewster up in the parking lot waiting for the crew."

Waiting for the crew? As she watched a geyser of salt water break over the stern of the stricken ship, Donna wondered how anyone could possibly be airlifted under these conditions.

Time couldn't be measured. Each second, at this point, held the grains of eternity. She watched the helicopter hover over the ship, then it moved off to fly around in a circle. When it swung back into position, Donna saw a long line descending against the gray sky, a rescue basket dangling at its end.

Again she had the crazy feeling that she was watching a movie being made, that this was only a Hollywood set, and the whole scene was being enacted in miniature.

She held her breath as the rescue basket was raised again, and she saw a human form clasped within it. Then again the basket was lowered, again and yet again, until finally the chopper took off with its first load, and the crowd on the beach watched it circling toward the area of the Snack Shack and the parking lot just beyond.

She heard the stranger next to Mark swear softly under his breath, then he said simply, "If I hadn't seen that, I wouldn't have believed it. Let's hope they can repeat it. They've got at least a couple dozen men to get off her.''

Donna wanted to tell him how fervently she echoed his sentiments, but her throat was so dry she had to swallow before she could speak.

"I wonder how they are," she said at last.

The tall stranger looked down at her curiously, and Donna felt he was really seeing her for the first time. She smiled wryly. She looked pretty sorry at the moment, wet and bedraggled. Although she'd dried off while working in the Snack Shack she felt damp all the way through again. Her face was exactly as nature had made it, without makeup. She'd given it a quick wash with soap and water before dashing out of the apartment, and the rain had done a further job of moisturizing her skin. She doubted if she'd ever looked less appealing than she did right now. Nevertheless, there was an interested expression in this man's deep gray eyes.

"I imagine the rescue team will be okay," he said. "I presume it's the crew you were referring to?"

She shuddered. "Yes. I can't imagine how anyone could be in one piece after riding through a storm on *that*." She nodded toward the freighter. "No one will remain on board will they?"

"Probably not, for the time being," the man told her. "Someone will be going back to her, though. Otherwise she'd be anyone's for the taking."

"What do you mean?"

He'd been gazing toward the ship again, but now his gray eyes swept over her face. "An abandoned ship is fair prey."

Mark Nickerson laughed. "I can't imagine anyone putting out to stake a claim in this kind of weather."

"You'd be surprised," the stranger retorted. He was looking at the ship with an unusual intentness, as if he had a personal interest in the freighter.

Donna studied him covertly. He intrigued her, provoking her curiosity. She'd known he was different the instant she'd looked up into his face after nearly bumping into him earlier. That initial impression was now reinforced. He stood out, at least in this crowd.

The hood of his parka covered his hair, so she had no idea what color it was, but she suspected he would have a touch of gray at the temples. She guessed his age to be close to forty, and he looked as if he'd done a lot of living.

His features were rugged rather than even, and Donna wouldn't have labeled him handsome. But he was very attractive and thoroughly masculine, though she imagined his brawn was equaled by his brains. There was a quiet confidence about him, and something more. A certain containment, as if he was used to doing things for himself, making his own decisions and having things pretty much his way.

At her side Mark announced, "I've got to get back to the shack."

"I'll come with you," Donna told him. Yet she found herself reluctant to leave this stranger. She didn't even know his name and she'd probably never see him again. She would have to round out the rest of his character and put together the story of his life purely from imagination. But she was going to file some notes on him for future reference, she promised herself. At some point in time—if she ever could get back to writing—he'd make a good character in one of her books.

IT WAS NEARLY NOON when Donna returned to her apartment. By then the beach parking lot was filled with all kinds of vehicles, and the police had begun to set up barricades to keep unauthorized individuals away from the scene of the shipwreck.

As it was, hundreds had already trekked along the wet sand, getting soaked to the skin, chilled to the bone, and windblown in the process, so they could get as close to the *Portia* as possible. Hundreds of pictures had been taken, most of which would look as grainy as the day itself when they were finally developed.

Donna had promised the Nickersons that she'd come back and help them later in the afternoon. She'd also offered Mark and his sister the use of her bathroom for a hot shower whenever they felt they couldn't stand the chill any longer.

She'd been longing to take a hot shower herself, and she lingered under the spray, appreciating as never before the feeling of being warm. Even her pine-scented soap seemed especially luxurious, and she lathered herself with it again and again.

Emerging from the shower, she dried off with a thick towel then slipped on an equally thick white, lace-trimmed terry robe that zipped to the neck.

She'd had enough coffee, so she made herself a cup of hot chocolate, leaving out the box of mix in case Mark or Althea wanted some later. Cup in hand, she wandered to the living-room window and noticed that the rain seemed to be letting up slightly and the visibility was better.

The wind wasn't howling quite so much, either. Donna doubted that the storm was over. Northeasters were usually good for a full three days, and this one had been in action for only a third of that time. But perhaps its force had decreased somewhat, at least for a while.

The *Portia* seemed unbelievably close to Donna, though she knew it was nearly a quarter of a mile down the beach. It loomed large...high and dry. Almost dry, anyway, Donna amended. The ship was fully broadside to the land, but its prow had cut deeply into the sand, and more than ever it looked like a huge, beached whale.

Even before Donna had left the Snack Shack, word had filtered in that the ship was owned by an English firm but was operating under Liberian registry. She'd been traveling light, having unloaded her cargo, but speculation was running rampant about how she had come to veer so badly off course. Evidently, from what Donna had been able to make out, by the time the captain might have been alerted about the worsening weather conditions in his path, the ship's radio had gone out. This was a double blow, because her radar also hadn't been functioning properly.

While Donna was still pouring out coffee, news had come that, miraculously, the twenty-seven members of the crew had escaped injury. Twenty-five crewmen, the captain and the first mate had been checked out by area medical personnel, and temporary accommodations were now being found for these men in various private homes and motels around town.

The Windcrest was not one of the motels being used and Donna was glad, even though being glad made her feel selfish. But her privacy was vital if she was ever going to break this mental block and the stranglehold it had on her.

Her Uncle Joe was planning to reopen the Wind-crest in mid-April, the time when New England schools had their spring breaks and people were apt to start flocking to the beach. The current schedule was for him and his wife Mabel to return to Devon around April 10. Meanwhile some of the motel units were being redecorated in preparation for the new season, but they were at the far end of the complex from the owner's apartment occupied by Donna. She seldom even heard the workmen.

Several times a week Cynthia Doane, a middle-aged widow who'd worked for Joe Brucker for years, came by to handle mail, taking care of advance reservations and a number of other details. Once in a while Mrs. Doane walked across to the apartment and Donna fixed tea and cookies for the two of them, but she always had to assure Cynthia that she wasn't writing before the older woman would come in at all.

Writing. Donna sighed deeply as she thought about the profession to which she was so dedicated.

She was a mystery writer, and until recently she'd been a successful one. Now, with a book deadline staring her in the face, she'd gone sour. The words wouldn't come. She was suffering from a bad case of writer's block.

That was the reason that she was in Devon at the end of March. Her aunt and uncle had offered her the use of the apartment in their motel while they were in Florida, and she'd come down in mid-February. She'd put in her usual hours each day, staring at the computer's blank screen, but nothing had happened. She'd asked for an extension on her book contract and it had been granted. At regular intervals her agent called to proffer a helping hand, and at the conclusion of these telephone dialogues Donna usually felt better—until she faced the computer screen again. Then that awful feeling of blankness would descend, and so far there'd been nothing she could do about it.

Her present funk had nothing to do with her divorce. That had happened five years ago. It had nothing to do with *anything*, which was the most devastating part of all. Somehow, whatever it was inside her that made her creative much of the time had stopped functioning, and though she knew this was not an unusual thing to happen to a writer, it was still terrifying.

Would her talent ever function again? She had no way of knowing. The creative processes were mysterious, even to those endowed with them.

She thought of Mark Nickerson. His sister had told Donna that at one time he had wanted to be a rock guitarist. He'd had his own group in high school, and he had been good. Donna hadn't taken Althea's unobjective word for this. She had heard some records Mark had made.

His creativity had been undermined by a combination of bad experiences in the Coast Guard and his fiancée's defection, and it hadn't come back. He had found a niche of sorts in running the beach shack with his sister, but Donna had to admit that this was settling for less, something she wasn't sure she herself could ever be happy doing.

She also knew she was becoming paranoid about her career. Afraid that she'd "lost it," she was reluctant to talk about her writing to anyone these days; it was like a secret locked within her. The situation hadn't been getting any better as time passed, despite the fact that she'd been given the opportunity to write a book in an environment most writers would envy. But her mind had remained locked. The weather-beaten man she'd met on the beach had been the first person to pique her creative curiosity in a long time.

As she finished her hot chocolate and contemplated making a sandwich before going back to help her friends, she thought about putting a description of him down on the computer later on, once Mark and Althea had decided to close up for the day. Then, walking past the computer, she confronted its blank, staring screen. *Why wait,* she thought. *Mark and Althea don't expect me back for at least another hour. Now's as good a time as any to get down my impressions of him.*

Donna switched on the machine, slipped a floppy disk into the first drive, and was about to give the computer some preliminary instructions when she heard a knock on the door.

Smiling, she shut off the machine. It must be Mark or Althea wanting to take advantage of her hot shower offer.

It was neither. The man standing on the threshold looked as startled as Donna did when their eyes meshed.

Recognition flashed, and he smiled. "So, we meet again. I'm afraid I've come to the wrong place, though. I thought this was Joe Brucker's apartment."

"It is," Donna told him. There was a roof overhang above the door, but nothing was keeping the rain away today. His parka looked sodden, Donna observed, and she invited, "Come in."

"I'll drip all over the place," he warned her.

"No more than I did." She moved aside to make way for him. "This is Joe Brucker's apartment ordinarily, but he's still in Florida. I'm his niece, and I've been using the place in his absence. I'm Donna Madison."

"Hugh MacDonough," he introduced himself. "Look, I really am dripping all over your rug." He was shrugging out of the parka as he spoke. "Could I hang this somewhere? I need to talk to you."

The apartment boasted a small area with a washer and dryer. "If you don't think it will shrink, I can put it in the dryer," Donna offered.

"I'll chance it."

She took the parka from him, and a moment later it was whirring in the dryer. As she went back into the living room she wondered why Hugh MacDonough had said he needed to talk to her.

He was standing at the window, looking out toward the ship, and she had the chance to assess him. He was big, there was no doubt of that, but not as brawny as she'd thought. He was wearing a plaid wool shirt that stretched across his shoulders then molded its way down to a surprisingly narrow waist. Broad chested, he was equally slim hipped, and the snug jeans he was wearing emphasized the lean tautness of his thighs and his well-developed calf muscles. As she'd thought from the first, he looked like a man of action, a man used to living and working out of doors, and to commanding. She couldn't imagine Hugh MacDonough taking orders very long from anyone.

He turned toward her, and she saw that his thick hair was a dark coppery red. From this distance she couldn't see any gray in it at all. "Would you like a cup of coffee—or maybe something stronger?" she asked politely.

He smiled. "I don't usually drink until the sun's gone over the yardarm, but I could use some Scotch if you have it."

She did. She poured a liberal portion over a couple of ice cubes, and as she handed the glass to him their fingers touched. His were chilly—obviously the thick mittens he'd worn earlier hadn't been enough to keep his hands warm today—and there was a roughness to his skin. She also noticed he didn't wear a wedding ring, which wasn't necessarily significant, she realized.

She sat down on the low couch, conscious that once again she was appearing totally unadorned before him. She'd scrubbed her face in the shower until it shone, and she'd twisted her long, dark hair into a coil on top of her head. She was barefoot, but at least her toenails were painted pale pink, she thought whimsically. She wished she'd had the chance to fix herself up a little before confronting this man again, and the thought surprised her. It had been a long time since she'd had the desire to make a deliberate bid for a man's attention.

She saw that Hugh MacDonough was frowning. Maybe he didn't like her brand of Scotch.

He met her eyes, and as if to deny this said, "That's exactly what I needed."

She saw that he'd tossed the drink down, so she asked, "Another?"

"No, thanks, I'd be on my ear, Ms Madison...or is it Mrs.?"

Men still had an advantage, Donna thought. There was no way she could ask him the same question without being obvious about it. "Ms," she replied.

"I'd expected to find your uncle here and this puts me in something of a bind," he admitted. "I've known Joe Brucker for a long time. Years ago, when I was a kid, some of my relatives had a place in Devon and they were friends of his. I know he usually doesn't open the motel until later, but when I saw lights in some of the windows I thought maybe he'd decided to start in early this year.''

"Not really," Donna said. "My aunt and uncle don't plan to be back from Florida for another three weeks or so, and they don't expect to be open for business until the middle of April at the earliest. I'm here by myself. Uncle Joe's been having some redecorating done and his receptionist comes over most afternoons, that accounts for the lights."

It was such a dark, gloomy, storm-swept day that Donna had put the lights on in her own apartment the minute she'd walked in the door.

Hugh MacDonough thought about what she had said, then asked, "Do you suppose Joe could be persuaded to change his mind?"

"What do you mean?"

"I'd like to take over the motel."

"You?"

He nodded. "Me. Maybe I'm being a bit premature about it, I'll have to explain that to Joe. But if my plans work out I could use at least a wing of the motel, if not all of it, for the next month, perhaps longer."

The question tumbled out. "Why?"

Hugh MacDonough nodded over his shoulder toward the beach, in the direction of the *Portia*. "So I can salvage that ship."

CHAPTER TWO

HUGH SMILED at the expression of astonishment that crossed Donna's face. "I'm not a pirate," he said gently. "That's salvage, not steal. I've salvaged ships all over the world. Matter of fact, I returned from Africa only ten days ago, where I conducted the most difficult salvage operation of my career. Everyone said the ship was beyond redemption. I admit she may never put to sea again, but in the loose term of the word, we saved her."

Donna was frowning, and Hugh couldn't blame her. He drew a long breath and forced himself to concentrate on the things he needed to tell her. Donna Madison was a distracting woman. He'd discovered that on the beach when he'd taken a second look into her astonishingly beautiful eyes, which were the deepest blue he'd ever seen, fringed with thick, jet lashes.

He'd noticed her eyes the minute she'd almost stumbled into him and he'd clutched her arms to prevent her from falling. Although his attention had returned to focus on the ship, when he saw her later he'd observed that the woman had looked half-frozen and damp despite the protective slicker, and she had been shivering visibly. But he had found her rain-washed face lovely, and her eyes had been startling against the faint pallor caused by the cold.

Hugh had wondered if the man at her side was her husband and had concluded that he probably was. When she'd turned away to accompany the thin, blond man, he had experienced an odd feeling of regret. There were people you met, all too occasionally, with whom you felt an instant empathy, and he had had this feeling with Donna, perhaps because of the way she'd gazed at the ship as if it were a living being. Although most of the ships with which he dealt were at least partially wrecked, a ship to him had always been something very much alive. The *Portia* had been alive to him that morning as she struggled against nature's overpowering force, almost certainly headed for catastrophe, and he sensed Donna had felt the same way.

Now she asked him, "Am I to take it that you intend to claim the *Portia*? Can you do that if some of her crew go back to her?"

Hugh shook his head. "No. And I wouldn't if I could. What you're talking about is a claim usually made when a ship is adrift on the high seas, left abandoned and afloat. Then it's anyone's prize. This is a different situation. I'll shortly be getting information from Boston about the ownership of the *Portia*...." Hugh paused and had the grace to look shamefaced.

"What is it?" Donna asked him quickly.

"I assumed Joe would be here, so I left word that I could be reached at the Windcrest."

"Mrs. Doane's in the office," Donna said. "I checked on my way back from the Snack Shack. She'll take the call." She hesitated. "I'll phone her and tell her you're here, if you like." As she made the offer she wondered how long it would be before he received his phone call, how long he might be staying in her apartment.

She had no wish to see him go. She wanted to hear more about what it was he was planning to do in connection with the *Portia*. She wanted to know more about the kind of work he did. She wanted to know more about *him*.

"I don't like to intrude," he said carefully, "but I would appreciate it if you'd ask to have the call transferred here. I phoned Boston from the booth outside the Snack Shack before I came over here, so I should be getting some word before much longer. If you had plans, though, I don't want to hold you up."

"I told Mark and Althea I'd come back and help them, but that can wait awhile longer." Donna went to the phone and quickly placed the call.

"Mark and Althea?" Hugh asked when she had finished. "Do they run the snack shop?"

She nodded. "They're brother and sister. That was Mark with me down on the beach, and you probably saw Althea if you stopped for coffee."

He smiled. "Does she have golden blond hair and big brown eyes, and is she fairly tall and quite slim?"

"Yes," Donna replied, nodding. He was perceptive. Perhaps a shade too perceptive. Or did he always notice pretty women?

Remembering his casualness about her during their initial encounter on the beach, Donna bit her lip. She wasn't used to being dismissed quite so easily.

"I wonder," Hugh began. "That is…after my call comes through, do you think it would be possible for me to get in touch with your uncle?"

"Uncle Joe? I'm surprised he hasn't phoned here yet," Donna remarked. "He must be out playing golf or he'd have caught something about the shipwreck on

TV by now. Aunt Mabel, on the other hand, probably has her head in a detective story.''

''That's right. Mrs. Brucker's a mystery buff, as I recall.''

''A real one,'' Donna agreed wryly. The subject of mysteries in general was a sore one with her at the moment, and her aunt was one of her biggest fans.

''So am I,'' Hugh admitted. ''When you're off in a remote place on an intense job there's nothing more relaxing than going to bed with a good mystery novel. I usually take a tote bag of them along with me on each job I start.''

Donna couldn't help but wonder if, among the books he'd carried, there had ever been some of her novels. She used the pseudonym Jeffrey Jewell in her writing.

''To get back to Joe,'' Hugh said, ''I'd like to ask him if he'd consider having a section of the Windcrest opened up for me, as I mentioned to you. I should know fairly soon whether I'll have the salvage job on the *Portia*. If my bid is accepted I'll be getting together a working team, and we'll need a close-to-the-scene planning center, as well as a place to sleep.''

Donna tried to be objective as she thought about what he was asking, but it was difficult. The idea of having this man as a neighbor—probably for the rest of her stay in Devon—was disconcerting, to put it mildly.

I'd never be able to get any work done, she told herself. Yet it would be tremendously exciting to have Hugh MacDonough and his men on her doorstep, to have a front-row seat on the salvage operation. Thinking of the giant ship grounded on the beach,

Donna couldn't imagine how anyone would even begin to approach a challenge of such magnitude.

"You mentioned making a bid for the salvage job. Is that what happens?" she asked. "Does the highest bidder get the contract?"

"Not exactly." He paused, wanting to choose the right words in explaining what was involved in his work. The motto of his profession was said to be No Cure, No Pay, and he wondered if Donna would understand what that entailed if he put it to her that way.

Hugh was proud of the work he did, and of the fact that as a professional salvor he was one of a very special breed of men whose task it was to travel the world around rescuing broken, beached ships. The top men in the business, like himself, were sometimes dubbed "part gamblers, part sailors, part logicians." To function effectively they had to be highly qualified in a variety of ways. Hugh, who would be thirty-eight on his next birthday, held an international chief engineer's license, good for any tonnage in any ocean. He had not earned it easily.

"I'll be making a bid to salvage the *Portia*, yes, and if it's accepted I'll be calling in the right people to do the job, all of them experienced men who've been on my payroll. But," he hesitated, "the risk—at least the financial risk—will primarily be mine, and salvaging is always a gamble. Salvors deal principally with insurance companies, and what it amounts to is very much like making a double or nothing bet. In other words, we bid with the insurers for the shipwrecked vessel. In return for our cash outlay and our work, we get the remains of the ship...whatever they may be. Sometimes what's left is broken up and sold for scrap. Sometimes the reclaimed vessel can be made seaworthy again. Sometimes the ship's good enough to sell to another company who'll put it in dry dock for inspection and then decide what to do with what they've bought. What happens essentially is that I offer the insurance company a certain sum of money with which they pay off the owners. Then I stand to either win or lose, depending on how much I can get back."

He grinned. "Our object," he said, "is to make a profit, and we usually do. But there are plenty of sad stories about salvors who have lost their shirts on a job. It's always a risk."

Donna shook her head. "I wouldn't think you'd be able to sleep nights." She was about to add that being a salvor seemed to her an even more precarious way of making a living than being a fiction writer, but she bit the comment back in time. For reasons she couldn't define even to herself, she wasn't ready to let Hugh MacDonough know she had a dual identity.

The phone rang, and Cynthia Doane said, "I have that call for Mr. MacDonough, Donna."

Donna turned the phone over to Hugh and slipped out to the kitchen. She was making grilled-cheese sandwiches and a pot of hot chocolate when she heard him moving behind her, and she turned to see him standing in the doorway, his arms crossed, watching her.

It was impossible not to be struck by him. His presence filled the room. Maybe she was imagining it in view of what he'd been telling her, but he *looked* like an adventurer. Daring, courageous, the kind of person who'd take a risk as if it were a casually proffered dare. There was something very special about him, and his bronzed, weather-beaten skin and rugged features only enhanced his appeal.

"Well," he said, "I guess I've stuck my neck out again."

"You've made your bid?"

He nodded. "I'm first, and I was told I have a good chance of doing business with the insurance company. The *Portia*'s owned by a British firm, but she's sailing under Liberian registry. She's something of a tub, to tell you the truth. She's nearly twenty years old, and she was under both Greek and Japanese ownership before the British firm bought her. But even a tub can be worth a mint these days."

Donna slid the sandwiches onto plates, then carried the plates over to the kitchen table and motioned to him to take a seat. "I hope you like hot chocolate."

There was a strangely wistful quality to his laugh. "I don't think I've had hot chocolate since I was a kid."

"I shouldn't touch it, myself," Donna said, sitting down opposite him. "It's high in calories."

A smile lighted his gray eyes. "You don't have to worry about calories."

It was a statement any man might have made under the circumstances, Donna conceded, yet there was an honesty in Hugh MacDonough's voice that reached out to her. She got the impression that he would call things the way he saw them, and she liked that.

"People like me always have to worry about calories," she replied lightly. "I don't burn up enough of them."

"You need more exercise then?" he challenged.

"I suppose so, yes. My work is...mostly sedentary."

"Chained to a desk?"

"Uh—yes, I suppose you could put it that way." Donna wished she hadn't let the conversation take this direction. Before she knew it she'd find herself forced to talk about her writing.

"Running's good exercise for someone who puts in a lot of desk hours, provided you don't go at it like you're about to run a marathon the same afternoon," he advised. "You're lucky. You have miles of Atlantic beachfront right at your doorstep."

"True." Donna paused. "I *have* been beach walking."

He grinned. "Walking, not running?"

She laughed, then shrugged. "Maybe I'm inherently lazy."

"That, I doubt. I'll test you out," Hugh offered. "If I get the salvage job, you and I can go off on a beach run first thing each morning."

He finished his sandwich, drained his cup of hot chocolate, then leaned back. "Thanks for that. It tasted terrific. I hadn't even realized I was hungry. I'd forgotten I skipped breakfast this morning. I tend to lose track of everything else when I get a ship on my horizon."

A ship on his horizon. Donna liked the sound of that. She surveyed him closely, noting the fine network of tiny lines around his eyes that indicated he'd put in a lot of time squinting up at the sun. There were lines around his mouth, too, but those, she suspected, were lines of discipline. Right now he was relaxed, but she'd already sensed a tautness about him. He was controlled, completely in command of himself. She wondered what it would take to throw him off-balance.

Had a woman ever thrown him off-balance? Undoubtedly, Donna decided. He was too attractive not to have had more than one woman infiltrate his life.

Ships, of course, were also referred to in the feminine gender. Which "she" would win with Hugh Mac-Donough if there was a contest involved—woman or ship?

The question came unbidden. "Do you live anywhere in particular?" she asked.

He looked startled, and frowned slightly. "What do you mean?"

"I imagine your work takes you all over the world."

"True."

"Where do you call home?"

He considered the question, then said slowly, "I don't. What I mean is, right now I don't have a home per se. Until my mother died—nearly four years ago— we had a family house in a little town up in New Hampshire, but I sold it. It was in Contoocook. I was born there, but growing up I mostly went back for winter vacations. My father died when I was pretty young and I went away to boys' schools, then college."

"Where to college?"

"Cambridge. M.I.T.—the Massachusetts Institute of Technology."

"So you started out in engineering, and then you became a salvor?"

"The fields are not that unrelated, and...well, the sea has always held a challenge for me. I think I told you some relatives had a summer place here on the Cape? The North Atlantic forms part of my earliest memories. Sometimes I wish I hadn't sold the Contoocook place. It was a lovely old house on the bank of a river. Probably I should have kept it, but there was nothing to draw me back there. Like most rolling stones—" he gave a rueful grin "—I've gathered very little moss."

While Donna was digesting this information, he turned the tables on her. "Where's home to you?"

"I have an apartment in Manhattan," she told him. "A condo in an old apartment house on West End Avenue."

"You live alone?"

"Yes. Yes...I do."

"Do I detect a note of hesitation, Donna?"

"No, I'm not hesitating. I've lived alone for almost five years. Since my divorce. Before that, my husband and I had a house in Ridgewood, New Jersey. That's where I was born and brought up, and my parents still live there."

"And your ex-husband?"

"George moved to San Francisco right after the divorce. He's in public relations, and he had a chance for a partnership in a firm out there."

"You're still...amicable?" Hugh asked cautiously.

She laughed. "We don't bite each other, nor do we seek out each other's company. George has remarried. The woman in question was the reason for our breakup. One of the reasons," she amended. "It's a trite story, Hugh. We were high-school sweethearts, we married too young, it didn't work, he finally fell in love with someone else."

"Are you always so succinct?"

"No. Only when dealing with things I've put behind me."

"Good enough. With me what's past is merely past. I like to begin today as if it's the threshold of a new tomorrow. Call me an incurable optimist if you like."

But he wasn't an incurable optimist, Donna sensed that. And if he was so ready to dispense with the past in favor of an unknown future, then the past couldn't have been all that satisfactory.

"I don't want to push you, Donna, but do you suppose I could place a call to Joe?"

"Of course," she replied hastily. "You know where the phone is."

He hesitated. "Look, it occurs to me that you must have a reason for having moved in here all by yourself at this time of year. Isolation, maybe? What I'm asking is if I'll be throwing you a bad curve if I try to persuade Joe to let me set up headquarters here in the Windcrest."

Donna considered the question. She knew he definitely would be a distraction, but in all honesty, she hadn't been able to write even with all the solitude in the world at her disposal. What concerned her most was that she wasn't eager to become involved with a man, especially one who admitted he was a rolling stone at heart.

However, she reminded herself, there was no reason to think that she and Hugh would necessarily become involved with each other, regardless of what her uncle's answer to Hugh's request might be. Considering this, Donna was able to face him and say honestly, "I think there's space enough here for all of us."

When Hugh had finished speaking to her uncle, he turned to Donna. "Joe wants to talk to you himself."

At the other end of the line Joe Brucker said, "Level with me, Donna. Is this going to spoil your game plan? I know you wanted to be there by yourself until Mabel and I get back."

"I know. But this is an emergency."

"There are other places around town where MacDonough and his men could hole up," Joe told her. "Not so close to the scene, I admit, not so ideal. Even so, you have first rights, Donna. How's the book going?"

She hesitated. "It isn't."

"I'm no writer," Joe said, "but I think maybe you're worrying too much about it."

"Well," she said cautiously, "maybe I have been. That's hard to say. I've certainly tried—"

"Which is what I'm telling you," her uncle interrupted. "Maybe having a bunch of salvors move in on the scene would be good for you. Some action. Sometimes you can be alone too much, Donna."

Donna heard another voice in the background, and her uncle said, "Mabel wants to talk to you."

Donna and her aunt had always been very close. "Don't pay any attention to Joe trying to play psychologist, Donna," said her Aunt Mabel. "We don't have to open up the place for Hugh MacDonough. It's entirely up to you."

Donna glanced across at the man in question and saw that he'd sat down on the couch and had picked up a magazine, but obviously he was having a hard time trying to focus his attention on it. He glanced up and met her eyes, and a wry smile twisted his mouth. She found herself thinking that she liked his mouth. It was well shaped and very expressive. Right now she could read his ruefulness.

"It'll be fine," she said into the phone. "Does Uncle Joe want to give me any instructions?"

Mabel posed the question and came back on the line to say, "No. Cynthia can handle the arrangements to have whatever space Hugh and his men need opened up for them. You don't have to concern yourself with anything."

"Okay, then, I'll tell Mr. MacDonough that."

Her aunt had a few more nonconsequential things to impart to her, and then she hung up. Donna turned to hear Hugh say, "Just what do you plan to tell Mr. MacDonough, Ms Madison?"

"Mrs. Doane will see to it that everything's ready for you," Donna said with a smile.

"So I take it your verdict is yes?"

"My verdict?"

"It was fairly obvious that yours was the last word, Donna. Joe gave me the impression that you're here because you want privacy. I did give you the chance to veto my idea, you know," he reminded her.

"Yes, you did."

"You can tell me it's none of my business, but if I'm going to be on the premises I'd kind of like to know why you wanted so much to be alone."

Donna hesitated, then settled for what was essentially the truth, realizing she couldn't hedge forever. "I'm trying to write a book," she said, hoping that he'd think it was her first attempt. Time enough later to tell him she was the author of several successful books.

"Really?" His interest was genuine. "I've always envied people who can write and wished I could myself."

"Have you ever tried?"

He shook his head. "No. It's not my kind of thing and I have the sense to know it. I have a lot of material that would make excellent stories, but no talent in that direction at all. About you, though. Do I gather from what you were saying on the phone that the book isn't going well?"

So he had been listening while pretending to scan the magazine. Donna couldn't repress a smile, but she sobered as she said, "The book hasn't been going at all."

Hugh frowned. "We'll try to keep out of your hair," he promised. "We won't be here at all unless our bid is accepted, as I explained to Joe. If it is, once the work starts we'll be down there with the ship most of the time. When you're on a job like this you're usually too damned tired at night to do anything but fall into bed. So I don't think my men will annoy you with any large parties, unless maybe they get carried away on a Saturday night. But then, we don't always observe the usual work week, either. We have to go with the tide and the weather a good part of the time."

He stood as he finished this statement, and Donna looked across at him anxiously. "Look, I don't want you or your men to feel you have to walk on eggshells if you move in here."

Hugh grinned. "I appreciate that. And if my men and I move in we'll thank you properly. Now I think I'd better take off and attend to a few preliminaries."

"You'll speak to Mrs. Doane on your way out?"

He nodded. "I'll alert her, and later I can be more specific about our arrangements if everything works out for us."

"When do you think you'd be moving in?" she asked him.

"As soon as possible. Right now I'm using a friend's apartment over in Hyannis. He's off fishing in Florida for a couple of weeks, and this was supposed to be a vacation of sorts for me."

He was moving toward the door, and Donna trailed after him. It was only at the last minute that she said, "Your parka." She turned to get it for him.

It was still warm from the dryer, and shrugging into it, he said, "Does that ever feel good. Thanks, Donna. I'll give you a call if you like, as soon as I know what the score is."

She nodded. "I hope you will."

She stayed in the doorway long enough to watch him dash through the rain, which seemed to be increasing again. Then she got dressed, choosing some of her warmest clothing because it was going to be cold in the Snack Shack.

A ship had washed up on the beach, and already it was beginning to change a lot of lives, Donna found herself thinking as she zipped up her slicker.

Hers included.

CHAPTER THREE

BY SATURDAY, most of New England seemed to have made up its mind to go to Devon over the weekend and see the *Portia*.

By then the selectmen, the town's park and highway departments, the police and concerned citizens involved with a number of civic committees had banded together to take steps toward coping with the effects of a well-publicized, twentieth-century shipwreck.

Donna watched with interest as acres of snow fences were erected to keep people from tramping over the fragile dunes and destroying beach grass that had been carefully planted as a front army in the constant battle against erosion. Sightseers were allowed access to the beach only via carefully marked paths, and the principal path was the one that went past the Seashell Snack Shack.

Mark had used all his contacts to get supplies trucked in to the shack on an emergency basis, and business was booming there and everywhere else in Devon. Already postcards of the shipwreck had been printed and were for sale all over town, as were brightly colored T-shirts depicting a huge silhouette of the beached freighter.

The *Portia* herself was high and dry on the beach, and the prospect of her ever being floated again seemed gloomy. Speculation in town was rampant, and Donna wondered if there was validity to it. She hadn't seen Hugh again or heard from him, and by the time the weekend arrived she wondered if his bid had been refused or if, after further consideration of the problem involved, he had decided to abandon his initial offer.

Donna spent Saturday working for the Nickersons, primarily because she needed action. Time and again she'd been tempted to go over to the reception office to ask Cynthia Doane if she'd had any word from Hugh, but she'd resisted the impulse. She didn't want to display that much overt interest in him. People in Devon, even Cynthia, were all too apt to take a clue and turn it into a full-fledged case.

The Snack Shack did such a booming business that Saturday that every hand was needed. Though darkness still came early to the Cape, people lingered. The Nickersons turned on their lights and kept on going, and Donna stayed with them.

She had a dinner engagement with Rod Eldridge, but midway through the afternoon she called him to ask if he'd give her a rain check. She and Rod, who was manager of the Devon Bank and Trust Company, had an easygoing relationship. She'd met him years before when she'd been in Devon visiting her aunt and uncle. At that time Rod had been married, but he'd since been divorced.

She liked Rod. He was attractive and interesting and a good companion. Romantically he didn't stir her at all, but then no man had for a long, long time. George Farrish, her ex-husband, had done a job on her in that respect. Because of him she'd had enough of marriage, enough of commitment. Rod understood that what she wanted was companionship. She liked going out with someone congenial, someone with whom she was able to relax and enjoy dinner or a movie or a play without things becoming intense.

An hour or so after she'd called him, Rod appeared at the Snack Shack, having gone down to the beach to take a look at the freighter. As he sipped a cup of coffee he surveyed Donna and said frankly, "You look bushed. Why don't you wind up here and go home. I prescribe a hot bath and a stiff drink and then bed." He smiled. "I'll give you a call tomorrow. Let's plan to get together for dinner then."

Donna was more than willing to follow his prescription. She was bone weary from standing up and working so long, and though she was wearing thick, warm clothes she still felt cold. She had a hamburger and coffee, accepted Mark's thanks for her help, then trudged across the parking lot to the motel. Once in her apartment she drew a hot bath, added a liberal measure of herb-scented bubbles, and soaked long and luxuriously. She had just donned her terry robe and was about to fix herself a hot drink when she heard the knock at the door.

She had a strong sense of déjà vu as she went to answer the summons, and opening the door she confronted Hugh MacDonough.

He towered over her. He was wearing jeans and a short, heavy tweed coat. The yellow light outside Donna's door cast a pale glow over him, enhancing his ruddiness.

"Hi," he said. "I hope I'm not intruding."

"No," Donna replied hastily. "No, not at all."

As she moved back to let him pass, she was forced to admit how much she'd wanted to see him again.

She'd been trying to downplay the fact, but now she yielded to her own delight, hoping she wasn't telegraphing visible messages.

"I tried to call you a while ago," Hugh said, entering her living room as if his being there was the most natural thing in the world.

Donna followed him. "I was working over at the Snack Shack. They had a crowd crisis."

"I can imagine," he said dryly. "Half the world seems to be milling around Devon. I checked with Mrs. Doane and she said people can't believe the Windcrest isn't open. I'm glad I got my request in when I did."

What did that mean? She must have looked quizzical, because Hugh went on to say, "I've been so damned busy these past couple of days. I wanted to call and tell you I got the bid, but I couldn't seem to get around to it."

Until she heard this, Donna hadn't fully realized how much she'd wanted his bid for the salvage job to be accepted. Her eyes sparkled as she exclaimed, "That's great!"

He grinned. "I'm glad you feel that way. I was afraid you might reconsider your willingness to share the premises once you'd thought things out. I could understand it if you had second thoughts about having people poking around here when you're trying to work." His next question threw her. "Why didn't you tell me you were Jeffrey Jewell?"

Donna stared at him, dumbfounded, and he laughed. "I had to call your uncle again and your Aunt Mabel answered the phone. She and I used to exchange books. Then for a while I was all over the globe and I didn't see much of the Bruckers. I've been a fan of yours ever since your first book was published. Why all the mystery about your identity, Donna?''

''There isn't any,'' she said, but she was almost stammering as she spoke.

''It's okay,'' Hugh said easily. ''You don't have to explain—at least not now. But one of these days I'm going to trot over with my collection of your books and ask for your autograph on each and every one of them.''

He paused before going on. ''I came over primarily to tell you I'll probably be moving in Monday, but meantime I was wondering if you'd be free to have dinner with me tomorrow night. I owe you one. It was only due to your agreement that I was able to book space here. And besides, I'd like to celebrate.''

Donna had not told Rod specifically that she'd have dinner with him Sunday night but had agreed that they'd work something out when he called. She hesitated, torn because she wanted to accept Hugh's invitation, yet rather glad she had an escape route in Rod. She might need one! Hugh, now watching her with those knowing gray eyes, was going to be living practically next door. There was no way they wouldn't be meeting frequently unless they went out of their way to avoid each other. Donna had no intention of doing that, yet instinctively she began to draw back a little. Hugh MacDonough, in their brief encounters, had made an unusual impact on her. She already knew that if she was never to see him again she wouldn't forget him. Meeting him had been memorable, but she was still at the stage where she could have the memory and go on living happily without him.

How long would it take to progress from stage one to stage two—and beyond—in a relationship with this man?

"I have the funny feeling you're going to tell me you have a previous engagement."

"A somewhat tentative one," Donna admitted. "I had a dinner date for tonight but I begged off because I've been working all day and, frankly, I'm done in. But I did say that maybe I could make it tomorrow."

"In that case I'll just have to defer my celebration a little longer."

The disappointment in his voice was real, and Donna responded to it. "I was about to fix myself a drink. Would you join me?"

"I'd like that," he answered readily.

Donna dispensed with the thought of tea or coffee and fixed Scotch on the rocks for both of them, adding water to hers. When she went back to the living room she saw that Hugh was standing at the window, staring out into the darkness.

"Funny," he said. "You can just about make out the lights on her mast, but I think they'd escape you if you didn't know she was there. It would be easy to believe the whole thing's an illusion and that the *Portia*'s somewhere out at sea."

"Do you think she'll ever go to sea again?" Donna asked, handing him his drink.

He shrugged. "At this point I couldn't hazard an honest guess. And before we find out for sure, I'll guarantee you'll hear every rumor in the books about what's going to become of her. That's always the way it is."

Donna sat down in an easy chair, and Hugh took a place across from her on the couch. "Sometimes when

I read in the papers about what I'm supposed to be doing, I find it difficult to believe I'm on the job being written about. I don't blame the media. Rumors run rampant and they make good copy. Of course, sooner or later they're disproved, and the truth finally comes out. What the truth about the *Portia* will be I have no way of knowing, nor will I until her entire situation has been evaluated. We'll need to make a thorough study of her in order to gain an idea of the methods we're going to use in trying to set her free. It'll take time, and a hell of a lot of work.''

She smiled. ''I seem to hear a certain relish in your voice.''

''I can't deny that. Each job is such a challenge. Each time it's different, you have to contend with different factors, and that's what makes it exciting. I guess the thrill will never entirely wear off for me, though when I get down to action it becomes a matter of hard, often downright grueling work. Sometimes I ask myself why I got in the salvage business and swear I'll never go after a ship again.''

His eyes met hers directly. ''Isn't that the way you sometimes feel about your books?'' he asked.

Donna flinched, then said honestly, ''Yes. I look forward to each new project, and for the most part my enthusiasm continues to run high. But right now, besides swearing that I'm never going to write a book again once I finish the one I'm working on, I'm wondering how I'm ever going to get through this one. I'm under contract and I've already had to ask for an extension on my deadline....''

She stopped. This was the most she'd said to anyone about what was happening to her. Even to the

Nickersons she'd merely commented that she'd struck a snag in what she was doing.

"What's happened to put you off course?" Hugh asked, as if there was nothing unusual about her predicament.

She smiled ruefully. "I never really got *on* course with this story. I worked out a proposal that was accepted—"

"What does a proposal involve?"

"A plot outline, really, including a good idea of the characters, the complications, and so on. With mysteries it's especially important for a writer to know exactly where the story's heading. It's vital to pick up the clues as you progress. But you, as a mystery buff, must know that."

"Not necessarily. I'm one of those people who read mysteries for the plain, unadulterated pleasure they give me. I don't even try to guess who committed the crime. Sometimes I get an idea despite myself, but I'm happy to say that more often than not I'm wrong."

"Happy?" she asked curiously.

He nodded. "Yes. I suppose it's the eternal kid in me, but I like to be surprised."

She laughed, then added dryly, "I doubt if you'd get many surprises from my current work, the way it's going. I got about four chapters down on a disk and then I bogged completely. I've been thinking about wiping them out and starting all over again."

"You can't do that with wrecked ships," Hugh said. "Once you're committed to a course of action it can be almost impossible to switch. Not until you've followed the first course to a conclusion, at least. If what you've planned to do bombs, then of course you have to try something else. But you hope to God that won't happen." He smiled. "I'd say writers have more latitude."

"Maybe too much latitude," Donna agreed.

It was surprising her to find she could talk with him so easily about writing, at least on a superficial level. Lately it had been all she could do to discuss the book with her agent when she called. She'd begun to feel a total failure and to think it might be better to scrap her plot idea entirely and pay back her advance to the publisher. At the least she could ask that the book be postponed indefinitely, in which case she could try to come up with a totally different story line that might unlock this head of hers.

"Do you try to work a certain number of hours each day?" Hugh asked.

"Usually. I like to get started early and then print out what I've done. Then I have some lunch and rest awhile and edit what I've written. Sometimes I get started on further new material, sometimes I quit for the day. But the problem lately..."

"Yes?" he encouraged.

"I haven't gotten anywhere at all." Donna spread her hands in a wide, helpless gesture. "Nothing comes out. The words have dried up."

"I doubt that," Hugh said simply. "You need to set them free, that's all."

THE STATEMENT RETURNED to haunt Donna.

"You need to set them free, that's all."

Hugh was right. But despite her writing experience she had no idea how to go about liberating her thoughts, her mind.

Hugh left shortly after finishing his drink. Donna turned on the TV and watched a sci-fi movie, but by the end of it she was nodding in her chair. The combination of working in the Snack Shack and breathing in the cool ocean air, plus the unaccustomed Scotch nightcap, made her so sleepy she drifted off as soon as her head touched the pillow.

Saturday had been a bright and beautiful day, and Sunday turned out to be the same. Crowds continued to stream into Devon, and the beach parking lot became as crowded as it was on the Fourth of July. Donna helped Mark and Althea during the day, then went out for an early dinner with Rod.

They ate in a quiet French restaurant, and Rod ordered the best fare on the gourmet menu, as he always did. He knew food, he knew wines, he was a sophisticated man, interested in many things and well informed about most of them.

Donna had chosen a slim, beige wool dress for their dinner engagement, accenting it with gold and topaz accessories. But she didn't match up to her dinner partner, who was wearing a custom-tailored, three-piece, pale gray wool suit, with a matching shirt and a tie striped in pearl gray, pink and maroon.

The color scheme complemented his coloring. He had almost black hair and hazel eyes, and though on the slim side, he was well proportioned. Donna had often thought that if he wasn't a banker he could be a model.

As they enjoyed their food and the excellent Beaujolais he'd chosen, the talked principally about the *Portia*. In Rod's opinion the ship was giving the town's preseason economy a terrific boost that was going to be widely beneficial.

"Cape China is putting out a full line of *Portia* mugs, and maybe ashtrays and souvenir plates, as well," he informed her, speaking of a local gift shop. "There are five different companies making *Portia* T-shirts at this point, and I don't know how many photographers are having postcards and posters and bumper stickers printed up. A local author called me at home today and made an appointment to come in to the bank tomorrow. He wants to do a book about the *Portia* with color pictures to illustrate it, and he's going to try to wangle a loan from us to finance it. Personally I don't think it's a bad idea."

Rod refilled their wineglasses. "Something like that will sell like hotcakes."

To her surprise, Rod didn't mention anything about a salvage operation beginning in the near future, and Donna kept silent. Evidently word hadn't been passed along yet in the business community about Hugh MacDonough having secured the contract to try to get the *Portia* off Massasoit Beach.

After dinner Rod suggested they stop somewhere for a liqueur, but Donna told him honestly that she was too tired. It was a healthy kind of fatigue, entirely different from the lethargy she'd been experiencing lately, caused by her failure to get down words after hours of staring at the computer's blank screen. But it was just as authentic.

Rod kissed her good-night, as he always did, and his kiss didn't move her any more than it ever did. He drove off, and Donna let herself into her apartment. She kicked off her shoes and was heading for the bedroom to undress when she heard the knock at the door that was beginning to sound familiar.

"Donna," Hugh said apologetically, "I'm sorry to bother you but do you suppose you could let me have some soap and a couple of towels?"

Donna looked surprised. "Have you moved in?"

He nodded. "Yes, and I guess I shouldn't have. Mrs. Doane gave me the keys yesterday, but I told her I didn't think I'd be able to make it until tomorrow. So she thought there'd be plenty of time to stock my unit."

Donna's mind was racing. He was here...already. She had to get used to the idea.

"What about your bed?" she asked.

"My bed? Oh, you mean sheets? There aren't any, but I don't mind that. I can sleep on the mattress for tonight, and there are a couple of blankets."

"Aunt Mabel and Uncle Joe would have a fit. Cynthia really should have seen to it that the place was made up for you."

"It's not her fault, it's mine," he insisted. "I would like to take a shower, though," he admitted somewhat sheepishly. "So if you could part with a towel and a bar of soap..."

"I can also part with some sheets. I'll come over and help you make the bed."

"No, no," he protested. "That's asking too much."

Donna was already moving to the large closet off the bathroom that contained a supply of sheets, pillowcases, towels and other essentials. She was all too aware of Hugh's presence behind her.

Flustered, she pulled out bath towels and face towels and a couple of washcloths, then turned to find him even closer than she'd thought he was. She felt her skin tingling and an invasive warmth swept through her. She was sure she was flushing like an adolescent—or was about to—and this amused her.

Next thing, I'll find myself tongue-tied, she thought wryly.

"Here," she commanded, a little more brusquely than she might have were she less affected by Hugh MacDonough. "Hold out your arms and I'll give you a pile of these things."

"You don't need to raid your linen closet, Donna," he protested. "All I want is enough for a single night."

"Towels," she said, laying those she'd chosen across his outstretched arms. "Here, I'll give you one fitted bottom sheet and one top one, two pillowcases and...what else was it you wanted?"

She was continuing to stack things on the growing pile as she spoke, and she was also trying not to look at him. But when he didn't answer her question her eyes swerved upward to lock with his. "Soap," he said, then added softly, "you're beautiful."

Donna was taken aback. She hadn't expected to hear anything like that at a moment when things were so prosaic. And what could be more mundane than handing a person a supply of clean linens?

"Why are you looking at me like that?" Hugh said gently. "You must have been told you're beautiful any number of times, Donna. Your mirror must tell you you're beautiful every time you glance into it."

She didn't seem able to wrest her eyes away from his. "Hugh, please..."

"Come on, Donna," he chided. "You must know you're as desirable as hell in that dress you're wearing. In anything you wear, for that matter. It was all I could do to keep my hands off you the first time I saw you in that white terry thing. It's even harder now." He laughed. "But you've seen to it that my arms are full of sheets and pillowcases, haven't you?"

She could feel the color stinging her cheeks, and she felt as awkward as an adolescent. Even worse, words were failing her, just as they did during those awful hours when she sat staring at the computer's screen. She didn't know what to say to Hugh. She tried to think of something clever, something flip, something sophisticated, even something stupid, but nothing came.

There was a hamper outside the bathroom door. Before Donna realized what he was doing, Hugh had set down the pile of linen atop it. Then he moved toward her, first touching her shoulders with his hands then urging her toward him, and she felt the strength of his arms as they enfolded her.

He held her against him, then raised one hand to fondle her hair, his lips following his fingers to kiss the tendrils that curled back from her forehead. There was a question in his voice as he asked, "Donna?"

She tilted her head back to look up at him and saw the diffused emotion in his smoky gray eyes, the latent desire, the wanting that matched the warm, provocative feeling swirling through her body.

I've come in out of the cold night to the warmth of the fire, she found herself thinking. But fire was dangerous, she reminded herself quickly and she had no doubt he was the kind of man who could burn a woman very easily, even involuntarily.

"I want you," Hugh said, his voice low. "Oh, I know it's quick, you don't have to tell me we're still strangers. I'm not going to try to rush things, Donna. You don't have to warn me about that, either." He drew a long breath. "I'm willing to take my time, but meanwhile..."

As she continued to look up at him, Hugh's mouth descended to hers, and the effect of his kiss was overwhelming. A needle of compressed emotion threaded slowly through her, transfusing her with desire every inch of the way.

Her response was instinctive; she could not have held back from Hugh. Her mouth became soft and pliant, her lips parting to speak a silent language that needed no translation. Time seemed to stand still.

Then slowly Hugh released her, clutching her for a moment until she steadied, just as he'd held on to her during their first encounter on the beach.

He laughed shakily and turned back toward the pile of linens she'd given him. Picking them up, he said, "I think I'd better make up my bed by myself tonight, Donna. Otherwise I'd have to have you in it!"

CHAPTER FOUR

THE FIERCE NORTHEASTER and the resulting shipwreck the previous week had seriously altered Donna's routine, but on Monday morning she was
determined to get back on schedule again. First on the
agenda would be a brisk beach walk, followed by a
good breakfast. Then, a session with the computer.
Maybe today the words would find their way onto the
screen.

She had recently been stirred physically, in a very
potent way. Maybe the reaction had shaken up the
creative cells in her brain, she thought whimsically as
she put on a warm, fleecy running suit then topped it
with a rose-colored quilted parka.

It was cool out, but the newly risen sun was a golden
orb in the east and the day promised to be a glorious
one. For the first time since the *Portia*'s ill-fated arrival, the beach parking lot was deserted, but that was
only because of the early hour. Even though it was a
Monday, Donna was sure the sightseers would be descending before the morning was far advanced and
they'd keep coming until dark.

The Snack Shack was closed, and the Nickersons
wouldn't be opening up for another couple of hours.
The park and highway departments' vehicles were not
even around yet. Donna drank in great drafts of the
bracing air as she headed out along the path toward

the water. She was planning to get to the hard-packed sand at the tide line then walk briskly, swinging her arms, maybe even trying a little—just a little—jogging. But before she reached her goal she heard a man call, "Wait up!" and she turned to see Hugh coming after her.

He was wearing a gray wool turtleneck with a heavy green wool jacket over it, faded jeans and scuffed running shoes, and he looked absolutely wonderful.

"Look," he said, catching up to her, "I'm not trying to butt in. If you want to go for your walk alone, just tell me and I'll have the grace to bow out." He smiled rather sheepishly. "Not willingly, though."

She had to smile back at him. "I'm not up to a real run, if that's what you have on your mind."

"I don't have anything on my mind except getting some fresh air and trying to clear some of the cobwebs out of my head," he assured her. "But I'd like your company." He grinned like a small boy caught swiping icing off a cake. "I was looking out my window and I saw you starting out. I raced like hell to get something on so I could join you."

"I can't ignore all that effort," she teased. "So come along. If I can't keep up with you, don't blame me, that's all."

"I don't think I could ever blame you for anything, Donna," he said, and her pulse quickened. The deep resonance of his voice did something to her, and the tenderness in his tone struck her even more than the words themselves.

"Look," he went on, "about last night. Did I come on too strong?"

After he'd left, Donna had found herself close to wishing he'd come on even stronger. She shook her head slowly and said, "No."

"You don't sound too sure. I…"

He paused, and she glanced up to see that his lips were pressed together in a tight line and he was staring straight out to sea. She could have understood his absorption if he'd been looking down the beach toward the stranded ship, but he wasn't.

"Hugh," she ventured, "don't make too much of it."

"No?" he queried, without looking at her. "Once I was in my own unit I nearly gave up and went back to your place. I felt so damned lonely all of a sudden."

His glance swerved to her, and there was a cloudiness to his deep gray eyes. "In a way I'm used to being lonely," he said simply. "In my work I usually wind up in strange places. I've always made friends fairly easily. Friends? I should say acquaintances, of course, but the friendships—or acquaintanceships—seldom last long, because inevitably I move on." He shrugged lightly. "I've moved on ever since I can remember. I suppose I always will. Sometimes I feel I've missed a lot. Other times I think I've had—still have—the best of all possible lives."

Donna stiffened. Was he warning her about involvement with him? Was he reminding her that he'd already said he was a rolling stone? Did he want her to know he was a loner? A charming, charismatic, tremendously appealing loner?

If that was the case, at least he was honest. Yet she couldn't find it in her to appreciate his honesty. Hugh MacDonough had come over the horizon of her life and she found herself so glad he had.

If his game plan is always to love and leave, I don't want to know about it. Not yet.

Would you rather be deluded, a small voice asked.

It was a question Donna didn't want to deal with. Not on this glorious spring morning, with Hugh so close to her she could almost feel his warmth.

They moved on, trudging through the ruts of deep sand, which were made all the more pronounced by the hordes of people who had come to see the beached ship over the weekend.

"Footprints, footprints everywhere," Hugh mused. "Something like this could cause an ecological disaster."

"The park department has worked overtime to get all the snow fences up," Donna said, trying to put things between them on a less personal level...at least temporarily. "Hopefully, they'll keep more of the beach grass from being trampled. Mark Nickerson was saying there has already been considerable damage."

"It won't take long for everything to get back to normal if a stop is put to the trespassing right now," Hugh said. "What I'm more worried about is the effect our own equipment is going to have. We'll minimize the upheaval as much as we can, that goes without saying. But we're going to have to take some pretty heavy stuff through here."

They'd come to the break in the dunes, which flanked either side of the sandy path, and could more clearly see the huge ship that dominated the horizon, just to their right.

Glancing toward the *Portia*, Hugh said, "The crew's back aboard her. And they've gotten the diesel off her, thank God."

"Fuel?"

He nodded. "There were nearly two hundred thousand gallons of diesel fuel aboard her when she hit the shore. If there had been serious leaks in her hull, the oil could have created a major spill. As it is, if we had had another storm there's no telling what might have happened. Her hull still could have split apart, which would have meant that oil would have leaked all over the place, and that would have been a real disaster. But—" he grinned down at her "—there's endless potential for catastrophe inherent in any shipwreck. The *Portia*'s no different."

"You sound so cheerful about it," she protested.

"There's no point in being gloomy. I have my work cut out for me and I know it. She's not going to be the easiest old girl in the world to straighten out. She's flat bottomed, I wouldn't rate her 'A' for stability. Because she was empty her propellers were riding high, and in a sense she was a sitting duck. I've talked to Alex Bruce—he's her captain—and he says that for a while out there at sea she was going around and around in circles and they couldn't control her."

They'd come to the hard-packed sand, and they turned toward the ship. After a moment Donna asked, "Do you really think you're going to get her off the beach?"

Hugh's face creased in a pained smile. "Don't sound so skeptical. I need all the votes of confidence I can get. I've handled more difficult jobs," he added, but there was no conceit, no hint of boasting in the statement. He was voicing simple fact. "Each time you face new challenges. I suspect the *Portia*'s not going to give us an easy time of it. Few ships do."

"There are all kinds of rumors going around town about what's going to happen to her."

"I know. Most of them aren't very optimistic, either." He grinned. "I try not to listen to them."

"Do you have your own plan of action?"

"I have a number of plans working their way around the back of my mind. Some of my crew will begin arriving later today. Once we've got our act together here we'll be getting down to strategy."

Gazing toward the ship, he said, "There's a chance we may be able simply to tow her off the beach with tugs. Or we may be able to use ground tackle and her winches so she can pull herself off. Those are the two most desirable possibilities. There are a number of less attractive alternatives."

"What if nothing works?" Donna asked practically.

"Are you always such a pragmatist?" His expression was rueful. "Okay, if all else fails we may have to cut her up and tow away what's left of her. But as far as I'm concerned that's going to be a last resort. I'll do my damnedest to get the old girl off the beach in one piece. I want to see her riding out there in deep water again."

They were close to the ship yet still not abreast of her, when Hugh said, "This is far enough. Let's turn back, if it's okay with you. I'll be spending more than enough time around her in the near future."

She smiled. "I have an idea you're going to like her company."

"That depends on how she responds to me," he countered. "A man can't really relate to a woman unless he gets a certain response from her."

He'd gotten enough of a response from *her* last night, Donna thought. She felt herself go warm again, and Hugh laughed. "I like it when you get that embarrassed, little-girl look." Then he sobered. "I'm glad you're going to be around. Very glad. Before we settle the *Portia*'s destiny, I have a feeling I'm going to need all the moral support I can get.''

''THE TOWN'S BECOMING A ZOO,'' Mark complained by midafternoon. ''Souvenir junk all over the place and people pouring in to see the *Portia* like she's the main act in a circus.''

Once again Donna was helping out in the Snack Shack. The Nickersons had expected that business would level off on a weekday, but they'd been mistaken. The *Portia* was undoubtedly one of the biggest attractions the New England coast had had to offer for a long time.

Althea and Mark both knew Donna was in Devon to write a book, and they respected her privacy. They hadn't asked her to pitch in and help them again. She'd come of her own volition.

Over the course of the morning she had become increasingly aware of the crowds converging on the scene every time she went to her apartment window, which was too often. Finally she'd given up trying to work. Once again the words were not coming, and it had been a relief to have an escape route.

Mark was offering a limited menu. ''I'm not getting into fried clams and scallops and stuff like that,'' he'd announced. ''But we can do hamburgers and hot dogs and french fries without too much of a problem.''

Donna was stationed at the front of the shop, and she spent the afternoon taking orders and then trying to keep the orders straight. At least, she thought gratefully, it kept her mind occupied.

She was perturbed, because after the walk along the beach with Hugh that morning she'd felt rested and invigorated and more hopeful about her creative powers than she'd been in quite some time. Yet she hadn't been able to concentrate on her story line at all. Instead, her thoughts had kept wandering to the *Portia*.

She became aware that Althea had gone over to the far corner of the shack, turning her back on potential customers, and was deep in conversation with a tall, thin man with a shock of dark hair and burning blue eyes.

"Alex Bruce, captain of that blasted boat," Mark said in her ear, nodding toward Althea.

Mark had growled out the words, and Donna looked up at him in surprise.

"Althea's let us in for more than our share," he explained as he passed along a series of hamburgers and hot dogs to Donna. He didn't elaborate. There wasn't time, she realized, as her fingers flew in the effort to get the orders to the customers waiting for them. But she promised herself she'd get Mark to explain what he meant as soon as there was a chance to do so.

Meanwhile she eyed the *Portia*'s captain curiously. He was an attractive man in a lean, dark way. He was wearing jeans and a heavy, Arran sweater, and he didn't look much like her idea of a ship's captain. He needed a shave, and he looked as if he could do with some sleep, as well.

Donna reminded herself that the man had just been through an ordeal in which he could very well have lost his ship to the mercies of the sea...and possibly had. There was no telling whether or not Hugh's salvage attempts would prove to be successful.

"We didn't see much of Bruce at first, but he's been hanging around here the past three days," Mark muttered resentfully as he slid along another assortment of hamburgers and hot dogs to Donna. "Wonder you didn't notice him before."

She hadn't, but there'd been so many people to deal with.

It was plain that Mark didn't like the *Portia*'s captain, and Donna mulled this over as she poured coffee and tea, made chocolate frappés and passed out cans of soft drinks.

She was keeping out a weather eye herself. She hadn't seen Hugh since they'd gone back to the motel together after their early-morning walk. But when she'd left her apartment to come over to the snack shop, she'd been aware of a surge of activity around the Windcrest Motor Inn.

Now she wondered if Hugh and his men were already settled in and perhaps engaged in preliminary conferences about the salvage operation.

"No, it's too soon for that."

She didn't realize she'd spoken aloud until Mark looked across at her, puzzled.

"Did you say something?" he asked.

"Not exactly," she hedged.

"Look, Donna, are we keeping you from something? I'll give Althea a shout if you just say the word."

Donna was sure Mark wanted nothing more than to divert his sister's attention from the *Portia*'s captain. But she wasn't about to get into that one.

"I want to keep on doing what I'm doing," she assured Mark.

The sunlight began to fade by midafternoon and was replaced by charcoal-colored clouds that scudded across the sky. By then, Althea had returned to work, but she was preoccupied as she helped Mark cook for the customers who kept on coming, despite the fact that it was well past the lunch hour.

Without the sunlight, the Snack Shack became chilly, and Donna paused during a lull to fix herself a cup of tea. She was sipping it as she glanced down the path to the beach and saw Hugh MacDonough coming along with two other men.

He came up to the counter and flashed a smile at her. "Have you taken a regular job here?"

"Only temporary," Donna assured him. "This rush can't last forever. You wouldn't believe how busy we've been. It doesn't seem possible this is a Monday in March."

"The ship's a magnet," Hugh said, looking out over the parking lot, which was still crammed with cars and people even though the afternoon was becoming grayer and grayer. He turned to the men at his side. "Brent Hancock and Jim Babson, Donna," he introduced them. "My right hand and my left hand, though I'm not going to say which is which."

The men laughed and Donna laughed with them. They were big and ruddy men, both of them older than Hugh, but they had that same, bronzed, weather-beaten look about them. These were men who were gamblers at heart, men who were willing to take risks, men who lived lives far out of the ordinary, she found herself thinking. Were they all loners?

"Can I get you something?" she asked.

"Coffee would be fine," Hugh told her, and she filled three cups with the hot beverage.

"If you guys want to go along," Hugh suggested to his companions, "I'll catch up with you later."

The men took the hint, and a moment later Althea came over to say, "I'll handle things for a while."

Mark had set redwood picnic tables and benches out on the sand by the shop, something he ordinarily didn't do until the Memorial Day weekend. Hugh led the way to one of them, and Donna sat down gratefully.

"I'm not used to standing on my feet for hours at a time," she admitted. "They're sending messages to me."

"Wait till you start running," Hugh remarked. "It'll build up the muscles. Donna…"

"Yes?"

"Would you be free to have dinner with me tomorrow night? I think I should stick with the men tonight. Brent and Jim came in late this morning, two or three others should be arriving by dinnertime. I doubt we'll get much groundwork covered, but we have to make a start at it. Anyway, we need to settle in."

"I'm sure you do."

"I'd like it very much if we could have dinner together tomorrow, though. You've been very decent to me."

Donna had never had a man tell her that she'd been decent to him, and the adjective sounded strange to her ears. Nor did she like the idea that Hugh Mac-Donough was asking her out to dinner because he felt he had a small debt to pay.

Hugh, she saw, was eyeing her closely. "What I meant to say was that I appreciate your kindness. I'm not especially good with words, Donna. I don't have your talent in that direction. But the honest truth is that I want to be with you. I want to be alone some-place where I can talk to you. If I can arrange a background of soft lights and sweet music to go along with the conversation, that'll be fine."

She smiled. "All right."

He nodded. "Good. Suppose I knock on your door tomorrow night around seven?"

"Fine," Donna replied, and she knew she would have to refrain from counting the hours.

DONNA HAD NO IDEA where Hugh would want to go to dinner, but she was determined to dress up, regard-less. She wanted to wear something very special for him.

Her royal-blue dress had a lustrous jacquard pattern and dramatically full, pleated dolman sleeves. A belt of the same fabric tied at the waist, and for her only jewelry she chose the lapis and gold drop ear-rings she'd bought in a New York antique shop the winter before.

She arranged her hair in a swirling chignon, took more pains with her makeup than she normally did, and added a touch of Giorgio as the final note. But although she knew she looked fine, she was unac-countably nervous by the time Hugh knocked on the door. She felt like a teenager embarking on her first date. As she went to the door, she reminded herself with an effort that she was a twenty-eight-year-old di-vorcée. There was no logical reason for Hugh Mac-Donough to have this kind of effect on her.

When she opened the door to him, though, the ef-fect he had on her intensified. Staring up at him, she wondered how she'd ever thought he was too rugged to be handsome. Tonight he looked absolutely devastating. He was wearing coffee-and-cream slacks, a brown tweed jacket, a gold-colored shirt and a striped tie that picked up all the right color variations.

They stared at each other for a long moment, then Donna laughed nervously and said, "Would you like a drink before we go out?"

"Let's save it for the restaurant," Hugh suggested. "I've made reservations at Paddington Station. I hope that's all right with you?"

Paddington Station was currently one of the most popular restaurants on the Cape, and Donna had been wanting to go to it ever since she'd been back in Devon. It was in the Barnstable area, a drive of twenty miles or so up the Cape, and so far it had not occurred to Rod Eldridge to suggest they dine there. Now she was glad he hadn't.

Hugh was driving a deep brown Mazda, and she admired the competent way he handled the sleek car. He seemed to do everything with his own brand of ease, and she wondered if this extended to salvaging ships. Or maybe because his work was so difficult, everything else seemed relatively simple to him.

They didn't talk much on the way to the restaurant, but theirs was an easy silence. Donna found herself relaxing with Hugh, and she was determined to get over what she was calling stage fright. True, she hadn't traveled the world as he had, and she had no doubt he was infinitely more experienced than she was in almost every way. But she'd made her mark in her chosen career, she supported herself and she lived well, and until a point last Wednesday when she'd found herself clinging to a stranger's arms in the face of a violent northeaster, she'd thought she was pretty self-sufficient.

At the restaurant they were led to a choice corner table. The atmosphere was delightful, the furnishings and decor that of an English Victorian railroad station. The lights were soft and the music in the background was sweet and timeless. It was a romantic setting, and as Hugh smiled at her and Donna returned his smile, she knew this was going to be a very special evening.

They lingered over an excellent dinner, then moved on to the adjacent lounge, where there was music for dancing.

"I've been told that I have two left feet," Hugh warned, but when he took her into his arms and started to guide her around the dance floor, she found that he danced with the same expertise with which he seemed to do everything else.

Donna had never considered herself a particularly good dancer. Her ex-husband had been excellent and had always shown her up in this respect. But she followed Hugh's steps easily, as if they'd been programmed to yield together to the rhythms of the haunting melodies.

"I like this kind of mellow music," Hugh confessed. "I like to listen to the new stuff, but I don't move well with it."

Donna laughed. "Neither do I." She gave in to the impulse to rest her head against his shoulder, the rough tweed of his jacket brushing her cheek. He smelled of soap and something faintly spicy, and he was so warm, so intensely male.

The hand clasping her waist tightened slightly, and he said huskily, "I want to make love to you, Donna. I swore after Sunday night that I wouldn't rush things,

but I want to make love to you so damned much. *Am*
I rushing things, Donna?''

She nestled closer to him, and her words were muf-
fled. ''I don't know. I honestly don't know, Hugh.''

''It's so hellishly presumptuous just to come out and
say, do you want me? I wanted you so much last night
it was all I could do to stay away from your end of the
motel. To tell you the truth, I'm damned if I know
how I'm going to keep my distance. On the other
hand, I respect you, and I'll respect what you want,
whether or not it's what I want. But...''

To her surprise, he started to laugh. ''I'm talking
too damned much.''

He was right. He was talking too much. Donna's
beautiful mouth curved into a smile he couldn't see as
they swayed to the music, and she let the moment wash
over her, a moment without words. She let herself respond to the man and the music, and let her emotions
take control.

For once she wasn't worrying about what was going
to happen next. When the dance was over, she clasped
her hands in Hugh's and thought that this small in-
terval had come as close to perfection as anything she
had ever known.

The intimacy between them was like a warm cloak
as they drove back to Devon. Most of the lights in the
motel were out as Hugh slid his car up in front of her
apartment ell. ''It looks as if the troops have gone to
bed. I hope so. Donna...''

He sounded troubled and Donna, still in her own
paradise, looked across at him questioningly. ''What
is it?''

''I've put myself in something of a bind,'' he said
unhappily. ''Right now Brent Hancock's sharing my

unit with me. Tomorrow we're taking over some of the rooms that have just been redecorated, so this is temporary. I'll have my own quarters after tomorrow, but just now..."

She sensed his struggle to find the right words. "I'd hate like hell for Brent to wake up and find my bed hadn't been slept in." It was a moonless night and Donna couldn't see him clearly, but he sounded miserable. "It's you I'm thinking of," he added. "The guys can be pretty...earthy. I wouldn't want them to get any ideas. I..."

His words faded, and she stepped in to rescue him. "It's all right, Hugh."

"The hell it's all right," he exploded savagely. "I've never wanted anything in my life as much as I want you right at this moment." His anger abated, replaced by laughter. "I'm taking a lot for granted, aren't I? I'm acting like you've already invited me to spend the night."

She hadn't, of course. But in her heart of hearts, Donna knew that she would have.

CHAPTER FIVE

THAT WEDNESDAY history seemed determined to repeat itself. A new northeaster swept over the Cape, a macabre reminder of the *Portia*'s grounding just one week earlier.

Watching the driving rain through her living-room window as she sat in front of her computer, Donna could imagine Hugh's frustration. This kind of weather could only delay his getting started on the salvage operation.

Well, Hugh had his frustrations and she had hers.

She stared at the blank computer screen, but the story she was supposed to be working on remained as remote as ever. Other thoughts intruded, completely eclipsing it. She kept thinking of the *Portia*, and Alex Bruce, the ship's captain. She could visualize the dark intentness of his expression, and the way he and Althea had talked together, seemingly oblivious to everyone else around them.

Donna had not had the chance to ask Mark what he'd meant by saying that Althea had let them in for more than their share. But she felt sure that the share he'd been speaking about had something to do with Captain Bruce and his ship, and she was curious.

Alex Bruce was an arresting character. The word *character* came to Donna inadvertently and started a whole new train of thought.

There was something vaguely sinister about Alex Bruce, she decided, recognizing as she did so that this was probably her imagination at work. There were times when her imagination overextended itself and she attributed to people characteristics that didn't truly belong to them at all. Once she'd been vastly surprised when a cherubic-faced old lady had turned out to be a bank thief. On another occasion, a man who'd worn a patch over one eye and looked like a pirate had developed into one of the kindest individuals she'd ever known.

Whether true or false, as far as his inherent character was concerned, it was fun to think of Alex Bruce as the villain in the piece.

What piece?

Donna sat tapping her fingers reflectively on the silvery bar that edged the computer keys, and, as if self-motivated, her fingers wandered onto the keys and she began to fill the screen with sentence after sentence of impressions.

Suppose, just suppose, the *Portia* had been carrying contraband cargo. Donna didn't stop to figure out what kind of cargo it might be, that could come later. But suppose the ship had gone aground with something still aboard her, something only Alex Bruce, as her captain, knew about.

Suppose it was imperative for him to form a close association in Devon with someone who could be of help to him. He would zero in on Althea as his ally, use all of his considerable charms on her, and she would fall in love with him.

Trite? Donna paused, considering the plot line she was following, and was forced to admit that at first glance it might be considered trite. But right now she was merely trying to get down an idea in broad sweeps. Later, as the ideas evolved, she could make everything plausible.

She worked on, developing Alex Bruce. He became something of a renegade, highly intelligent but unscrupulous. In her basic referral to him she listed him as "A.B." The initials were obvious, but no one else would be looking at what she was doing. Later, as a camouflage, she could give him a name, but right now she wanted to let her thoughts flow, let her fingers fly over the computer keys without restraint.

After a time she decided to give her wandering thoughts some stability and save what she'd put down on a disk. She pondered about a name under which to store what she'd written and decided that "Portia" would do very well. She programmed in the instruction. "Break—Save—Portia-O," the "O" standing for outline.

She sat back and let the computer do its work. It wasn't long before red lights blinked outside her disk-storage spaces, indicating that the information she had fed into the computer had been recorded. For posterity? Donna chuckled at the thought. She had no illusions that what she was toying with was material worthy of being saved for posterity. But fooling around this way was a lot of fun. She couldn't remember when she'd last really had fun writing anything. She'd achieved quite a success with her first mystery novel, and it had been imperative to follow that success with another, till finally she'd gotten onto a treadmill of sorts, unable to let up at all.

She made herself some coffee and went back to the computer, but despite her recent splurge of creativity she still couldn't get back to the book she was supposed to be writing. Finally she set her notes for it aside again and let herself brood about the *Portia* and Alex Bruce and Althea, sinister forces, a great storm that had caused Bruce's ship to wreck...

She began to make further jottings on the Portia disk, and it was after noon when she came to a halt, her back starting to ache from sitting in the same position so long.

She was hungry and didn't want to be alone, so she put on some foul-weather gear and crossed to the Snack Shack. Despite the wind and the rain there were still a number of cars in the parking lot.

Mark had put up heavy plastic curtains across the edge of the shack, making a small tunnel inside where people could stand and eat. He was handling the place alone, Donna saw, but business was desultory. He gladly fixed her a hamburger and watched as she heaped it with mustard and catsup and pickle relish and chopped onions.

"You do go for all the trimmings, don't you?" he observed.

She laughed. "I guess I do. Where's Althea?"

"Back at the house," Mark said grimly. "She's using our kitchen to brew up a few gallons of stew."

She stared at him. "Did you say a few gallons?"

He nodded curtly. "She's feeding the crew of the *Portia*. Didn't you know?"

So that's what Mark had meant when he'd said Althea had let them in for more than their share. "Are you saying she's been feeding them all along?" Donna demanded.

He nodded. "Since the Coast Guard got the oil off the ship. Until then, the men were staying around town in motels or private homes, except for the captain and the first mate, I guess. Now all twenty-seven of them are back on board, and Althea's acting like she's Joan of Arc. Anyway,'' Mark concluded, obviously disgruntled, "she's taken it upon herself to save their stomachs, if nothing else. Yesterday she fried up eighty-one eggs and packed them in Styrofoam containers and delivered them to Tony Ramirez, the first mate. She did that before she came over here to work. Later she took time off to make eighty-one sandwiches for their lunch. Evidently she allows three per man of everything she makes.''

There was no business at the moment, so Mark took advantage of the lull to pour himself a cup of coffee. "I'm getting pretty damned sick and tired of it. It's one thing to be a good Samaritan and another to be a damned fool. The restaurants in town have pitched in and they're willing to help out in feeding the *Portia* crew, but Althea's acting like a prima donna about it. She's rubbing some people the wrong way. Maisie Burns was the first one to feed the men. She owns the Spice and Nice. Her husband, Bill, is on the rescue squad and he was at the fire station when they began to get calls last Wednesday about the ship going aground.

"Wednesday night they fed the men right at the fire station, and Maisie did all the cooking," Mark went on. "She still wants to help out, but Althea's turning a deaf ear to all offers. And I know why. You saw her with the captain yesterday, remember?''

Donna nodded. She remembered very well.

"He's conning Althea and she's falling for it," Mark stated bluntly. "I don't know what the hell's come over her, but I don't like it.''

"Maybe Althea just wants to be helpful," Donna suggested.

Mark snorted. "Tell that to someone else, Donna. It was one thing to be helpful, as you put it, when the ship first grounded. Now that there's power back aboard her and the men are on board, they're perfectly capable of handling their own affairs, and that includes doing their own cooking. If they need help, they'll holler for it." Mark looked grim. "Althea's problem is that she can't get Bruce off her mind. She's edgy all the time she's working here, waiting for him to show up. It's a pain, because we've been so pushed. You know how busy we've been. I don't know how we'd have gotten along without you," he added gruffly.

"Feel free to call on me whenever you need me," Donna offered. "This weather isn't going to last forever, and you'll be swamped again."

"I know. Ordinarily I'd be glad. But right now I can't wait to see the last of the *Portia*."

Donna couldn't join Mark in that sentiment, she reflected, as she dashed back through the rain toward her apartment. As long as the *Portia* remained on the beach Hugh MacDonough would be around. Once the ship was freed...

She didn't pursue the thought.

She was at the edge of the sidewalk that bordered the motel when she saw the Mazda coming to a stop at the opposite end of the Windcrest. Hugh got out of the car and when he saw her he waved and came toward her with long strides.

They moved up the sidewalk together and stood under the wide roof overhang. Hugh was wearing the thick, hooded parka he'd had on the day of the shipwreck, and Donna was wearing the same slicker. He smiled slightly. "I have a feeling we've been through this before."

"Uncanny, isn't it?" she agreed. "Two storms like this, just a week apart."

"And what are you doing out in this one? You haven't been on the beach, have you?"

She shook her head. "No. I went over to the snack shop to get something to eat. I was too lazy to fix anything."

He looked tired, she noticed. There were dark shadows under his eyes, and tension lines etched his mouth. "How's the book going?" he asked.

"It still isn't."

"Maybe you ought to get your mind on something else," he suggested perceptively.

Donna wanted to tell him how close to the mark he was, but she resisted. Instead she asked, "How are things going with you?"

"Slow. Five of my men are in residence at this point, and I'm going to hold off bringing in the rest of the crew until we have more of the details worked out. I suppose you've been hearing all the rumors floating around," he added wearily. "The Coast Guard was even quoted in one of the local papers as saying that there's always the chance we may not be able to get her off or even to dismantle her, in which case she'll become a permanent fixture on Massasoit Beach." Hugh grimaced. "That kind of opinion helps a lot. Usually the Coast Guard's more than helpful, and I give them full credit for the way they got the oil pumped off the ship. They had a hell of a hard time doing it. They had to snake rubber hoses across the sand to tanker trucks about a quarter of a mile away. At one point, the pumping machinery broke down. So often when you're doing something like that, one damned snag after another crops up."

He gazed out at the slanting rain. "It's a damned good thing they got the oil out of her, though. As I told you before, a second storm could have created a real problem. At that, there wasn't too much time left over before this second northeaster struck. It took about thirty-eight hours to complete the pumping job. They were pumping out more than five thousand gallons of oil an hour.

"I'm beginning to think I'll be glad when this one is over," he added slowly. "Maybe it's a case of too much too soon. I just got back from the job in Africa and I was intending to go to Bermuda or someplace for a couple of weeks after Charlie got back from Florida." He smiled down at her. "Ah well. So much for the best-laid plans."

Donna didn't know how to answer that.

"Well, back to the drawing board. We're still trying to work out a million different details." He kissed her lightly on the forehead. "See you later."

Later. Donna had no idea when later might be. Her concentration was shot, though, and she would do no more work today.

She had to do some grocery shopping, so she drove over to a large supermarket in Orleans in the middle of the afternoon. It was miserable driving, and by the time she got to the plaza she was wishing she'd stayed home and settled for a can of soup.

Since she was at the store, she stocked up on food, but once she drove back to the Windcrest, it was no fun lugging the bags of groceries back and forth from the car to her apartment. When she finally accomplished this, she stashed her purchases, took off her clothes—everything she'd been wearing felt dank—and slipped on a deep red housecoat.

She was brewing a cup of tea when that knock at the door came again, and she swallowed hard. Hugh? It could be Cynthia or Rod or Mark or Althea or a number of other people, she reminded herself.

But it *was* Hugh, and he looked even more tired than he had when she'd seen him earlier in the day.

"I'm getting to be a pest," he said by way of introduction. "But I have a hell of a headache, and I can't find an aspirin anywhere."

"Come in," she invited.

He took the aspirin she proffered. "I'd suggest a drink, but you really shouldn't, not right after taking aspirin. If you'd go for a cup of tea..."

"I'd love a cup of tea, Donna," he replied frankly. "I'd like to just sit down and look at you, for that matter. That color's terrific on you," he added, indicating her housecoat. "It puts a glow in your cheeks."

He was following her into the kitchen as he spoke, and he pulled up a chair at the kitchen table then sat down and propped his elbows on the tabletop. "You're a sight for sore eyes. I've been looking at so damned many columns of facts and figures I can't see straight. Brent and Jim don't seem to be operating on the same wavelength with each other, and neither of them is operating on the same wavelength with me, which is rare. We seldom disagree about the methods to be followed."

Donna was standing near the stove, waiting for the water to boil. "I suppose the ultimate decision is yours?"

"Yes, it is, but I'm not damned fool enough to listen only to myself. There are a lot of factors to be considered. The Cape sand presents a special problem. There's a granular quality to it, it's constantly shifting and sliding. The ship has dug into it, and the longer it stays here the more of a sand buildup there's bound to be."

He managed a tired grin that tugged at Donna, bringing out all sorts of long suppressed instincts in her. She yearned to comfort him, to hold him close to her, all of which sounded very motherly. But she knew only too well that the last thing in the world she would wish for was to be a mother to this man.

She wanted to be with him. She wanted him. Desire flared, and she drew back from it, forcing herself to concentrate on making the tea.

"Forgive me for burdening you with my problems," Hugh said. "You're good to talk to, do you know that? Good to talk to, good to look at..." His voice trailed off as he stirred sugar into his tea.

He was only too well aware of Donna's reaction to him, and he knew from long, hard experience that this was not something he should encourage. She was a very attractive woman, and right now it was heaven to be with her, letting him lean back and be comfortable and talk out his worries with her. But it was idiotic to have come right out and told her so.

He had met a wide variety of women in his time, and he knew intuitively that Donna was a very decent person. It would be wrong to take advantage of her, yet such an easy thing to do. She stirred him...hell, he'd be a liar not to admit to himself that she stirred him more than any other woman had. But that fact alone gave its own warning.

The last thing he needed right now was a serious involvement with a woman. For that matter, he never needed serious involvements with women and usually went to great lengths to avoid them. Serious relationships and the career he'd chosen for himself didn't mix.

One woman at a time was enough, and sometimes more than enough, he thought ironically. And right now the woman in his life was the *Portia*. As the day had progressed Hugh had come close to thinking he'd made a real mistake in bidding for her. He was as confident about his ability to salvage her as he'd been about each of the jobs he'd taken on over the course of his career, it wasn't that. But he'd been working too hard for too long, and he needed a break. If he'd had even a month's respite between the African job and this one he would have been in much better shape to handle things. As it was, he'd had less than two weeks away from a shipwreck scene.

His work was intensely demanding both physically and mentally, and it was the kind of work that took a hard emotional toll. He was thankful he hadn't made many wrong decisions in the course of his career, but the few he had made had been costly. He'd learned a great deal from each error, but every time he made a mistake it reflected upon the lives and fortunes of others, as well as himself.

"I guess I'm getting cautious in my old age," he said aloud, and Donna smiled.

"Your old age, Hugh?"

"I'm almost thirty-eight."

"Hardly ancient," she scoffed.

"How old are you, Donna?"

"Twenty-eight."

"There's nearly a decade between us," he said rather glumly, and she laughed.

"What a way to phrase it. Age is a very relative thing. At least I've always felt so. It depends so much on attitude, on the way a person looks at life. I should think your work, with all its excitement, would be enough to keep you young."

He shook his head. "Right now I feel it's my work that's about to make me old."

"Is the *Portia* going to be that much of a problem, Hugh?"

"I honestly don't know. It's too soon to say. I stepped into this thing very quickly," he admitted, "principally because I was just a few miles from the scene, so I got on it a lot faster than I normally would have. Often the shipowners will order their insurance company to hire a salvage consultant to look things over and decide what's to be done. In this case they accepted my bid because I was here. I've built up a reputation in my field, and they trusted my appraisal."

"Do you just roam around, Hugh?"

He looked puzzled. "What do you mean?"

"You said you don't really have a home," she reminded him. "Am I to take it you don't have an office, either?"

"I've misled you," he said lightly. "I'm president of MacDonough, Inc., and our offices are in Boston, Donna. I have a condo on Beacon Hill, a small one. It's really just a studio apartment, and I've never thought of it as my home. It's just a place to put my head between jobs and consultations. Matter of fact, I sublet it when I went to Africa and it's still occupied. That's why I was glad to have Charlie Evans's place to go to."

"I see." What he was saying made him seem more than ever a man without ties. Thirty-seven, and he appeared to have gotten through life thus far without making any real commitments. She wondered how strong his bond to his mother had been. Apparently he'd sold the family home in New Hampshire without any particular regrets after his mother had died. She was trying to remember if he'd told her he was an only child, as she was, and she thought he had. His father had died when he was quite young, and he'd gone off to be educated in private boys' schools.

Summing up the little she knew about Hugh MacDonough, Donna realized it would be easy to conclude that he was lonely and starved for affection. But was this really so? He struck her as the type of person who would go after affection if it ranked very high on his list of priorities.

Brimming over with questions, wishing she could suddenly come to know a great deal more about him, she was startled when Hugh pushed back his chair and stood up.

"I'd better get going," he said.

"Back to work?"

He stirred restlessly. "No. I've had it for today. I'd only botch up anything else I did. I'm tabling my powers of concentration, such as they are, until tomorrow." His smile was weary. "Have you heard the very latest about the *Portia*?"

"I'm not sure. I've heard so much."

"Well, Brent Hancock went uptown a while ago and he came back and told us the latest word is that since we're not going to be able to get her off the beach she's going to be sold to a hotel concern. They're either going to make a big restaurant or a motel or a combination of both out of her. Someone suggested a gambling casino, but the opinion was that the Massachusetts laws wouldn't bend that far.''

"I heard that," Donna admitted. She saw him run a hand over his forehead and asked, "How's your headache?"

"Better. I think what I need is to go get something to eat. It occurs to me that I skipped lunch today. As I think I've told you, I have a tendency to forget about everything else once I start working on a job.''

Donna hesitated only briefly. "I was going to put together a meat loaf for dinner. I know that doesn't sound very exciting, but I'd be happy to have you share it with me.''

"Never invite me to do anything with you unless you really want me, Donna," Hugh advised her, "because my answer will always be yes.''

THAT NIGHT, for the first time in a long while, Donna wished she had a house with a lot of charm and a wood-burning fireplace. She wanted to be able to sit in front of a blazing hearth with Hugh as they shared predinner drinks and snacks, with beautiful music filtering in the background.

As it was, she had to settle for candles on the kitchen table, and she found an FM station on the radio that didn't interrupt the records they played with too many commercials.

She decided not to change out of the red hostess coat but added some crystal earrings and flat silver sandals and a dash of Giorgio. Her inner excitement brought a special light to her eyes as she waited for Hugh.

It was still pouring outside when he arrived, and the wind moaned softly as it gusted around the motel.

Knowing his preference for Scotch, she'd made Rob Roys and served them in the living room, bringing in a platter of hot hors d'oeuvres to go along with them.

Hugh was wearing beige cord slacks and a deep blue chamois shirt, and maybe it was her imagination, but Donna thought he looked more rested.

He was definitely more relaxed as they sipped their drinks, and before long he started talking about places he'd been, things he'd done, stories that fascinated Donna.

Locked together in the intimacy of the motel-apartment with the second northeaster expending itself around them, listening to the beat of the rain and the keening of the wind, it was easy to imagine they were all by themselves, alone in their space with the rest of the world beyond their borders.

Donna found herself watching the play of expressions on Hugh's face as he talked. A slow sensual feeling began to build in her, and she had to force herself to pay attention to what Hugh was saying.

The buildup started at the very core of her, radiating outward until she was possessed by a tantalizing need for this man. She shifted restlessly, unable to sit still.

As she watched him she became aware of the sprinkling of reddish hairs on the back of his large, beautifully formed hands, and of the latent strength about him. He exuded such a blend of physical and mental power, confidence and knowledge, that right now he looked as if he could move the *Portia* off the beach all by himself.

Donna's eyes traveled over his body, and she felt a warm flush rising with the tide of her desire for him, suffusing her, making her hot yet leaving in its wake a funny, shivery feeling.

"Why are you staring at me, Donna?" Hugh asked suddenly, and she couldn't answer him. She was sitting on one end of the couch, he on the other. Instinctively she'd kept a distance between them, but now he bridged it. Carefully he pried her fingers apart to release her cocktail glass, then put the glass down on the coffee table. Gently, very gently, he touched the hollow of her throat and said softly "I can feel your pulse beating."

His fingers moved to caress her neck, then he cupped her chin in his hand, looking deep into her eyes. "You do want me, don't you?"

She nodded mutely, mesmerized, knowing she was falling under his spell but having no wish to resist him. On the contrary, she wanted him desperately.

"I think we've both been stalling ever since the day we met—for our own reasons—but I don't think the reasons hold anymore, Donna. There's something very special between us. You do know that, don't you?"

Again she nodded mutely. Yes, she knew that. Whatever might happen between the two of them, this was their time. It might be their only time, she knew, but she was willing to take the chance. This moment belonged to Hugh and to her, and she was not going to let it slip away.

She moved closer to him, cupping her hands behind his head, letting her fingers plunge deeply into his thick hair as she pulled his head down until she could meet his lips with hers. Her kiss was an affirmation, and he drank hungrily of what she had to offer.

The coffee table in front of them became an obstacle. They rose together, moving away from it, locked in each other's embrace. Passion flared through Donna as her senses reached a point of no return. They moved to her bedroom, which was lighted only by a small lamp with a rosy shade. Donna clung to Hugh, fumbling with the buttons on his shirt, impatient to feel his flesh under her fingers.

He smiled indulgently, helping her, but as she touched him the smile died, overcome by his own urgency.

He undressed her, wanting to be slow about it, wanting to prolong every exquisite moment, but he was thankful she had on only the red hostess robe, a wisp of a bra and the skimpiest of panties. His eyes devoured her, and although women had played a role in his life for a long time he felt a need for her, and an awe, such as he'd never known before. She was so beautiful.

Again he helped her as she fumbled with the brass buckle on his belt, and then he stood before her, a proud, virile man in the prime of his life and power, and there was no more waiting.

They fused, caressing each other, and the chemistry that had been tugging at them from the very beginning became overwhelmingly potent. Donna had never been swept away like this by a man, and the experience of matching his tempo, of moving with him toward total fulfillment, was so overwhelming she was transported out of herself and into a new dimension of sheer emotion.

Hugh carried her with him to the ultimate of moments, and their sharing comprised not only fulfillment but a beauty so intense it brought tears to their eyes. The experience washed over them, a wave that gradually subsided.

Then slowly they touched, caressing each other intimately, and desire began to spiral again. This time, unhurried, was even better—better than Donna would have believed anything could ever be.

CHAPTER SIX

DONNA WANTED HUGH to stay with her that night, but remembering his earlier qualms, she wondered how their evening together was going to end.

They shared the candlelight dinner at the kitchen table, then went back into the living room with the remainder of the bottle of wine they'd opened and simply talked together.

Donna spoke more freely of her marriage to George Farrish than she had to anyone else. She wasn't ashamed to let Hugh know that for quite a while she'd been bruised by the failure of her marriage.

"It made me feel I was a failure myself," she confessed.

"Because the man was an idiot?" Hugh shook his head firmly. "I'd guarantee that you put everything you had into trying to save your marriage. You're that kind of a person."

A sad smile curved Donna's mouth. "I didn't know what to put into my marriage after a time. I certainly didn't know how to hold George. I guess it amounts to the same thing."

"You married too young," Hugh said. "Youthful marriages work for some people, they don't for others. I'm convinced that if I'd married when I was in my twenties it would never have worked. There are too many green pastures on the other side of the fence beckoning to me, and I'm not speaking solely of sexual experiences. I felt I had to do my share of living. I couldn't have been loyal to a woman, because in those years I didn't know what I wanted...."

His words drifted off, and after a moment he said reflectively, "I'm not sure I still know what I want...on a permanent basis. I've had only myself to account to for so long that it's hard to think of taking another person into constant consideration."

Donna laughed rather shortly. "I've developed the same syndrome. For five years I've had only myself to think of. I can do what I want to do, go where I want to go, eat when I want to eat, write when I want to write...."

"I don't sense any great enthusiasm in your voice when you say that."

She shrugged. "Well, like you, I'm not sure what I want. Maybe because I *was* married and it broke up, I'm even more uncertain than you are about where to go from here. I don't want to make another mistake. And how can you ever be sure?"

He looked at her speculatively. "I take it you've shied away from commitments since your divorce?"

"Yes, I have," she answered honestly.

He nodded. "I tend to run scared, too. I guess when it comes to commitments you never can be sure. It would be nice to think that if two people were meant to be with each other forever a great blinding white light would suddenly flare up so they'd know, without reservations, that what they had would last through eternity. But I doubt there are ever any real guarantees."

He spoke without cynicism, seeming merely to be making an observation. But Donna couldn't help but feel that some of his rationale must stem from experience.

At some time in his life had Hugh lost his faith in women? That sounded overly dramatic, she decided, and set the thought aside. Hugh, she suspected, was merely calling things as he saw them. At least he was honest. He'd been honest with her all along, and though the distance they'd traveled together had not been that lengthy, Donna trusted him. She *had* had an experience that had caused her to believe, deep down inside, that she could never again trust a man. She liked men, she enjoyed their company, and she was a normal, healthy woman insofar as her sexual needs were concerned. But since George she'd kept her relationships with men on a superficial level, and she'd never given herself to any man, even George, as she'd given herself to Hugh tonight.

As she thought about this, desire began to flower again, and she moved inadvertently. She wanted Hugh to stay with her tonight. She wanted him to share her bed. She wanted them to make love with the rain pelting down on the roof over their heads and the wind playing a wild melody around them.

Hesitantly she glanced across at him. They'd fallen silent, and Hugh seemed lost in his own thoughts. But her eyes drew him, and he smiled at her. "Tired?" he asked.

"Not really."

"I am," he admitted, and added reluctantly, "I'd better be getting back to my own room, Donna."

He read her disappointment and said gently, "I'm not doing what I want to do. I'm thinking of you."

Was he, Donna wondered. Could it be that he didn't want his colleagues to know he'd formed a relationship with a woman so quickly? To have escaped serious entanglement to the age of thirty-seven must have taken some doing on the part of a man like Hugh.

Donna tried to keep her tone light. "I don't sit around nights worrying about my reputation, Hugh. I became an adult a long time ago."

"I know, I know," he said. "But I wouldn't for anything in the world do anything that might backlash on you."

She felt he was putting that rather strongly, but her pride kept her from saying anything.

She went to the door with him, feeling his restraint when he kissed her good-night. He was holding back, she could sense his effort. She knew that if they went even a step farther before he left her, neither would have the willpower to resist the other.

Hugh left before she had time to put that step into action.

IT WAS STILL RAINING the next morning. Donna was sitting in front of the computer screen, jotting down notes about the *Portia* and Hugh's salvage bid and the effect the ship had had on a preseason Devon when, once again, there was a knock at the door.

Assuming it was Hugh, she quickly stored what she'd written then pulled out the disks and turned the computer off. She wasn't ready to have him see what she was doing.

Althea, not Hugh, stood on the threshold, however, and she looked distraught.

"Donna, I'm sorry," she began immediately. "I know I'm interrupting your writing, but I have to talk to you."

"You're not interrupting anything," Donna said quickly. Though her subterfuge made her feel slightly guilty, she was glad she'd switched the computer off. She would have hated for Althea, even more than Hugh, to have seen her notes on A.B.

Althea sank down on the living-room couch. "Mark insists on opening up the damned shop today, which is ridiculous. No one's going to come down here in this downpour. Anyway, I'm bushed."

Was this Althea's problem? The reason she'd trekked over here in the pouring rain? Donna doubted it, and she bided her time, waiting to hear more.

"Mark is furious at me," Althea confided after a moment. She had shrugged off her foul-weather gear but still looked damp and cold and generally miserable.

"Look," Donna suggested, "how about something hot to drink?"

"No, don't bother."

"It's no bother," Donna insisted. "Come on out to the kitchen. It seems warmer there."

The kitchen was on the protected, west side of the apartment, and it was very snug. As she put the kettle on to boil, Donna reflected that it was getting to be a habit, making coffee or tea or hot chocolate or pouring out a drink for someone who needed a particular kind of port in a storm. Until now, though, it had been Hugh to whom she'd been serving her soothing beverages.

Hugh. All she had to do was think of the man and her heart started beating to a different rhythm.

She forced her attention back to Althea. "Why is Mark so angry?" she asked, even though she suspected she already knew the answer.

"I've been fixing food for the crew on the *Portia*," Althea said, "and he doesn't think much of it. He feels there are a lot of people around town willing to pitch in and help, and he doesn't think the men need that much help any longer anyway. Maybe he's right, but what I can't explain to Mark is that this is something I've really wanted to do. It gives me a personal sense of satisfaction. I can't say I exactly feel fulfilled running the Snack Shack," she concluded bitterly.

The Seashell Snack Shack made a very good living for Althea and Mark, Donna knew that. Her friendship with Althea went back a number of years, well before Althea had gotten into the business enterprise with her brother. In those earlier years Donna had come to Devon to visit Joe and Mabel Brucker and had met the young Nickersons. She and Althea had liked each other from the start, and they'd kept up with each other since. Donna had long known all about Mark's failed romance and his reaction to it. She hated to see Althea displaying the same kind of bitterness.

It occurred to her that Althea and Mark were too involved with each other. They lived in the big old Nickerson homestead in the Heights section of town, an area about a mile up the beach from the Windcrest Motor Inn, where the houses sat atop high dunes overlooking the Atlantic. Many of these places had originally been sprawling, wood-frame summer "cottages," the cottages actually being very large houses, with wide verandas offering the best of all possible views. Mark and Althea's house had originally been a summer home for the Melville Nickersons, who had moved to Boston at one point, where their branch of the family had originated, then had bought property back on the Cape once they'd prospered.

Mark and Althea had been fairly young when they'd lost their parents, and for a time an elderly aunt had presided in the family home. But Aunt Beth had died quite some years ago, and Mark and Althea lived alone.

They were with each other too much, Donna thought. Sharing the same home, the same business. Even husbands and wives seldom were able to do that successfully.

She found herself wishing that someone would stumble into the Seashell Snack Shack with whom Mark would fall violently in love. Violently? It would have to be reasonably violent, she thought with an inner smile, or Mark would pass off a potential candidate for his affections as quickly as he did most things.

Feeling something of a fraud, because she was sure she knew exactly why Mark felt as he did, she asked Althea, "Why does Mark object to your helping out the *Portia*'s crew if you like doing it?"

"Oh, he says it's because it leaves him shorthanded at the shop," Althea retorted, "but I don't buy that. I've done the cooking in my own house. Our house," she amended angrily. "Damn it, there are moments when I wish our family had left it either to Mark or to me, but not to both of us. We're hooked to each other financially through the house, through our business..."

Donna pulled the kettle off the stove, turned the stove off, then got two wineglasses and filled them with a liberal quantity of sherry.

Althea raised her eyebrows. "At this hour?"

"Sure," Donna said. "Look, Althea, Mark's had quite a bit on his plate since the *Portia* came aground. He wasn't ready to open for business. He—"

"You don't have to defend him," Althea interrupted. "I know Mark's a good person, Donna, and I love him very much. I just feel so...hemmed in sometimes, that's all. And this whole thing with the *Portia* has made me realize how chained I am."

"We're all chained, to a point," Donna said quietly.

"You're not," Althea retorted. "I'd say you're as free as anyone I've ever known, and I envy you."

She was free, Donna admitted, but the admission didn't bring with it any particular sense of joy. Her parents had never tried to chain her. They lived their own lives. Her father was still active in business and her mother was a prototype club woman. They had a good rapport, she enjoyed visiting them now and then, but invariably when she got back to her West End Avenue apartment in Manhattan she was glad she had her own space.

She'd been married to George Farrish for nearly four years, though, so she knew what Althea meant. The difference was that she'd been legally and morally bound to George. A brother was a different matter.

"Does Mark ever date?" she asked suddenly.

Althea, preoccupied, looked up surprised. "Mark? Whatever makes you ask that?"

"I just wondered."

"Mark's a woman hater, didn't you know? He was burned, and he vowed he'd never again put his trust in a female. He's lived with his pledge for quite a while now, and I can't see him turning out as anything but a sour old bachelor. I just don't want to be a sour old maid.''

Donna laughed. Althea was very pretty, and a certain charm and a wistful quality went along with her blond loveliness. "I don't think you have anything to worry about."

"Don't you?" Althea's beautiful brown eyes were bleak. "My Aunt Beth lived with Mark and me for years after our parents died. You remember her, don't you?"

Donna nodded. Beth Nickerson could have posed for a Norman Rockwell portrait of a typical New England spinster.

"Well, the house was always ours, but she was given a life tenancy in it—I think that's the legal term. I suppose maybe if she'd lived I would have had more chance to get away. As it is..."

Donna eyed her curiously. "Are you saying you feel responsible for Mark?"

"I suppose in a way I do," Althea admitted. "He can be so helpless sometimes, despite that hard shell of his. But then so can most men, wouldn't you say?"

Was Hugh MacDonough ever helpless? The adjective didn't apply to him, Donna decided, and she found herself wishing that it did, at least once in a while.

"I wish the damned rain would stop," Althea said irritably. "That might help. This weather's getting on my nerves."

Althea had been born and bred on Cape Cod, where this kind of weather was not all that unusual. But Donna wasn't about to point that out.

She saw that Althea had drained her sherry, but she wasn't about to pour another glass of wine for them.

Already the off-hour indulgence had made her feel slightly giddy.

"I guess I'd better get over to the shack," Althea said reluctantly.

In the doorway she turned. "I wish the *Portia* had picked some other beach to get wrecked on. I wish the damned ship had never come here." She considered her words briefly, then shook her head. "No, I don't mean that. Actually, I wish it would stay here forever."

She forced a smile. "Don't mind me, Donna. I guess Mark's right. I have been working too hard."

"Look," Donna said, "I can take over at the shack for you today if you like, and you can go home and get some rest. There isn't going to be much business anyway, unless the rain stops."

"It's okay," Althea said, and started out.

Donna stood in the doorway, watching her go. Then her eyes roved toward the opposite end of the motor inn, and she stiffened.

Hugh was walking along under the roof overhang with a tall, slim woman who looked like a fashion plate in a belted beige raincoat. Donna caught a glimpse of coppery curls and a cameo complexion, and she had no problem diagnosing the feeling that suddenly twisted deep inside her.

Jealousy. Pure, unadulterated jealousy. There was no other word for it.

At that instant Hugh glanced up and waved cheerfully, and Donna decided she'd like to strangle him. He look complacent, completely at ease, in command of himself as always, and perfectly happy, which was the worst of all.

She nodded somewhat formally and went back into her apartment, but a moment later she was at the window again, peering out at the parking lot.

Hugh and the woman were walking toward a small beige compact. The woman had thrust a hood over her head that was the same color as the car, and she walked like a model, with an easy confidence.

She slid in behind the wheel, and Hugh leaned over to talk to her through the front window. He was bareheaded, but he didn't seem to mind getting his hair wet.

There was absolutely no reason to feel so sick at heart because Hugh had been spending some time with another woman. Donna chided herself for her childishness, but a sore spot developed in the center of her chest and it wouldn't go away.

Turning away from the window she decided there was no point in going back to the computer with the idea of jotting down impressions. She doubted if she could concentrate on putting the alphabet down in correct order.

After a time, restless and hating her own company, she got in her car and drove over to Hyannis. She browsed around in the Cape Cod Mall, then put in a couple of hours in a cinema, watching a movie she'd never particularly wanted to see and didn't enjoy any more than she would have expected.

When she got back to her apartment, she discovered a sheet of white typing paper folded in half and tacked to the door.

Hugh's writing was exactly the way she would have imagined it to be: big and bold, slightly slanting, very masculine and self-assured.

"I have a tremendous hankering for Chinese food," he had written. "I'll be in my unit. Give me a buzz if you share the mood, will you? I'll wait till I hear from you."

Donna felt like a schoolgirl who'd just been given an unexpected holiday. She restrained herself long enough to take off her raincoat and kick off her shoes before she called him. But she doubted very much if she could have held off a second longer.

He answered on the first ring, and it occurred to her that he must have been sitting practically on top of the phone.

"I'll bet you know how to use chopsticks," she accused when he said hello.

"I'm an expert. How about you?"

"I tried to eat with them once and I nearly starved to death."

"I can teach you in one easy lesson how to be so proficient you'll even be able to cut up your egg roll," he promised. "Rainy nights always seem to bring out a yen for Chinese food in me. Does this mean you share the yen?" he added teasingly.

"I could make a bad joke out of that," Donna warned. "But it's the Japanese who call their money 'yen.'"

"But there are many kinds of yens, dear Donna. For example—" his voice lowered "—I haven't been able to get you off my mind for an instant. It's like having a video turned on right in front of me with the screen filled entirely with you. I had a hell of a time trying to figure out some relatively simple things with Brent and Jim. Then—" He broke off. "We can catch up on the details of our respective day when I see you."

He called for her fifteen minutes later, bringing his car up to the edge of the sidewalk right in front of her apartment. It was still raining hard, but Donna couldn't have cared less about the weather. She scampered down the sidewalk and smiled up at him as she slid into the right bucket seat.

"Where were you?" he asked as they started off. "I was trying to reach you off and on all afternoon."

"I went over to Hyannis to a movie."

"By yourself?"

"Yes."

"I wish you'd called me. I would have played hooky. I would have been glad to play hooky. I couldn't get down to anything today. I gave an interview to a reporter from the *Boston Globe* and if she quotes me accurately I'm going to sound like an idiot."

She. Had *she* been coppery haired and fair skinned?

"This girl—her name is Terry O'Connor, incidentally—is staying in Devon," Hugh told her. "She's been assigned to follow our progress with the ship. I told her it may be quite a while before she gets much copy. It takes time to mount a salvage operation. So meanwhile she's going to fill in with interviews. She plans to talk to Alex Bruce tomorrow and that should make a good story. Have you met Bruce?"

"No."

"He's an interesting guy. Scottish. A highly experienced mariner. What happened to the *Portia* was plain bad luck, but he's worried that some of the blame may be attributed to him. The fact of the matter, as I well know, is that sometimes these shipowners—particularly those operating with foreign registrations—sail the ships to death. They don't keep them up the way they should, they don't make repairs when they should be made. They don't want the ships to put up in dry dock, they want them at sea making money. The *Portia* is certainly a case in point. Her radar wasn't working and her radio went out. The Coast Guard does its best to keep an eye on the ships in our waters, but they can't monitor the world. Anyhow..."

Hugh smiled across at her. "I don't intend to spend this night talking shop with you. Was it a good movie?"

She smiled back at him. "No. Matter of fact it wasn't. Matter of fact it was terrible."

He laughed, and Donna loved the sound of his laugh. Like the rest of Hugh, it was free and uninhibited and rang clear.

IT WAS GETTING HARDER and harder for Donna and Hugh to say good-night to each other. He came back to her apartment after dinner and for a time they watched a hockey game on television.

Donna had never been much of a sports enthusiast, and hockey was totally unfamiliar to her. But Hugh swiftly explained the rudiments of the game in a way that made her understand what was going on, and then he caught her up with him in his enthusiasm for the sport.

As a child growing up, Donna had always been encouraged more toward cultural than physical activities. She had been exposed to the opera, the symphony, the ballet, good literature, art, New York's museums—the list was a long one. But she knew nothing of baseball or football or any of the other sports that captured the interest of millions of Americans on a regular basis.

Hugh, on the other hand, obviously knew a great deal about a great many things. She admired his versatility and was a little envious of it. She felt that in comparison she must seem awfully dull.

But at least she caught on fast, Donna consoled herself. Tonight she'd learned to eat with chopsticks, and by the time the final quarter of the hockey game had been played she was becoming as excited as Hugh every time the goalie on "their" team deflected the puck.

The game came to an end, and Donna groaned inwardly. The situation between them was becoming awkward. The proximity of their living quarters was actually hindering rather than helping them, especially since five of Hugh's men were now living at the other end of the motor inn.

Donna was as conscious as he was of the presence of Brent Hancock and Jim Babson and the others. There was no doubt that having them so near was inhibitive. Also, she reminded herself, for all the potent chemistry flowing between the two of them, she and Hugh were still strangers. Each time she was with him she felt she knew him better, but "better" wasn't nearly enough.

"I'd better be off," he said now, slowly.

Donna appreciated his obvious reluctance because it matched her own, yet she felt curiously restrained. She couldn't bring herself to try to do anything that might keep him with her.

It seemed crazy that a man with whom you'd scaled the heights of passion only the night before could simply bend down and give you an almost brotherly good-night kiss, she thought ruefully. But that was the way it was, and after Hugh had left, Donna chided herself for having been so nonaggressive. She had her share of feminine wiles, and tonight she should have pulled out a few of them.

She dreamed about Hugh that night, fantastic dreams that could have been background for a science-fiction story. She and Hugh were far away in another world. There was no one near them, yet in the background she kept hearing the unending rote of the sea, its roar falling on her ears like a message of disaster.

Donna woke up, her pulse pounding. The rain had stopped but the sound of the sea was real enough. Windswept, the water thundered onto the beach, its echo vibrating in the night.

Normally it was a sound Donna loved, but tonight it frightened her, and it was a long time before she could get back to sleep again.

CHAPTER SEVEN

WHEN DONNA AWAKENED the next morning the sun was shining. She wasted no time in putting on some warm clothes and heading for the beach.

This time she turned away from the *Portia* once she'd reached the hard-packed sand and walked north. The dunes to her left became steadily higher as she moved along, giving her the illusion that she was alone in a world made up of sand mountains and an endless sea.

The tide was coming in, and once or twice Donna had to scamper quickly to avoid the swirling water. She knew it would be cold, very cold. The ocean temperature hereabouts was seldom much above sixty, even in midsummer.

The air was fresh and cool, and she could taste the salt on her lips. As she walked at a steady, even pace, she tried to put her thoughts in order. During that long, wakeful spell last night it had occurred to her that her aunt and uncle would be returning to the Windcrest in only a couple weeks. It would be time for her to move out of their apartment, then time for her to go back to New York.

Time to say goodbye to Hugh?

She hoped not.

In any case, she couldn't expect to stay on in the apartment once her aunt and uncle returned to Devon.

It was their residence, and there wasn't room for three people, especially when one of them was attempting to write a book.

She'd marked time after coming to Devon. The days had dragged and she'd felt so stagnant. But since the *Portia* had been cast up on the beach, all that had changed. Now she felt as if she was in a race with the clock.

The clock! Donna glanced at her watch. She'd come out here on the late side this morning, and her conscience was beginning to needle her. Right now she should be facing up to that blank screen.

As she started back, the *Portia* was on her visual horizon, and she found herself thinking about its captain and the embryo plot in which she'd enbroiled him.

What sort of fictional contraband could the ship have been carrying? Drugs? Jewels? Military secrets on microfilm?

She worked her way through a variety of possibilities and didn't like any of them. By that time she'd reached the path that went past the Snack Shack. Mark was opening up for the day and she stopped to speak to him.

"Want some help later?" she offered.

He grinned. "I'm not about to say no. Althea will have my head, though. She says we're keeping you from your book."

"On the contrary," Donna told him, "I'm soaking up atmosphere when I work here. Tell Althea it will all be put to good use."

"You're planning to write a book about the *Portia*?" Mark asked.

"Who knows?" Donna retorted lightly. But Mark's question crystallized something that had been nagging at her. "Suppose I come over just before the lunch hour?" she suggested.

"That would be great, Donna, if you really feel you can spare the time."

"I'll be here," she promised.

As she went back to her apartment, Donna felt a curious sense of exhilaration. She sat down in front of the computer and programmed in the impressions she'd been making about the shipwreck and Alex Bruce and...yes...Hugh, as well. Then, without reading over what she'd already done, she let her thoughts flow.

She still wasn't sure what sort of contraband she wanted the *Portia* to be carrying, but she didn't want it to be anything big in size. She wanted Alex Bruce to have something on board the ship that could represent a real danger when she was wrecked.

Donna paused at this point. A danger to what? To Alex? To the ship? To the crew? To the environment?

If the *Portia*'s hull had leaked, there would have been an oil spill that could have done considerable environmental damage. Hugh had pointed that out. She suspected that everyone involved with the ship, the Coast Guard, the Devon town officials, as well as the salvors, had been even more deeply relieved than Hugh had indicated once the diesel fuel had been pumped off.

Suppose the contraband was something radioactive, which, if released, could present a major hazard to all of Cape Cod, maybe even the whole New England coast?

Donna let her imagination roam but she was hampered in pinpointing this phase of her plot by her own lack of technical knowledge. She wondered briefly if she might be getting into the realm of science fiction, which wasn't her field. But, no, radioactivity was a real threat, and there was not anything particularly futuristic about it.

I'm going to have to do my homework, Donna told herself, and then sat stock-still.

She *was* going to write a book about the *Portia.* A mystery. What had started out as some idle fun, spurred partially by the need to do something—anything—that would help cure her case of writer's block, had turned into an exciting challenge.

More motivated than she had been about anything for a long time, Donna went to the phone and called her agent.

Rebecca van Horton was not overwhelmingly enthusiastic when Donna outlined her plan to her.

"You already have an extension on *Knifepoint,*" she reminded her client.

"I know, I know, and I'll get back to it," Donna promised impatiently. "But you know I've gone stale on that story, Becky. I've been trying to get myself into gear on it for weeks now, and nothing's worked. This...well, I'm so excited about it, I'm brimming over with it."

Becky van Horton was in her late forties and had been a successful New York agent for twenty years. She was a sophisticated woman who had seen many writers come and go, and she was only too familiar with the fragile egos most of her clients possessed. It was easy to kill an idea that could turn into a very good book at the inception simply by making a wrong remark. But Donna Madison was a professional. She'd weathered her share of rejections in her early days, and generally speaking it was possible to talk to her frankly.

Becky sighed. "Donna, you're getting yourself into something with this radioactive bit. You're going to have to do a lot of research, make sure of your facts. There are Ph.D.s in science all over the place, and if you're not absolutely accurate your publisher will be inundated with nasty letters and—"

"You're saying this isn't my kind of thing, is that it, Becky?" Donna interrupted.

"I'm saying I want you to be sure you really want to do this before I start talking to your publisher about your change in plans," her agent stated firmly.

"I want to do it," Donna retorted, equally firm.

Becky sighed again. "Okay. Send me down an outline of what you have in mind, and I'll try to take it from there."

Donna became so absorbed in getting a basic plot line down on the computer that she had to tear herself away from the apartment at quarter to twelve to go over to the shack.

Walking across the parking lot she almost wished she hadn't promised Mark to help out today. She wanted to get down as much as she could about her proposed story, and to do a separate profile on the character of her villain, who would be Alexander Bruce under another name.

It was a shock to see the real Bruce standing at the counter sipping coffee. Donna let herself in the side door, slipped on an apron, then made her way up to the counter to report in to Mark, but it was all she could do not to stare at Alex Bruce. She wanted to drink in everything about him she possibly could.

He was freshly shaved and looked more rested, and he'd combed his black hair. He was a very attractive man, but there was a strange intensity about him that was communicable. It bothered her.

The lunch crowd was beginning to descend, and Donna was forced to get busy taking orders. But she knew now that she had to meet Alex Bruce, talk to him, get to know something about him. She also knew that there was no way she could leave Devon when her aunt and uncle came back to take over at the Windcrest.

For as long as the *Portia* remained stranded on the beach, she was committed to this locale.

BRENT HANCOCK AND JIM BABSON both stopped by for hamburgers and french fries at noon, but Hugh didn't. As she served them, Brent told her, "Hugh's gone up to Boston. He had a chance to hitch a ride with that reporter from the *Globe*. She had to report in to her office."

Donna was glad that a new wave of people swept in at that moment, so she didn't have to make a reply.

She remembered that Hugh had said the *Globe* reporter was going to interview Alex Bruce. She'd have to start getting the paper to read Terry O'Connor's stories, she decided.

By two o'clock the major rush had slacked off, and once again the parking lot looked like a carnival scene. A lot of people had brought their own picnics along with them, and those with station wagons were having tailgate parties. A small concession had been set up in front of the bandstand where concerts were held in summer, and a brisk business was being conducted in the sale of souvenir items. Children were running around wearing *Portia* T-shirts, which by now were being offered in every color of the rainbow. Another enterprising vendor was selling *Portia* balloons.

Surveying this, Mark said, "There's no end to it. I'd almost be willing to give up making the extra money if they'd all go home."

Donna grinned. "I notice you said 'almost,'" she teased.

He laughed. "It's that inherent Yankee thriftiness. I can't wash it out of my system. Have you had anything to eat?"

Donna had been so busy she hadn't thought about food. She was also still possessed by that inner excitement about her story idea, and, in its way that was food itself.

"Not yet," she said.

"I'll broil you up a special Nickerson burger," Mark promised, and he did. He added chopped onions and a variety of seasonings to a large hamburger patty, and the result was delicious.

Munching it, Donna said, "No matter what you say, Mark, this is a great experience." She was looking out at the crowded parking lot and watching a bright red balloon that had suddenly become airborne. "I don't expect any of us will ever see anything quite like it again."

"I don't think I'd ever want to," Mark replied. At the moment there were no customers and he was sipping a Coke. "That woman from the *Globe* wants to interview me."

"What great publicity!"

"Yeah, I suppose so," Mark said diffidently. "I don't know. Most of the time we don't even need any publicity. The crowds come by themselves."

"It never hurts to promote your name when you're in business," Donna insisted.

"I guess you're right. That's what Althea says."

"Where is Althea?" Donna asked. It had been a while since Althea had been around. She'd left almost immediately after the major lunch-hour rush.

"She's gone over to Hyannis to get some stuff," Mark said.

Donna wanted to ask whether Althea was still cooking for the *Portia*'s crew but she decided to table the question, knowing it was a sore subject with Mark.

After a time he said, "There's no point in your hanging around here any longer, Donna. I can handle the stragglers from now on. Look..."

She turned to him. "Yes."

"Althea and I really appreciate what you're doing," Mark said simply. "We mostly hire college kids to work in the summers, I guess you know that. That's one reason why we usually close earlier in the fall than we'd like to. Once the kids go back to school, help is hard to come by. We would have been out flat if you hadn't pitched in as you have. Have you counted up how many hours you've put in here?"

Donna shook her head. "No."

"Neither have I," Mark admitted ruefully. "And the thing of it is...well, I told Althea the least we could do was pay you or something."

"You don't need to pay me, Mark," Donna told him. "I'll keep coming over and helping out as long as you need me. There's one thing, though..."

"Yes?"

"Well," Donna said, "you could do me a favor. I think I'm going to look for a place to stay."

He frowned. "You're moving out of the Windcrest?"

"Aunt Mabel and Uncle Joe will be back from Florida soon," Donna explained. "I'd planned to leave once they returned, but…well, I want to stay and see this through, Mark." She nodded in the direction of the ship.

"Wouldn't your uncle let you have one of the units in the Windcrest?"

"I'm sure he would, but they're not equipped for housekeeping, and I need more space than that anyway. I was wondering if you or Althea might know of a cottage I could rent for the next couple of months. I'd be out of it by June, so I wouldn't interfere with anyone's summer rental."

Mark grinned. "How about ours?"

"I hadn't realized you and Althea have a cottage."

"Well, actually it's a wing attached to our house by a breezeway, but it's like a separate apartment," Mark told her. "Years ago my grandmother used to live there summers when my folks came down from Boston for the season. Aunt Beth never liked the idea of renting to anyone, but after she died Althea and I fixed it up and we've been renting it summers. There's a living room, one bedroom, a kitchenette…"

Donna's eyes sparkled. "That sounds perfect, Mark."

"Then it's yours."

"I don't believe this," she said happily. "Look, we'll have to get down to the rent and the utilities and all of that—"

"No charge," Mark said firmly.

"Oh, no," Donna protested. "I couldn't accept that."

"Then I can't let you come here and help us out no matter how much we need you," Mark insisted stubbornly.

"Come on, Mark," Donna tried to appeal to him. "It's not the same thing at all, you know that."

"Althea and I are not using the apartment," Mark pointed out. "We have a rental beginning June 15. Till then it's vacant. What you'd use in utilities wouldn't amount to a fraction of what your salary would be for all your work here. And..."

Mark hesitated, and Donna asked curiously, "What is it?"

"It would be good for Althea to have you around," he said rather obliquely.

She considered this. "Well, we'll talk about it later."

The more she thought of it later, at the intervals when she got up and stretched or walked around a little to break the routine of sitting in front of the computer, the more Donna realized what a perfect solution moving into the Nickersons' cottage would be. She only wished Mark wouldn't be quite so stubborn. She wanted to pay a decent rent. That seemed only fair to her.

Late in the afternoon Althea stopped by, and her enthusiasm at the idea of having Donna as a close neighbor was enough to make Donna decide not to be stubborn herself.

Mark had been right. It would be good for Althea to have her around, for whatever reasons.

That night she went out to dinner and a movie with Rod. Back at the Windcrest again, she was aware that the far end of the motor inn was in darkness. Maybe

Hugh had stayed in Boston. If not, he and the rest of his crew were either out or asleep.

Donna went to bed counting the hours since she'd last seen him. A full twenty-four, and she'd missed him during every minute of them.

BRENT AND JIM came to the shack again for lunch the next day, and once again Hugh wasn't with them. This time they didn't say anything about him, and Donna was not about to ask. His absence was beginning to hurt.

She was startled, toward the middle of the afternoon, to hear a familiar, teasing voice ask, "How about a hot dog?"

Donna looked up into Hugh's dark gray eyes, and she started visibly.

"Hey, I didn't mean to scare you."

"You didn't scare me," she retorted quickly. "I...I just wasn't expecting you, that's all. Did you say a hot dog?"

"Yes, I said a hot dog."

As she relayed the order to Mark, Donna was aware that Hugh was watching her closely. She tried to be businesslike. "Coffee?"

"No," he said deliberately. "I'll have a chocolate frappé."

Donna put together the ingredients for the milk-shake and set them whirring in the machine. She kept her back turned to Hugh, which was valid enough under the circumstances, and besides, she didn't want him to see her face.

She was running through a whole gamut of emotions, and she tried to tell herself she was overreacting.

Behind her Hugh said, "I went jogging both yesterday and this morning. I thought I might run into you."

She sensed a slight edge to his voice, and she turned toward him. "I went for a walk each morning," she said, a bit defiantly.

"I started out around six. I guess you weren't even up."

"No. No, I wasn't."

"I guess I got the idea you were an early riser from that first morning when I saw you starting out for the beach," he confessed, then grinned. "To tell you the truth, I've been setting my alarm clock so I wouldn't miss you."

His eyes caressed her. "Why are you mad at me, Donna?"

The devastating simplicity of the question made its impact, and she felt foolish. "I'm not mad at you, Hugh."

"Oh? What are you, then?"

She hesitated, then she came out with it. "I've missed you," she admitted.

She saw him draw in a sharp breath, and his mouth twisted in a peculiarly eloquent way, as if he was experiencing pain. For a brief moment, he shut his eyes. But then he relaxed, opened his eyes and looked directly at her. "Don't you think I've missed you, sweetheart?" he said gently. "You're never far away from me, Donna. I feel you all the time, at the edge of my thoughts. I told you it's hard to keep my mind on my work. That still goes. Yesterday I had to go up to Boston and I rode along with Terry O'Connor. She wanted to talk to me some more about what's going to happen next with the *Portia*, and I thought if I drove along with her it would kill two birds with one stone. I took the bus back to Hyannis and I called you. I was hoping maybe you could meet me over there and we could go out for an early dinner together. I didn't reach you, so I got hold of Brent..."

"I went up to the pharmacy," Donna remembered. "That was after I finished working here. And last night I went out to dinner."

"I knew you were out somewhere. I went over to your apartment after I got back." He looked at her pointedly. "You and I...I think we're beginning to suffer from a communication gap, Donna. We've got to do something about that."

Mark came over, bringing Hugh's hot dog personally, and the two men spoke briefly of the weather, which was very good at the moment, and of the *Portia*.

"We're going to start moving in some heavy equipment next week," Hugh told them. "I've been in conference with the selectmen and the conservation committee. It'd been decided that the best bet will be to use the entry to the beach at the far end of the parking lot that's reserved ordinarily for four-wheel-drive vehicles. As I understand it, they've already put a ban on four-wheel drives going out on the beach."

Mark nodded. "That's what I heard."

"About a quarter of the parking lot is going to be blocked off for us," Hugh continued. "We'll be using four forty-foot trucks to haul in stuff, as the plan now stands, and there'll be a lot of equipment around. As a start we'll be bringing in a front-end loader, a back hoe, welding machines, pumps, compressors..."

"The *Portia* must be dug in pretty deep at this point," Mark observed.

"You can say that again," Hugh agreed. "Each day's a drawback, as far as we're concerned, because of the sand. What's happened is that thousands of tons of sand have formed a long finger to her seaward side. Then there's a regular mountain up under her bow. I've been telling my men this is going to be as much an excavating problem as it will be a tugging one."

Hugh finished his hot dog and drank the last of the frappé. He turned the conversation to the crowds that had come to the beach, and he and Mark applauded the job the town had done in handling the sightseers. Then he said, "Well, back to the grindstone. I'll be seeing the two of you."

"Why don't you take off, Donna," Mark suggested unexpectedly. "Althea's out at the house but she'll be along shortly, and I think we've done most of our business for today. Anyway, you've been here long enough."

Donna didn't protest, but as she started across the parking lot with Hugh by her side she wished Mark had been more subtle. He seemed to be pairing her with Hugh, which was amusing in its way but also embarrassing.

Once they were out of earshot of the shop Hugh said, "Something's been worrying me, Donna, though I suppose it's none of my business. How close are you to Althea Nickerson?"

"Althea and I have known each other for ages," she replied, surprised. "We met way back in our elementary school years when I came here to visit Uncle Joe and Aunt Mabel."

"I don't like to see her getting involved with Alex Bruce," Hugh muttered.

"Oh?" Donna queried.

"I think I told you this isn't my first encounter with Bruce," Hugh continued. "We've met on other occasions in various places. I like him personally. He's an extremely interesting guy. I think I told you that, too."

"Then why are you against Althea becoming involved with him...if she is?" Donna asked.

"For one thing, he's married. He has a couple of kids, his wife lives in Glasgow. That's where Bruce is from. Also, Bruce is a man with a dark past, and I'm afraid it's never going to stop pursuing him."

Donna glanced up curiously. "What's that supposed to mean?"

"A few years back he got in some serious trouble. It involved a ship he was captaining, and some highly suspect cargo. There was a murder involved, and Bruce was implicated."

Donna couldn't believe it. Hugh was filling in her plot for her...with a true story!

"Bruce was dragged up before a marine court of inquiry. He wasn't convicted, they couldn't prove their case. But he was left with a cloud hanging over him. A lot of people thought he'd never get a job, at least not as a captain. But he wound up working for companies like the one that owns the *Portia*. The major shipping companies wouldn't touch him. Later there were rumors that he'd developed an alcohol problem. It goes that way, you know," Hugh observed. "Once a man's character is blackened—whether rightly or wrongly—people tend to try to complete the job."

"Do you think Alex Bruce was guilty?" Donna asked.

"No," Hugh said slowly. "I do happen to know that there was a hell of a lot of evidence against him, even if it wasn't enough to convict him. But I still have a gut feeling that he was telling the truth, if you want to go by that."

They had arrived at the Windcrest. "I have to work tonight, Donna," Hugh said. "Damn it, time's going to close in on me and I want so damned much to be with you. Maybe this sounds crazy to you, but do you suppose we could go for a walk on the beach in the morning and then go out to breakfast together?"

She smiled at him. "I don't see why not."

"Okay, then. You be ready by seven o'clock, all right?"

"I'll be ready."

Donna was still smiling as she went into her apartment. Tomorrow morning seemed a long way off, but she had something with which to occupy herself in the interim.

She'd already determined that in her book Hugh and Alex Bruce were going to be brothers. Alex would be injured, either at the time of the shipwreck or shortly thereafter. He'd further be devastated, psychologically, because he'd know that the wreck of the *Portia* might be all that was needed to put an end to his career, and that another marine court of inquiry might cause him to spend the rest of his life in prison.

Hugh would become determined to prove his brother's innocence. Needless to say, he would be successful.

Hugh would be her hero—Donna couldn't think of a more fascinating one—and Alex would be a victim rather than the villain. Remembering the *Portia*'s dark, intent captain as he'd stood at the shop's counter sipping coffee, Donna was far happier with this definition of his character.

She programmed in the proper disk on her computer and set to work.

CHAPTER EIGHT

THE NICKERSONS' APARTMENT could not have been more perfect for Donna. Like the main house it was gray shingled and overlooked the magnificent, deep blue North Atlantic. A wooden staircase cut down the face of the dunes to the beach, but it was surprising how distant the *Portia* looked from here. The Windcrest was only about a mile away, but in her uncle's apartment, Donna had felt as if the ship was right on top of her.

Althea took her out to see the apartment one afternoon during a lull, and she had no doubt about taking it.

"Except that I really wish you'd let me pay you something," Donna said as she and Althea were driving back to the Snack Shack in Althea's car.

"No way," Althea stated firmly. "Mark wouldn't think of it." She smiled impishly. "Let him have his way on this. It's good for him to be generous once in a while."

Donna smiled back, but she was again aware of a tension in Althea despite her outward cheerfulness, and the shadows under her brown eyes had not been there before the *Portia*'s appearance. She wondered if Althea would be moved to confide in her once they were living under the same roof, and she wasn't sure how she felt about that.

For one thing, Alex Bruce was already intertwined in her mind with his prototype in the book she was going to write, and for the sake of their friendship she didn't want to write Althea into the plot. If she knew too much of the relationship between Alex and Althea—assuming that Mark and Hugh were both right and there really was a relationship—it would be hard to keep her friend out of the story.

It would be hard anyway, Donna had to admit. She'd already paired the two mentally, and Althea as a character would work so well in the plot.

"Damn," she said under her breath, and Althea glanced across at her.

"What?"

"Nothing," Donna replied evasively. "I was just thinking, that's all. Look, maybe I could cook dinners for you and Mark."

"We're not going to get into any commitments," Althea said firmly. "If you want to cook dinners some nights and we're around, that's okay. I'm sure Mark would welcome someone else's cooking. He gets pretty tired of mine, which, I admit, isn't all that exciting. But we're not going to get down to any share-the-load schedules, Donna. That's not the purpose of this. The reason you're moving in is so that you can stay on in Devon and finish your book."

In a way that was true, but Donna felt guilty as she thought about it. Ah, yes, she was going to finish her book. Except that it would not be the book Althea was thinking about.

THERE WAS NO POINT in remaining on at the Windcrest until the Bruckers returned. Donna realized that later in the afternoon, as she was getting ready to go out for dinner with Hugh.

This time he'd had a hankering for Italian food, and it had taken little effort on his part to persuade her to try an Italian restaurant in Orleans with him.

As she was slipping on a soft turquoise wool skirt and a full, pullover blouse that belted at the waist, Donna decided it made sense to move to the Nickersons' as soon as possible. She was reaching the point where she was going to want to put in a lot of time on the book, and the sooner she was settled the better.

On an impulse she called her Uncle Joe and told him what she was contemplating.

At first he was taken aback. "There's no reason why you can't stay on at the Windcrest, Donna. Matter of fact, Mabel and I have been talking about that. You can have the apartment. We can fix up a couple of adjoining units, and Mabel says as long as she has a pot to heat some water for coffee in the morning she'll be satisfied. She doesn't get the chance to do much cooking during the season, anyway."

"I wouldn't think of that," Donna said. "I know you have to have your codfish cakes and beans every Saturday night and Aunt Mabel's the only one who can fix them the way you like them. So don't tell me you don't need a kitchen."

"I'm not that much of a traditionalist," Joe protested, but he was laughing as he spoke.

By the time Donna had finished talking with him, she'd convinced him that it was a good idea for her to make the move. And, she reminded him, they'd only be a mile apart.

It wasn't until she'd hung up the receiver that she started thinking about that mile.

It would be the distance separating her from Hugh, and she wasn't sure whether that would be to their mutual advantage or disadvantage. She found herself hating to tell him that she was going to be leaving the Windcrest, and she decided not to go into the subject until they'd had their dinner and were on their way back to the motor inn.

La Gioconda was typically Italian in atmosphere, with clusters of empty Chianti bottles in baskets competing with plants for decoration, lots of red and green and white in the color scheme, and Venetian murals adorning the walls.

"I feel like someone should break into strains of 'O Sole Mio,'" Hugh observed once they were seated.

It was a pleasant ambience and their waitress was obliging. Hugh ordered wine and an antipasto for two, then he leaned back in the booth they were sharing and rubbed his eyes.

"Too much paperwork," he admitted. "I tend to be farsighted, and I guess the time has come when I need glasses for close-up stuff."

"Why don't you get your eyes examined?" Donna suggested practically.

"It's one of the things I keep putting off."

"Now I suppose you'll be so busy you won't have time to make an appointment?" she chided.

He grinned sheepishly. "I'll try to remember to phone an optometrist tomorrow. Cynthia Doane should be able to recommend someone. She seems to know everyone around here."

"She does," Donna assured him. "That's why Uncle Joe has so much faith in her."

The subject arose much sooner than Donna wanted it to, as Hugh asked, "Won't Joe and Mabel be getting back here pretty soon?"

"Late next week," she answered, which was what her uncle had told her.

She was staring at her napkin, still folded on the table, as she said this, and Hugh got the wrong impression.

"You're not going to leave once they get here, are you, Donna?" he asked, and was surprised at the anxiety he felt as he waited for her to answer. He didn't like to even think about Donna leaving Devon. The thought had occurred to him way back that maybe she'd have to give up the apartment when the Bruckers returned, but he had thrust it aside. Now he faced how much he wanted her to be there while he was salvaging the *Portia*. For the first time in his life, he felt he needed someone else's moral support.

He also wanted more than moral support from Donna. Each time he'd left her at night to go back to his lonely, empty motel unit, he'd upbraided himself for being a fool. Yet he'd been sincere in telling her that he didn't want his men to think they were having an affair. The men he worked with were like himself in many ways. Men who'd traveled the world, living in all kinds of places, meeting all kinds of people. Brent Hancock had been married and divorced twice. Jim Babson had waited till he was in his forties before he married, and his wife was nearly twenty years younger than he was. Hugh had met her. She was pretty but somewhat empty-headed. He couldn't blame Jim for his growing suspicion that she was fooling around with other men when he was away, which was too much of the time.

Hugh had nearly gotten married himself once, about ten years ago, but his fiancée had wanted him to give up his career and take a position in her father's Boston engineering firm. He'd been offered the post of vice-president with a plush salary. He'd turned it down, and had received his engagement ring back by messenger the next day.

He hadn't blamed Nancy. She was his age, almost twenty-eight at the time, and had her own career as a lawyer. She wanted to continue to live in Boston, where she was making a name for herself in legal circles, and wasn't willing to be tied to a husband who would be away for weeks if not months at a time. Nor was she the type who would have traveled with him, even if he'd offered to take her.

For that matter, he'd never thought of offering a woman the opportunity to go where he went, and he doubted very much if he ever would. It would be far too heavy a demand. Too many of the places in which his work was involved were well off the beaten track. Ships seldom wrecked themselves in the world's more desirable locations. The *Portia* was an exception in that respect. Hugh could think of few lovelier places than Devon, Massachusetts.

He looked at the beautiful woman sitting opposite him and wondered how he could possibly expect her to stay on here just so he could turn to her at times when he was so damned tired or discouraged that at best he'd be poor company.

What *did* he expect of her?

He had no right to expect anything. In the long run he had nothing, but nothing to offer her. Yet despite this attempt at logic it occurred to him that she was taking an awfully long time to answer his question. So long that he felt a bolt of pure fear.

Donna was going to leave. Another few days and she'd be gone. Hugh, who was so used to being a loner, wondered how he could cope with the job that faced him without Donna around.

He phrased the question differently and added a couple of new ones. "Donna, are you taking off once your aunt and uncle get back? Where are you going? New York?"

"No," she said. "I'm not going back to New York, I'm not leaving Devon. But I am moving out of the Windcrest, Hugh."

"Where to?" he demanded.

"I'm moving in with Mark and Althea," she explained. "I'm going to take over an apartment that's like a cottage, really. It's entirely separate from their house, a little place all its own. I was out there today looking it over, and I'm thrilled with it."

Hugh suddenly looked like a thundercloud, and she was perplexed. "There really isn't room in the apartment for three people, Hugh. I talked to Uncle Joe just before I met you today and he wanted me to keep the apartment. He said he and Aunt Mabel would take over a couple of units. But I'd never let them do that. Anyway, this place will be far more perfect to write in. I've enjoyed my window seat on the *Portia* and everything that's been going on, but the carnival atmosphere gets kind of distracting sometimes. I hear something and I get up to go see what it is, and that doesn't help my train of thought."

"So," Hugh said slowly, "the book is working for you again. You didn't tell me that."

The statement was close to an accusation, and she was surprised. She hesitated. The book he was referring to wasn't working at all, and she still wasn't prepared to tell him about her new project.

Before she could speak, Hugh asked, "Why are you moving in with Mark Nickerson?"

"I'm not moving in with Mark," Donna retorted promptly, taken aback by his attitude. He sounded so suspicious, almost jealous. Remembering her reaction to seeing him with Terry O'Connor the other day, she grinned. It was nice to think that in some areas they reacted the same way.

"What so funny?" he asked crossly. She wanted to go around to his side of the booth, run her fingers through his thick, dark red hair and kiss him square on the lips.

He was acting like a spoiled brat. She loved it. And in a sweeping moment she knew that she was at the edge of falling in love with him.

She wasn't prepared for the revelation. Her grin faded, and she stared at him apprehensively.

Hugh still sounded cross. "I only asked what was so funny. You don't have to look at me like I bit you."

Donna forced herself to rally, but her pulse had begun to throb. She could feel it pounding in the hollow of her throat. Her voice husky, she replied, "Nothing's funny, I guess. That is, if I didn't know better, I would have said you were jealous."

"And what makes you think you know better?"

"You're not the jealous type, Hugh." And until now she would have believed that to be true of him.

"Anyone who's able to feel an honest emotion is also capable of being jealous," Hugh said roughly. "I'll admit I'm jealous of Mark Nickerson. I have been ever since the first day I met you. You were with him down on the beach, and I thought at first the two of you were married.''

"Married. Mark and me?'' Donna laughed. "That's the silliest thing I've ever heard, Hugh. Mark's a woman hater.''

"You could fool me. He doesn't act much like a woman hater when he's around you.''

"We get along,'' she conceded. "I'll even go so far as to say that I think Mark likes me. But not in any romantic way.''

"What about this character you go out with all the time?'' Hugh persisted. "Now that we're on the subject we might as well clear the slate. What about the banker?''

"Rod? He's a friend, that's all.''

"That's all? What's your definition of friendship, Donna?''

The waitress had placed the antipasto platter between them and provided them each with a plate, but Hugh ignored the food.

Donna reached over and speared an anchovy with her fork, stalling for time. "I can't come up with a definition of something like friendship on the spur of the moment, Hugh.''

"No? You're a writer,'' he challenged. "Writers are supposed to be good with words, aren't they?''

"There's a difference between writing professionally and...and defining relationships,'' she hedged.

His next question startled her. "Are you moving out of the Windcrest because of me, Donna?''

"No,'' she said quickly. "Why should you imagine such a thing?''

"Well, I've interrupted you at times when I suppose you were working, or thinking about working. I told you I was afraid I was becoming a pest."

Hugh had been direct with her in the past. Now Donna was direct with him.

"What's the matter, Hugh?"

He stared at her for a moment, and his eyes were almost the color of charcoal, reminding her of clouds on the Cape on a stormy day. Then his lips twisted in a wry smile and he said frankly, "I don't want you to go, that's all."

"I'm not really going anywhere," she reminded him. "The Nickersons' house is only a mile from the Windcrest."

"You'll be going away from *me*," he pointed out. "Oh, I don't mean to sound like a damned fool, but having you close...it's meant a lot to me, Donna. And my work in Devon is just beginning. These next few weeks are going to be rough." There was a bitter-sweetness to his smile that tugged at Donna's heart.

"I guess I just wanted to know you were there," he admitted. He tried to change his tone. "That's the second anchovy you've eaten. I'm surprised you like them, so many people don't. I happen to be very fond of anchovies myself, and if I don't get into the act you'll have gobbled them all up before I get any."

He served the antipasto for both of them and began to eat with his customary appetite, but Donna felt as if a small veil had descended between them and she wanted to rip it away.

"Mark and Althea have made it plain that my quarters in their house will be my home, to use as I wish." She paused. "You'll come out there, won't you, Hugh?"

The veil vanished, and Hugh grinned across at her. "I was wondering if you'd ever ask."

DONNA HAD NEVER ACCOMPLISHED a move quite so easily as she did the one from the Windcrest to the Nickerson house. She'd traveled light when she'd left New York, and the only two heavy objects she had to move were her computer and the accompanying printer.

Hugh helped her with them one cloudy afternoon. He'd just set up the computer and printer in an alcove off the small living room when it began to rain.

Glancing out the window, he said, "Well, we made that just in time."

Donna nodded. She was thinking that for the rest of her life whenever she heard rain she would think of Hugh, and of their making love during the course of that second northeaster.

He held out his arms to her and she walked into them. She rested her head against his shoulder and he pressed her close. She loved his warmth, she loved the smell of him, the feel of him. She loved simply being with him.

"I nearly forgot something," he said.

She drew back. "What?"

"We have to christen your new abode properly," he told her, and guided her toward the kitchenette.

Somehow, without her noticing, he'd put a bottle of chilled champagne in the fridge. Now he opened it. They couldn't find wineglasses so they filled water glasses and toasted each other. Still touching his glass to hers, Hugh said, "I think maybe it was a good idea for you to move. You were right. There's a certain privacy to this place...."

She laughed out loud. "There's nothing subtle about you."

"No, I suppose there isn't," he admitted. "I tend to say what I have on my mind, which at moments has gotten me into all sorts of trouble." He put down his glass. "Donna?"

He didn't have to go any further. Again Donna had the strong feeling that this was their moment, and she had no more intention of letting it escape than he did.

The small bedroom was furnished with maple and bright chintzes. There was a thick quilt on the bed, and Donna and Hugh undressed, then snuggled under it. She hadn't thought she needed to turn on the space heater, as Mark had suggested, but there was a chill to the air, a chill soon dispelled as Hugh slowly began to caress her, his touch evoking a brand of fire that warmed her all the way through.

It was so right, their coming together, so perfect. They savored each other, taking their time. This was their world, and they both intended to make the most of it. Hugh explored every inch of Donna, his kisses following in the wake of his fingers, and long before he was finished she was frantic with her need for him.

They moved together, sharing their pleasure, and when fulfillment came it was mutual.

As the afternoon waned, Donna lay within the circle of Hugh's arms listening to the rain beat down on the roof. She wished she could stop time. She wanted to suspend this moment, she wanted to cherish it forever.

HUGH HAD PREDICTED there was no way Donna would ever get up in time to meet him for a morning walk once she moved, but she was determined to prove him wrong.

The first morning in her new abode she set her alarm clock for six. She dressed in jogging clothes, donned running shoes and was parked outside the Snack Shack when Hugh came along at seven, as he'd said he would. The sight of her caused him to raise his eyebrows in mock surprise, but she merely slid out of the car, and they set off together.

Donna was not about to get into running. Years before she'd twisted her right knee playing field hockey in school, and although it usually presented no problems, she decided to use it as an excuse. Hugh, though skeptical, was willing to go along with her. Besides, he said, brisk walking was almost as good as running, and a lot better since it meant he could exercise and enjoy her company at the same time.

Their early-morning walks, put aside only on rainy days, set a pattern for them, but there wasn't time for much talking during the course of them. It was simply a matter of being together, of getting in tune for the day.

Back at her apartment Donna followed a routine of fixing coffee and toast and then settling down with her computer. By the end of her first week at the Nickersons' she had an outline complete enough to send on to her agent, and she planned to follow it soon with a full-fledged proposal, complete with sample chapters and a résumé of the balance of the plot. In the proposal she would also clearly define her characters.

At the end of that first week the Bruckers arrived home, and Donna had a joyous reunion with them. The next night Joe suggested that Hugh join them at

dinner, and they went to a lovely old inn that overlooked one of the Cape's many harbors.

Joe and Mabel were both tanned and well rested,
and they were obviously delighted to see Hugh. Hugh
and Mabel got into a discussion of recent mysteries
they'd read, which gave Donna a few uncomfortable
moments. She didn't want any inquiries about her own
writing.

Fortunately there weren't any. Mabel and Joe were
both still fascinated by having seen the *Portia*.

"How are you ever going to get her off the beach?"
Joe demanded of Hugh as they lingered over dessert
and coffee.

"I may personally swim out and tug her to sea,"
Hugh responded, but there was a certain terseness
about the way he said it that made Donna regard him
more closely. He looked tired, but then he usually
looked tired lately.

"Planning the whole damn thing's sometimes worse
than doing it," he'd told her.

The day after their dinner with the Bruckers,
Hugh's equipment began arriving in Devon and the
whole complexion of the beach parking lot was
changed.

Donna had been breaking away from her work
shortly before noon each day and going over to the
Snack Shack to help out with the lunch rush, so she
was on the scene when the trucks drove by.

She hadn't appreciated just how big forty-foot
trucks would look on the lot until she saw four of
them, loaded with equipment.

Hugh had been spending an increasing amount of
time on the ship with Alex Bruce, Tony Ramirez, the
first mate, and some of his own men. Donna flinched

when she asked how he managed to get aboard and he told her, with a grin, that the only route was via a forty-four-foot Jacob's ladder strung over the side. While she wasn't paranoid about heights, she'd never relished them and had often been teased that she'd never make a mountain climber. The side of the *Portia* looked as high as a mountain to her, especially in the seaside environment, and she shuddered at the thought of Hugh's daily need to navigate the ladder, often more than once.

Hugh was often involved in planning sessions at night, and Donna came to count more and more upon seeing him during their early-morning walks together. There was no phone in her apartment, and although the Nickersons had urged her to make free use of theirs, she knew Hugh wasn't likely to call her casually.

There were times when she felt remote from him, when being just a mile from the action seemed a very long distance. Working at the shack each noon kept her in touch, and often some of Hugh's men came by for lunch. But Hugh was seldom with them, and she realized that right now he was too busy.

As April progressed, the sightseers continued to stream to Devon, and during the midmonth school vacation the town was jammed. There wasn't a room to be had for miles around, and Donna told the Nickersons ruefully that they could easily have rented her apartment early. But both Mark and Althea scoffed at the idea.

It was the Monday after the school vacation that Althea tapped on Donna's door early one morning.

It was very early, in fact, and Donna was getting ready to meet Hugh for their walk.

Althea looked so tired and strained that Donna asked anxiously, "Is something wrong?" But Althea shook her head.

"Alex is coming to dinner tonight," she said without preamble. "I thought it would be nice if you and Hugh could join us. I wanted to ask you now so you'd have a chance to ask Hugh this morning."

The question came automatically. "What about Mark?"

"He won't be here," Althea said. "He's already told me that. I don't think it's just because of Alex, though. He said he has something else to do."

This was the first time Althea had mentioned her brother and Alex Bruce in the same breath. But then she and Althea had had little time in which to talk to each other, Donna reflected as she set out to meet Hugh. The Nickersons had been very busy running their business of late, and Donna hadn't seen much of them except when she was at the shack herself.

She wondered what Hugh would think of the invitation when she put it to him, but he only said, "That's fine with me. I'm sure I can get away tonight...for a change. Naturally I'd rather have you to myself," he added, "but beggars can't always be choosers. And I've been feeling pretty much of a beggar these days. Sometimes it's like you're a million miles away from me, Donna."

She felt the same way. But she realized that as the salvage operation intensified, it was going to be more and more difficult for Hugh to find time to spend with her.

They'd reached the hard-packed sand at this point in their walk, and Donna looked toward the *Portia*, looming large against the horizon. She felt a twinge of something close to jealousy. In a way the ship was like a rival.

"How's it going, Hugh?"

He followed her gaze. "We're getting the act together. Shortly we'll be bringing in a large barge, plus a couple of oceangoing tugs. We've worked out an elaborate pulley system. We've moored four massive anchors, which are wired via the deck to the ship's electric winches. There will be a derrick aboard the barge, and the idea will be to have a pulley tandem, one working from the deck winches and the other from the sea derrick. They'll combine to pivot the *Portia*'s bow roughly one hundred degrees seaward. Our hope is to drag her off the sand on a high tide."

Donna had a general idea of what he was talking about, but the language was unfamiliar to her, and he smiled as he looked down at her. "It sounds complicated, but actually the principle is fairly simple."

"And what's the principle?" she asked.

"Weight can be nearly halved for each strand of rope or wire that goes over a pulley. In this case the blocks placed on the ship herself, plus the offshore pulling derrick, will work in a way that will reduce the ship's weight—with water ballast—from more than five thousand tons to about five hundred tons."

"I think I get the idea," Donna replied vaguely.

"It's pretty much a matter of playing tug of war until she responds," Hugh elaborated. "Tug of war, calculated to a fine art, that is." He sighed. "I only hope it works."

CHAPTER NINE

"YOU'VE MET Alex Bruce, haven't you, Donna?" Althea asked.

It was six o'clock, and Donna had walked along the breezeway that connected her apartment with the main house and had come in via the kitchen door. Hearing voices, she'd gone on to the living room, to see Alex kneeling in front of the fireplace, touching a match to some kindling.

He straightened. "I've seen Donna," he said with a slight smile, "but we've not been formally introduced."

Donna found his Scottish accent charming, and so was his smile. He was wearing navy slacks and a white sweater, which enhanced his dark good looks. She could understand why Althea might be infatuated with him.

He strode toward her, his hand extended. His handclasp was firm, and he looked Donna right in the eye. There was nothing evasive about him. Nor, in Althea's living room, did he seem as intense as he'd appeared to Donna the couple of times she'd seen him.

"Hugh's been telling me a bit about you," he said. "I understand you write thrillers?"

"Yes," Donna replied, able to answer the question without wincing. She did write thrillers. She was writing one right now. She wondered, though, what this man might say if he knew how prominently he figured in her plot.

Alex returned to his fire, and Donna asked Althea if she could use some help with the dinner.

"Thanks, but everything's under control," Althea responded with a smile.

Althea looked lovely tonight, Donna observed. She was wearing a pink dress that matched the flush in her cheeks, and her shoulder-length gold hair was a mass of curls.

The doorbell rang, heralding Hugh's arrival, and as she heard him greet Althea, Donna felt so flustered she imagined her cheeks must be as pink as Althea's. Hugh came into the room, radiating that marvelous vitality that was such a part of him. Tonight he didn't appear tired, as he had so often lately. He looked as if he'd just shaved, his dark gray eyes were clear, and Donna had never seen his hair combed quite so neatly.

The evening got off to a good start. They sat in front of the fireplace sipping wine and munching cheese and crackers, and Donna was surprised at the easy camaraderie that developed between them. She had expected Alex Bruce to be a far more difficult person to get to know.

Still, despite the outward charm, it seemed to her that she could detect shadows when she looked at him more closely. He appeared to her to be someone who was bearing up very well—but definitely bearing up. A man who carried the burden of his past, made all the more heavy by the latest catastrophe with the *Portia*. From what she'd been hearing around town, there was still a chance that the ship's captain might be blamed—at least to some extent—for the shipwreck.

Alex was as accomplished a raconteur as Hugh. He entertained them with fascinating tales of his experiences as a ship's captain, and Hugh told some tales of his own. The two men spoke easily of their previous meetings, and if Alex feared that Hugh knew more about him than he wanted Althea to learn, he didn't show it.

Althea had prepared a French Canadian meat pie for their dinner, and both men pleased her by requesting seconds. By the time they'd finished the chocolate mousse she'd made they were happy but groaning, and Hugh said to Donna, "Remind me to take off and jog in the morning. I'll have to leave you to your beach walking."

"Don't you get enough exercise climbing up and down that Jacob's ladder?" Donna taunted, and Alex smiled.

Alex stoked up the fire and they had their coffee in front of it. It seemed natural to Donna for Hugh to put his arm around her shoulder as they sat next to each other on the couch, and instinctively she snuggled toward him.

Althea was sitting in an armchair near the fire and Alex dropped to the floor at her feet. Donna noted a latent moodiness in his expression, highlighted by the flames' red-orange glow. Then she saw Althea reach out and tentatively stroke his hair. Alex's hand snaked upward and Althea clasped it. For a moment their fingers clung, then Alex released his grasp and Althea sat back, her lovely face suddenly sad.

There was a poignancy to the scene that was revealing to Donna. She'd been afraid, even this evening, that Alex was toying with Althea's emotions. Now she strongly suspected that these two people had fallen in love with each other.

She glanced up at Hugh and was sure he'd also witnessed the small byplay between Althea and Alex. Hugh's face was closed, more closed than it needed to be, which was one indication, and his mouth was drawn into a tight line.

It was Alex who first mentioned leaving. He announced, rather abruptly, "I guess I'll have to be going back to the ship."

"Let me get a sweater," Althea said immediately.

It occurred to Donna that Alex didn't have a car, and she glanced at Hugh, wondering if he might offer him a ride. They would be heading in the same direction. But Hugh said nothing.

Althea came back into the room, a sweater that matched her dress thrown over her shoulders. It was Alex who suggested, "I could ride along with Hugh, you know, instead of dragging you out."

"Hugh doesn't have a four-wheel drive, at least not with him," Althea stated.

"Nor should you have to go down on the beach in yours tonight," Alex told her.

"It's not that far, Alex, and a lot easier distance to cover with wheels than on foot," Althea insisted.

Alex smiled across at Donna. "She always wins. She appeals to my inherent laziness. I must admit I get tired of trudging back and forth through all that sand." He added, "I'm glad finally to have met you, Donna. I'll be seeing you tomorrow, Hugh?"

Hugh nodded. "We'll soon start digging you out of that sand you're talking about," he promised.

"I hope to God you succeed," Alex said soberly. "Sometimes I come close to believing what one hears around town. That the *Portia* may be beached here forever, that is.''

His eyes lingered on Althea as he said this, and Donna wished she could read his thoughts.

Even if the *Portia* was to remain high and dry on Massasoit Beach forever, unlikely though that was, Alex Bruce would inevitably be moving on.

Was that what he was thinking?

Hugh waited until the door had closed behind Althea and Alex, then asked, ''Do you want me to put another log on the fire? Or shall we go over to your place?''

''Why don't we go over to my place?'' Donna suggested. She picked up their coffee cups and carried them out to the kitchen. She and Althea had already stashed most of the dishes in the dishwasher and had taken care of the major part of the cleanup.

''There really isn't that much left to do,'' she commented aloud, looking around.

''Then come along,'' Hugh said. ''Though I doubt Althea's going to be back very soon.''

''It's rather cold to sit outdoors in an open beach buggy, and that's what the Nickersons' four-wheel drive amounts to,'' Donna pointed out.

''Maybe she'll go aboard ship with him.''

''Up that ladder?'' Donna protested.

''Who knows?'' Noting her shocked expression, he said quickly, ''No, I don't think Alex is about to try to have Althea climb the Jacob's ladder in the middle of the night. But it was pretty plain to me that the two of them were hungry for each other. Don't you agree?''

''Yes, I agree. And I felt sorry for them, Hugh.''

"Sorry for them? They're adults, Donna," Hugh said bluntly. "They know what they're letting themselves in for. At least it would seem so to me."

Donna was moving around the kitchen, putting away a few of the things that could be put away, stalling in a sense. "Do we ever really know what we're letting ourselves in for?"

"That's a hell of a question to ask *me*," he said, so bleakly that she turned to him. She was startled to see an expression close to anguish in his eyes.

"Everything in Alex's life is so damned temporary," Hugh went on, "and in mine, too. I'm only beginning to realize just how temporary. In Alex's case, he does have a wife and children to go back to."

"Has he told Althea about them?"

"You're in a better position to know that than I am," Hugh replied roughly. "It's not the kind of thing a man normally confides to another man. And it's Alex's business. I'm not about to butt into it. On the other hand, I hate to see Althea hurt."

"But she's bound to be hurt, isn't she?" Donna said softly.

"Yes, it looks so."

"Sooner or later, he'll leave her. He'd leave her even if he didn't have a wife and children to go back to, don't you think?"

What she was saying had a dual significance. Except for references to Alex's wife and children she could have been speaking about Hugh and herself.

Sooner or later he was going to leave her. He'd never pretended otherwise.

His face tightened. "Maybe you'd rather I went along, Donna."

His tone was cold, and she felt miserable. Her voice was small as she said, "Not unless you want to."

"I never want to leave you. Don't you know that?"

She shook her head. "Oh, Hugh." She was making a major attempt to understand him. Sometimes she thought she understood him so well, and other times she was sure she never would.

"Please," he said. "Let's get out of here."

Donna nodded, and with a last look around she slipped through the kitchen door ahead of him. The cool spring air was an astringent to her cheeks as she led the way along the breezeway and opened the door of her apartment.

She'd left on a couple of lights. Hugh crossed the threshold and seemed to fill the room.

His voice husky, he said, "Donna," and she turned to him. She went into his arms, but it was sorrow that swept through her tonight, not passion.

Hugh sensed this and sighed, and the sigh echoed through his own emptiness. He stared down at the top of Donna's head, smelling the sweet fragrance of her dark hair. She'd been in his life such a short time, and it scared him to think how much a part of it she'd become.

He knew exactly what she'd been referring to when she'd said that sooner or later Alex would be leaving Althea, and not only because he had a wife and children in Scotland to go back to. She might as well have added that she knew sooner or later he'd be leaving her, and there was no way he could have said anything to the contrary without lying to her.

How could he possibly not be called upon to leave her at some point in the future not all that far away? He knew as well as she did that this was something bound to happen, and though he wrestled with the knowledge, there was nothing he could do to change the facts of his life.

Somewhere in the world there would be another shipwreck, and he would go wherever it was. He would live wherever it was until he'd salvaged another ship, and then there would be another shipwreck and, again he'd move on.

He'd moved on for years. He knew, dismal though the prospect was to him at the moment, that for the rest of his life he'd be moving on. He was committed to his work. It was a part of him.

"I don't think this is a night for us, Donna," he said gently.

She stirred in his arms, and he could sense her resentment. He couldn't blame her. They'd had all too few nights that had been theirs, and from now on time was going to be his most valuable commodity. He belonged to the *Portia* until he got her off the beach. Until then he had no choice but to make the ship the first woman in his life.

DONNA DIDN'T ASK Hugh to stay with her that night. Even as he held her in his arms she felt so...bereft. She didn't doubt that he could arouse her, yet hers would be a false kind of passion tonight, and she didn't want that.

She turned on the television after Hugh left, but nothing appealed to her. Restless, she switched on her computer, and very soon she found her fingers flying as she wrote about Alex Bruce, about Althea, and about Hugh.

Tonight's dinner—changed and augmented to suit her plot—could be a scene in her book. And, yes, she was going to have to write Althea into the story. Althea belonged there.

Donna lost track of time as she worked, and she was startled when someone rapped on the window by her makeshift desk.

Hugh wouldn't have come back. She was sure of that. And even if he had come back he would have knocked on the door rather than tap on the window.

Apprehensive, Donna drew back the curtain and found herself staring into Mark Nickerson's scowling face.

When she opened the door for him, Mark strode into the living room. Looking around, he said, "I thought Althea might be here with you."

Donna had no idea how long it had been since Althea had left to take Alex back to his ship. A couple of hours at least, she imagined.

"You wouldn't happen to know where she's gone, would you?" Mark asked.

There was no point in hedging. "She went to take Alex Bruce back to the ship. I don't know where she might have gone from there."

"Hell!" Mark burst out.

He looked harried, and despite herself Donna felt a twinge of sympathy for him. She couldn't blame him for being worried about Althea's involvement with Alex Bruce. She was more than a little worried about it herself.

"Would you have anything to drink on hand, Donna? Anything *strong*, that is?"

The request was so out of character for Mark that Donna nearly smiled. "Would a brandy do?"

"Yes," he said, and added unexpectedly, "especially if you'll join me."

"Why not?"

A moment later they were seated at her small kitchen table, sipping brandy from the same two water glasses Hugh had used for champagne the day Donna had moved in there.

"If I'd had any sense I would have stayed here for dinner tonight," Mark said glumly. "Then I could have taken Bruce back to his ship myself."

Donna thought about this, then decided there were a couple of things Mark was going to have to face up to.

"Althea's a big girl," she reminded him.

His scowl returned. "I know that. But I just found out tonight that the object of her affections is married...and a father, as well. How does that grab you?"

"Who told you that?" Donna asked him.

"Terry O'Connor. I had dinner with her."

Donna could not have been more surprised.

"She's been wanting to interview me, you know that," Mark reminded her. "I was too busy at the Snack Shack for us to get down to anything there, so she suggested we have dinner together, on her paper's tab." A shadow of a smile crossed Mark's angular face. "How could any self-respecting Yankee refuse an offer like that?"

Before Donna could reply, he went on. "The thing is, the *Globe* has been spacing out the publication of Terry's material. They want to have something in the paper about the *Portia* each day during this interim time before the first serious salvage attempt is made. The story Terry did about Alex Bruce will be coming out in tomorrow morning's paper, and there's no way in the world I'm going to be able to keep someone from showing it to Althea. I'm not sure how she'll handle it.''

"I think she may already know that Alex is married," Donna ventured.

"What gives you that idea?" Mark asked, and added wearily, "You don't really think he's leveled with her, do you?"

"He may have, Mark," Donna said, remembering the way Alex had looked at Althea tonight, the eloquence of that moment when their hands had touched. Until tonight, until she'd seen the two of them together for herself, she would have been more than ready to agree with Mark that Alex was probably interested in little more than a brief affair while on foreign soil. Now she was no longer sure about that.

"I think he really cares for her, Mark," she said, and was met by a blaze of cynicism flaming from Mark's pale blue eyes.

"How naive can you be, Donna? You've been through enough yourself so I'd think you'd be more worldly-wise than that."

"It has nothing to do with being worldly-wise. Look, Mark, you've heard the old story that because there's one rotten apple in a barrel it doesn't mean that all the rest of the apples are rotten."

He groaned. "Spare me the clichés. How did you ever come up with that one, anyway?"

"I was just trying to think of an analogy that fit."

"Don't try so hard, Donna," Mark admonished. Then he smiled faintly. "I know you're pretty fond of Althea yourself and I appreciate that. I hate to think of what seeing this story in the paper in the morning is going to do to her if she doesn't know, that's all. She's a sensitive kid.''

Althea was less than two years younger than Mark, but Donna knew she'd always be a "kid" in her brother's opinion.

Mark left, slightly mollified, but Donna was on edge once he'd gone. She warned herself that she could be wrong. Alex Bruce might have said nothing to Althea at all about his marriage. If so, Althea was due for a terrible shock in the morning, and there would be no way of averting it.

DONNA SPENT a restless night, and she was more tired when she got up than she had been when she'd gone to bed. She drank a quick cup of coffee then drove down to the beach parking lot and slid her car into one of the Snack Shack's reserved areas. She'd been given carte blanche by Mark to use the space anytime she wanted to.

She waited, but seven o'clock loomed up on the car clock and Hugh didn't appear. The minutes ticked by, and Donna thought of going for a walk by herself, then dismissed the idea. Hugh would probably emerge from the Windcrest the minute she started out.

He didn't appear, though, and shortly after seven-thirty, Donna drove out of the parking lot and headed up to the center of town. She knew that Mark would be arriving on the beach momentarily to open up shop, and she didn't want to be around. Mark was too perceptive. He'd notice Hugh's absence and comment on it.

Donna pulled in at a small coffee shop and bought a copy of the *Globe* as she waited for an order of scrambled eggs and bacon to be prepared. She wasn't hungry, but she had the feeling that if she didn't eat now she wouldn't bother doing so for the rest of the day, and if she went without food, her energy would be sapped.

She scanned the newspaper, and as she turned a page she found herself staring at a large photograph of Alex Bruce. He was standing against the *Portia*'s hull, wearing a visored cap pushed back from his forehead so that his lean, attractive face was fully visible. It was a very good picture, and just looking at it made Donna aware again of the man's magnetism. She thought wryly that if she hadn't already fallen in love with Hugh MacDonough she might very well have been attracted to Alex Bruce herself.

It was a good story. Terry O'Connor was a competent writer and used plenty of color in her text. Alex emerged as the fascinating personality he was.

There was no hint that there were any shadows in his past, which meant that so far no one had stumbled on the facts Hugh knew so well.

But his marriage was mentioned. Terry gave a brief sketch of an off-duty Alex who lived in a small house in a Glasgow suburb with his wife, Heather, and their two children. There wasn't much to be gained from this word picture, but there it was.

Donna took the paper with her when she left the coffee shop and the next order of her day was to find Althea and talk to her.

She drove back to the Nickersons' house and saw that the van Mark usually used to drive back and forth to the Snack Shack was gone, but Althea's blue compact was still in the driveway.

Althea was in the kitchen, reading the *Globe* story. There was a sadness to her face as she looked up at Donna, but no shock.

So, Donna thought, more relieved than she would have imagined. Althea had already known about this part of Alex's life.

Althea saw the paper still clutched in Donna's hands. "I guess you've seen the story."

Donna nodded. "Yes, I have."

"It's a terrific picture of Alex, isn't it?" Althea said. "He's so handsome. I think he's the handsomest man I've ever met, and the nicest one. I don't know what Mark's told you, but nothing's been at all like Mark thinks it is."

"Mark hasn't told me much of anything," Donna told her hastily. "He's worried about you, that's all."

She wanted to say, he doesn't want your heart to be broken. But looking at Althea she knew it was already too late for that.

Donna didn't linger with Althea. She went back to her apartment, eager to start getting words down on paper again.

She heard Althea drive off after a time, and being alone in the old Cape Cod house overlooking the Atlantic only stimulated her creative juices. Her fingers flew on the computer keys, her characters coming to life. She was writing essentially about real people, yet as she dealt with them, they became clay to be molded in certain ways, so that in the long run they would be her own creations.

It was nearly noon when she heard a car door slam. She was appalled as she glanced at the clock. She'd intended to be at the snack shop by now, even though Althea and Mark had made it clear that she should come to help out only when she really wanted to.

She had to admit that today she didn't want to. Nor did she want to be interrupted by an unexpected visitor.

Donna told herself that if it was someone who had come to see the Nickersons they'd go away when no one answered the doorbell.

It wasn't anyone who had come to see the Nickersons, though. It was Hugh, and he'd obviously come to see her.

"I wish you had a phone," he said irritably. "I didn't want to barge in on you."

They'd parted on such a strained note last night, and then he hadn't shown up at the beach that morning.

If they kept on this way, they were going to ruin whatever time they did have together, Donna thought. There wouldn't even be any good memories to look back on.

She quickly corrected herself. No matter what might happen between Hugh and her, there were already good memories to look back on. Times that she would never forget.

"I couldn't make it this morning," he told her abruptly. "They needed me down on the beach to solve a couple of problems, but everything's going all right now, and there's no reason for me to stay around for the rest of the day. So how about coming along and picking out some frames for my glasses?"

This was the last request she would have expected to hear from him. "What?" she asked, as if her ears were deceiving her.

"You told me to have my eyes examined and I finally got around to it," Hugh explained. "I need glasses for close work. So how about you helping me get some that will be, as they say, becoming? Then how about playing hooky? Are you up for that? I'd like to drive out to Provincetown and take a look at the tip of the Cape. We could wander around some of the back roads. I haven't seen nearly as much of this place as I want to, and you know a lot more about it than I do. You can lead the way.''

He'd been brusque, but suddenly he mellowed, and his smile was so disarming that Donna felt as if her legs were about to give out from under her.

Hugh asked, very softly, "Please?"

He was standing so close to her that she could see the fine laugh lines etched at the corners of his eyes and the deeper lines around his mouth, the result of long-standing tensions associated with his work. He'd nicked himself when he'd shaved, and there was a tiny blot on his chin. This small imperfection made her aware that he was every bit as vulnerable as she was.

Looking at him, Donna made a decision. She was going to live in the present, for whatever time they had together. She was going to forget there was such a thing as a future. She was going to savor each hour with him, make the most of each moment.

Somewhere she'd read that this was the way life should be lived, anyway.

She lifted her chin and her blue eyes sparkled as she smiled up at Hugh.

"Let me put on some lipstick and I'll be ready to go with you," she said. *To Provincetown, or to the ends of the earth, or to wherever you want to take me,* she added silently.

CHAPTER TEN

CHOOSING HUGH'S EYEGLASS FRAMES proved to be hilarious. Donna wouldn't have expected that Hugh had much of the clown in him, but even the technician in the optometrist's office broke into gales of laughter as he tried on a variety of styles then affected a personality to suit each of them.

"I think I like you best as the executive type," Donna told him as he sat back and surveyed her with mock severity over a pair of heavy black frames.

"My clothes aren't right," Hugh complained. He was wearing brown cord pants and a tan chamois shirt, open at the throat. "I'll have to buy a three-piece suit."

Finally they settled for tortoiseshell frames, which, according to the technician, picked up the reddish tones in his hair.

"I'm glad I'll be coordinated," Hugh told the woman, flashing her his most winning smile.

As she watched the technician's response to him, Donna was sure that all through his life Hugh had affected women in this way, yet remarkably he seemed unaware of the scope of his charm.

There were crocuses in bloom in front of some of the houses on the way to Provincetown, a few early daffodils and the first golden, showering forsythia. Bright as sunshine, the flowers were harbingers of spring to Donna, and she began to live up to her promise to herself. It was easy to concentrate only on the joys of today in weather like this.

Hugh seemed to shed his cares with the miles, once they left Devon. Watching him relax visibly, Donna realized anew how pressured he was right now, and the pressure would be increasing until his salvage mission terminated in either success or failure. But, she warned herself, she wasn't going to think about that. She'd declared a self moratorium on looking ahead.

There was only one main highway to Provincetown but side roads branched off it, and every now and then Hugh turned onto one of them. Like a couple of youngsters pretending to be explorers in exciting new territory, he and Donna followed their instincts, inevitably winding up at beaches on both the bay and the ocean sides of the Cape.

Each beach was different in its way, had its own charms, and even offered its own variety of shells and marine life. Scallop shells were scattered liberally on one beach, oyster shells on another, clam shells on yet another. Donna found a plastic bag someone had left behind and began to beachcomb with such enthusiasm that Hugh finally asked, "What are you going to do with all those things?"

It occurred to her that he must have seen all sorts of shells on beaches all over the world. But she wasn't going to let herself think about the past, either. She had just picked up a smooth moon shell when he asked the question, and she replied, "I don't know. Maybe I'll make a collage with some of them, or decorate lampshades, or..."

He grinned. "Sure you will. I'll bet ten years from now they'll still be stashed in a box somewhere."

Ten years from now. Where would she and Hugh be ten years from now? Donna shut a firm door on the future.

In Wellfleet they stopped for cones in an old-fashioned ice-cream parlor. Donna chose maple walnut, which had been her childhood favorite, and Hugh chose chocolate.

They wandered along the winding streets in the little town as they ate their ice cream. Not all of the stores had opened yet for the season but a good variety had, and the two of them happily window-shopped.

Donna had a collection of small pitchers and was always looking for possible additions to it. She spied a small, amethyst crackle-glass pitcher that appealed to her in a thrift-shop window and was tempted to go in and price it. But she was sure that if she evinced interest in it Hugh would offer to buy it for her, and she didn't want that. The seashells she'd collected would be enough in the way of souvenirs. Besides, she wouldn't need souvenirs to remember this day.

Hugh's eye was taken by a small brass clock, and Donna wished she could divert his attention so that she could slip in and buy it for him, but there was no chance.

Probably it was as well. As they walked, he told her that he'd sold most of the family antiques after his mother's death.

"There was no one to give them to, no reason to keep them and no place to keep them in," he said rather flatly.

Donna tried not to think how rootless he was. A man with no real home and few possessions.

Looking at a stamp album in a bookstore window, she asked, "Do you have any hobbies?"

He shook his head. "Not really."

"I would have thought you might have taken up something like collecting stamps, you've traveled so much."

He smiled. "No. I would never have had time to sort them out and paste them into place. I had a stamp album once when I was in school. Lord only knows what happened to it."

"What about photography?" she persisted.

"What about it?"

"Haven't you ever had the urge to take pictures of the places you've been?"

"No, not especially. I haven't exactly chosen the locations of my travels, Donna. I could have done without going to a lot of the places I've had to go to. It makes a difference."

"I suppose so," she said, dubiously.

He laughed. "Why the questioning note?"

"No particular reason."

The timbre of his voice changed ever so slightly, but Donna was aware of it. There was a coolness to his tone as he asked, "What do you really want to know about me, Donna?"

She felt a little ashamed of herself. Admittedly she'd been probing, and she hadn't been too clever about it. She answered honestly, "I suppose I want to know everything there is to know about you, Hugh."

His smile didn't meet his eyes. "That might not be such a big order. My life isn't very glamorous, Donna, even though I suppose it may sometimes seem so. Most of the time when I'm on a job I'm so busy working I don't get a chance to do much else. Most of the accommodations given to me are not exactly in a category with the Ritz. At night I'm either poring over plans and statistics or else I'm so damned bushed I fall asleep right after dinner. More than once I've awakened to find a blank TV screen staring me in the eye.

"I'm not saying I've never been able to find someone to fill in the hours with me when I've been lonely," he went on, speaking with a deliberateness she couldn't fail to note. "Sure, there have been women in my life, and I'm grateful to a number of them for having come into it when they did. I guess I'm a loner, but not that much of a loner. I'm as human as the next man. But with very few exceptions there haven't been many people who have meant a great deal to me. That's a hazard of my profession, Donna. When you work out in the field most of the time, as I do, you don't have the chance to make many lasting ties."

She couldn't resist the question. "Have you ever wanted to make any lasting ties, Hugh?"

"Once," he said tightly. "Once I nearly got married, and it's a damned good thing she sent my ring back when she did. It wouldn't have worked. After I got over my hurt pride I saw that very clearly. She had her own career—she's a lawyer in Boston. There was no way she could have merged it with mine even if she'd wanted to. There was a lot of chemistry between us for a while, but we never had a chance. Once the glow had worn off we would have wound up in a divorce court, and I think that would have put me on a lifelong guilt trip. I always would have felt that I'd let her down."

His attempt at a smile tore at Donna's insides, and she felt wrenched with compassion for him.

Then he said simply, "I'm no bargain, Donna. I'd be a poor bet for any woman. But that's been my own doing. I chose my way of life and I love what I do. Until I'm a lot older than I am now, I'd be lost without a ship to salvage."

PROVINCETOWN WAS CROWDED, though the time of year was supposedly off-season. They left the car in the large municipal lot on McMillan Wharf and walked out to the end of the wharf to watch some of the fishing boats unloading their catches.

Commercial Street, Provincetown's narrow main artery, had fascinated Donna ever since she'd first visited it as a child. She and Hugh stopped for coffee and pastries at a small outdoor café, then wandered along enjoying the afternoon, the atmosphere and each other.

When Donna finally admitted to Hugh that she collected pitchers, after seeing a small cranberry glass one she couldn't resist in a shop window, he insisted on going in and buying it for her. She wanted to get something for him in return but knew that it would have to be something small. Hugh, she reminded herself, traveled light.

Finally she saw a tie tack made from the purple part of a quahog—hard clam—shell. This was the shell known as wampum, which reputedly had been used as a medium of exchange by coastal Indians and currently was popular in jewelry making.

The wampum was so reminiscent of the beach and their walks together that Donna couldn't resist diving into the shop displaying the jewelry and buying the tie tack for Hugh before he realized what she was doing.

As she handed him her small gift, he shook his head and said, "You shouldn't have," but the huskiness in his voice gave him away. "I'll always keep this, Donna."

"You don't often wear a tie, from what I've observed," she teased him, "so you may not have all that much use for it."

"I'll keep it with me, whether I wear it or not," he told her solemnly. She realized he meant this, and suddenly tears stung her eyes. She turned away from him quickly, drawing his attention to something in another store window, because she didn't want him to see how he had affected her.

Later on they had dinner in a tiny restaurant that specialized in seafood. The broiled fish they ate had been fresh caught that morning, and Donna pronounced it the best thing she'd ever had, with Hugh seconding her.

The moon was riding high in the sky as they started back for Devon. At Orleans, Hugh pulled off on a side road then drove over to the bay and parked overlooking the silver-mottled water.

"Game to go wading?" he asked her.

"If you are."

They slipped off their shoes. They were both wearing slacks, which they rolled midway up their calves. Then, as if they were adolescents, they scampered across the sand, Donna coming to a halt at the tide line.

The water touched her toes and she jumped. It was icy, but she wasn't going to let Hugh taunt her. After a moment her flesh adjusted to the temperature and she scampered through the shallows, the moon bathing her in silvery light so that she looked like an ethereal goddess to the man at her side.

His desire for her became a quicksilver thing, matching the moonlight, rising like the tide. He caught Donna in his arms, his mouth claiming hers, and there was a mystical quality to the passion that fused between them.

In her bedroom that night they made love, lost in their own world. And he didn't leave her. He stayed through the night, and this gesture made Donna realize that a point of no return had been reached for both of them.

Hugh did not speak of love in so many words, nor did she. But the bond between them was undeniable. Once she awakened to find him nuzzling her hair with his lips. He was saying something to her very softly because he thought she was asleep, but she couldn't quite make out his words.

THE DAY AFTER HER EXCURSION to Provincetown with Hugh, Donna went into the bank to cash a check. Often she simply used the drive-through window, but she'd noted as she neared the bank that there was a string of cars at it today, and she'd decided she'd make better time by parking and going inside.

She was wrong about that. As she turned away from the teller's window, Rod Eldridge appeared in the door of his office.

"Donna, come in here will you please?" he asked her.

His tone was so businesslike that she wondered if there might be something wrong with her account. Now and then she transferred funds from her bank in

New York to the bank in Devon. There was a chance
something had gone amiss.

She was puzzled when Rod motioned her to a seat
then closed his office door firmly before taking his
place behind his desk. He was wearing a three-piece
pale gray suit today, and looking at it reminded Donna
of Hugh's remark about buying such a suit when he'd
tried on the "executive type" glasses.

She smiled at the memory, but Rod didn't return her
smile. He asked frostily, "If I'm not probing too
much, I'd like to know what's going on."

Donna had no idea what he was talking about and
said honestly, "I don't follow you."

"Don't you?" Rod looked handsome in the tai-
lored suit, and it occurred to her that she'd seldom
seen him without a tie, and never with a hair out of
place. His hair was dark, sleek, perfectly contoured,
and she thought, as she had before, that he should
have been a model. He was wasted in a small-town
bank.

"I have the feeling you've been avoiding me,
Donna."

She hadn't been. The fact was she'd given Rod very
little thought at all lately, and the realization made her
feel slightly guilty.

"I didn't know you'd moved out of the Windcrest
until I met your Uncle Joe at a Chamber of Com-
merce dinner the other night and he told me you'd
rented the Nickersons' apartment. I thought perhaps
you might wonder why I hadn't called."

She hadn't wondered, and her expression gave her
away.

Rod eyed her narrowly. "I was at a bankers' meeting in Boston. I tried to reach you before I left but

there was no answer in the apartment at that time. After your uncle told me you'd moved I went down to the Snack Shack a couple of times because Joe said you were still helping out there. But you weren't around, and Althea told me you've been busy with your writing. At least,'' he said, ''I'm glad of that.''

It occurred to Donna that computer keys clattered. She hadn't thought it was a sound that carried, yet something must have alerted Althea to the fact that she was working once again. She hadn't gone into detail about it herself. She'd been purposefully evasive about her writing because she was far from ready to let anyone in on the secret of what she was working on. Only her agent knew, she thought whimsically.

Rod's gaze softened slightly as he looked at her. ''So, I take it you've gotten over your writer's block? That's what you called it, isn't it?''

''Yes,'' Donna admitted, ''that's what I called it. In a way I've gotten over it, yes. But...'' She paused. ''It's hard to explain,'' she finished lamely.

''Are you going to stay at the Nickersons' until you've finished your book, Donna?''

She couldn't answer him because she really didn't know. The Nickersons had the apartment rented as of June 15, so she had to be out of it by then. And by then the *Portia*'s fate would surely have been decided.

The logical thing would be to do as much as she could on the book here, then take the manuscript back to New York for editing and revision.

''*Are* you going to stay on here, Donna?'' Rod asked again, and she knew he wasn't going to give up without some kind of answer.

"I hope to get most of the book done here, yes," she replied vaguely. "I can stay with Mark and Althea until the middle of June, if necessary."

"Well, that's something of a relief. Donna, have you been avoiding me?"

"No," she said. "Of course not. Why would you think I'd want to avoid you, Rod?"

"It's a small town. I know you've been seeing Hugh MacDonough. Yes—" he nodded "—I've met him. The bank is handling funds for the salvage operation. MacDonough and I have had occasion to confer a couple of times."

"I see," Donna said rather weakly.

"Your uncle's evidently known MacDonough for a fairly long time," Rod observed. "Had you met him before he came here?"

She shook her head. "No."

This fact seemed to relieve Rod, and it relieved Donna when the buzzer on his desk sounded. With a grimace he picked up the phone and said, impatiently, "Eldridge."

He modified his tone as he recognized the caller. A person of importance evidently, Donna thought rather cynically. She decided maybe it was best Rod hadn't become a model after all. One of these years he'd probably wind up being the president of a big bank somewhere. Maybe in Boston. Perhaps he'd go into politics. She watched him, smooth and earnest as he talked into the phone, and decided he'd make an excellent politician.

She escaped the bank with a promise to Rod that she'd have dinner with him the following night. But she wasn't looking forward to it. She and Rod had operated on a casual footing until now, which was one reason she'd enjoyed going out with him as much as she had. His remarks that morning had given her the hint that he might be trying to throw a few strings in her direction, and she didn't want to be tied to him in any way at all.

On an impulse she drove down to the beach from the bank, though she hadn't intended doing so. But there was no good reason not to help Mark and Althea out today if they needed a hand.

As she strolled up to the shack she saw Terry O'Connor standing at the counter, consuming an order of fried onion rings as she spoke to Mark.

The reporter was wearing jeans and a *Portia* T-shirt, but she looked as attractive in this outfit as she had in her fashionable raincoat on the earlier occasion when Donna had seen her.

Mark introduced them, and Terry's unusual green eyes gleamed with excitement when she caught Donna's name.

"You're Jeffrey Jewell," she said, and Donna flinched. She'd come to Devon incognito, as it were, and she wanted to keep it that way.

"Hugh MacDonough told me about you," the reporter continued, apparently unaware of Donna's reaction. "I've been one of your biggest fans for ages. I can't wait for your next book to come out."

Donna was tempted to tell her this might be a while, but she held her tongue. She said something polite and inconsequential, then turned to Mark. "Need some help?"

"Thanks, but I don't think so," Mark told her. "I don't know why, but it's running slow today. My guess is that the crowds won't pick up again until the weekend."

"Too bad they can't run little excursions down the beach, so people can see what's going on down there," Terry said. "Hugh took me down in one of the four-wheel drives earlier today, and it's fascinating. He explained how he's planning to handle the salvage operation, but even with all of Hugh's engineering expertise I honestly wonder if they're ever going to be able to move the *Portia* around so they'll have a chance of pulling her off."

Donna heard only half of this. The thought of Hugh having taken this woman down the beach to the ship was so galling that nothing else registered. He'd never offered her the opportunity to share that much in his work.

"I'll run along if you don't need me," she told Mark, and nodded to Terry O'Connor. "Nice to have met you," she said politely. But she was smarting as she went back to her car and drove off.

THE BALANCE OF DONNA'S DAY was dominated by a sense of righteous indignation that gnawed at her. She felt closed in, and after a time she navigated the wooden steps to the beach and went for a long walk.

As she walked across the strip of lawn from the top of the steps to the house on her return, she saw Althea standing at a front window, beckoning to her. She wasn't sure she wanted to talk even to Althea right now, and it was with reluctance that she let herself into the main part of the house via the kitchen.

Althea was wearing a red cotton lounger and was holding her hands out stiffly in front of her. "I just put on some nail polish," she explained. "Alex and I are going out to dinner tonight. We thought we'd go to Provincetown and try the place you and Hugh ate at the other day. Hugh was telling Alex about it.''

"It was very good,'' Donna said, but her tone was dull.

She was conscious of Althea's surveillance, then her friend asked, "Are you okay? You're not sick or anything, you are, Donna?''

"No,'' Donna snapped, then modified her tone. "I'm fine.''

"Too bad Hugh had to go up to Boston and can't get back until tomorrow,'' Althea said sympathetically. "Otherwise, maybe the two of you could have come along with us.''

"Wouldn't you much rather be alone with Alex?'' Donna asked curtly, then, surprised at her own nastiness, wished she could retract the words.

Althea's eyes widened for just a second, then she said, "Yes, I would. But we'd both also enjoy having you and Hugh with us, Donna.''

She spoke with a quiet dignity, and Donna felt ashamed of herself. She said, contrite, "I'm sorry, Althea. I've been...out of sorts today.''

"Problems with your book again?'' Althea asked sympathetically.

"Well, yes, in a sense,'' Donna replied evasively. Suddenly she felt anxious to escape, she wanted to be alone. "I'd better be getting back to work.''

Althea nodded. "Oh, by the way, Hugh stopped by at the Snack Shack just before he left for Boston and said to tell you he'll try to call you here at nine tonight. He said he didn't expect you to stay around, he'd just chance it. Okay?''

"Why...yes,'' Donna said.

"You'll have the place to yourself," Althea continued. "Mark's going out with Terry O'Connor again.
She wants to go around in search of local color, I think
that's the way he put it, and she told him he could be
a lot of help to her. He knows just about everyone in
town."

Althea grinned. "It's almost too much to believe,
but I think Mark may be getting a soft spot for Terry."

DONNA TOLD HERSELF she was not going to sit in the
Nickersons' living room all by herself as nine o'clock
approached and wait for the phone to ring. But she
did.

She let it ring twice, then picked up the receiver. She
tried to keep her voice well modulated as she said,
"Hello?"

"Donna?" Hugh's relief communicated itself to her
over the wires. "Am I ever glad you're there!"

"Althea said you might call."

"I told Althea I'd try. I didn't mean to hold you up
from anything."

"You haven't."

"I had to come up here unexpectedly. Some of our
planning arrangements appeared to be running into a
snag and it seemed expedient to get up here and make
an effort to smooth out the logistics." He added softly,
"I miss you more with every passing hour. I want to
be with you. This is hell, Donna."

"Tell me about it," she said, her voice equally soft.

"Sometimes I think I must have dreamed last night.
Was it only last night?"

"Yes," she replied shakily.

"Look, I'll get back tomorrow as soon as I can. Be
waiting for me, will you, sweetheart? I want to be with

you from the minute I put my foot in Devon again for as long as I can. Plan to have dinner with me, all right?''

Donna grew sick at heart as she remembered that she'd promised Rod she'd have dinner with him. She heard the change in Hugh's voice as he asked, "What is it, Donna?"

He was astonishingly intuitive about her, even at long distance. "I'm afraid I made a date for tomorrow, Hugh. I didn't know what your plans would be."

The explanation sounded so feeble.

Too late she realized she should have said no to Rod. From now on, she vowed, she'd make no engagements with anyone until she knew whether or not Hugh was going to be free.

She could hear the desperation creeping into her voice. "Hugh, I think you know what I want to do. But...I...well, I just don't believe in breaking an engagement once you've made it without a good reason."

"Our being together wouldn't be reason enough, Donna?"

"It's not that," she protested. "You know it's not that."

"I don't own you, Donna," he said heavily. "At moments like this, I'm very aware of that."

"No one should ever own anyone else, Hugh. That has nothing to do with love."

The word hung between them like a shimmering pendant. It swung in a silence that seemed to go on and on. Then Hugh spoke, his voice so husky the words rasped. "Are you saying you love me, Donna?"

Was she ready for this? Donna wasn't sure. Nevertheless, she took the plunge.

"Yes," she whispered. "Yes, I love you, darling."

"Me too," Hugh said, the emotion in his voice even more pronounced. "It scares the hell out of me, but I love you, Donna. Dear God, how I love you!"

CHAPTER ELEVEN

DONNA SETTLED FOR A WALK along the beach in front of the Nickerson house the next morning, since she knew that Hugh was still in Boston. It was a dull day, and the heavy clouds were ominous. The sea had the kind of oily, slick look that often presaged the coming of a storm, and this worried her. Hugh didn't need any more bad weather.

She had never before thought so much about the weather, she reflected as she went back to the house. Until now she had never fully appreciated the tremendously powerful effect weather had on so many aspects of life and work.

New avenues in her life had been opened up by being here at the scene of the shipwreck, coming to know Hugh, and gaining at least a slight understanding of his work. She was grateful to him for that. He'd made her realize that, like many people, she'd been too insular in her thinking and needed to broaden her horizons.

She brewed a fresh pot of coffee and settled down in front of her computer, but it was hard to concentrate that morning. She was still shaken by the words she and Hugh had spoken to each other the night before.

She still couldn't believe he'd told her he loved her.

She felt shy at the thought of facing him again. Last night they'd said their goodbyes over the phone on such an emotionally charged note. She wished now that they'd made their declarations face-to-face. She wished she could have seen his expression, and they could have come together physically, after expressing their love in words.

How can I walk up to him and say hello, as if nothing has happened between us, she wondered.

The day moved on. After a few false starts Donna got into the story, and soon she was absorbed. She took a lunch break and fixed herself a peanut butter and jelly sandwich, and by the time she'd eaten it she couldn't wait to get back to her computer.

She felt that she was getting a real grip on Alex Bruce's character. She depicted him as a man who'd been belligerent as a youth, rebelling against parental authority—his father's, especially—in a strict Scottish household. He'd gone into the merchant marine initially as an act of defiance against his family, but he'd found the sea to be his true calling, and he'd risen to the top in the ranks of his profession. Then he had been falsely accused when a load of contraband—guns, to be used by a group of terrorists—were discovered on the ship he was captaining. A man had been killed and his body found in the dock area, a man tied in with the terrorist group that had been scheduled to receive the guns. There was a double cross involved, and Alex had been caught in the middle of it. He'd been accused of the murder, tried and sentenced. Now it was going to be up to his brother—a facsimile of Hugh—to prove his innocence.

Hugh's character was not coming as clear to Donna as Alex's was. She recognized her fear that she might pattern her fictional Hugh too closely on the real Hugh, and she didn't want to do that. She wanted to capture the essence of the real Hugh, yet create her own person. But it was becoming increasingly difficult for her not to put her hero down on paper exactly as he was in real life.

Late in the afternoon she finally shut off her computer for the day, satisfied with the major part of her output but still dissatisfied with her portrait of Hugh. She was using the name Keith for her hero in the book, and Alex had become Andrew. Andrew had assumed his own personality. She could say with honesty that he was no longer merely a copy of Alex Bruce. But Keith was still Hugh. Too much so.

The women in the story were somewhat hazy to her. There was Althea, called Flora in the book, and she'd named the woman with whom Hugh was involved Mary. But they were not yet flesh and blood to her, and she knew she was going to have to do some hard work in developing them.

Still thinking about her characters, Donna soaked in a bubble bath and then dressed for her dinner date with Rod. She was not in the mood to go out with him, and she wished she'd called him this morning and canceled her date after all.

Unfortunately Rod decided to take her to La Gioconda, but it wasn't until they had driven into Orleans and turned into the restaurant's parking lot that Donna realized this. Even then she was tempted to tell him she wasn't in the mood for Italian food, but she held her peace.

"I've been wanting to try this place," Rod said affably. "I've been hearing good things about it."

Donna remained silent.

Once she was inside, seated in a booth with Rod, the restaurant became so reminiscent of Hugh that a bittersweet longing for him swept over Donna.

She made an effort to be sociable for Rod's sake, but she couldn't wait to get through with dinner and out of the restaurant.

Rod didn't attempt to prolong the evening. He was tight-lipped as he pulled up in the little driveway that jutted out toward her apartment at the back of the Nickersons' house, and Donna couldn't blame him.

"I'm sorry, Rod," she said sincerely. "I know I was rotten company."

"I guess I should be the one to apologize," Rod said tautly. "But you should have told me you don't like Italian food."

"I do like Italian food," she protested.

"You could have fooled me," he retorted grimly.

Donna stared at him helplessly. She liked him, she really did. But right now there was no time in her life for any other man but Hugh. It was folly to try to pretend she could enjoy a casual date.

"Look," she suggested, wanting to make peace with Rod, "why don't I fix something for us here one night? I'll ask Mark and Althea to join us."

"Do we need chaperons, Donna?" Rod asked cynically.

"That wasn't what I intended."

He attempted a smile. "Okay," he said. "Call me."

Donna nodded and escaped into the house.

Loneliness closed in on Donna that night, and by morning she'd made one resolution.

She managed to reach Mark before he left for work. "Do you think I could have a phone put in?" she asked. "I wasn't going to bother, but I find I'd really like to have one."

"No problem," Mark replied easily. "There's already a phone line in the apartment. All I have to do is ask the company to hook it up. I'll call Jerry Robbins at the telephone office in town and ask him to send someone over."

Mark grinned at her. "Jerry's a good friend. He'll give this a priority."

Mark was right. The telephone man arrived before noon, and Donna, who had never liked telephones because they so often interrupted her flow of thoughts, had seldom been so glad to see anyone.

She took time out from her writing to call her Aunt Mabel, as if to prove to herself that the phone really worked.

"I was going to drive out to your place," Mabel admitted. "Joe and I were saying last night that we don't see half enough of you. I know you're busy..."

"And so are you, I imagine," Donna put in.

"The motel is full, that's for sure," Mabel said cheerfully. "Between Hugh's men and media people and members of the public who've taken early vacations so they can see the *Portia*, we don't have a bed to spare. I've managed to get a couple of the local women to act as chambermaids for us. It will be several more weeks before the college kids come down to go to work.

"Hugh had supper with us last night," Mabel went on. "He'd been up in Boston trying to unravel a lot of knots, as he put it. They're waiting for this enormous barge to arrive with a lot of equipment on it, and Hugh's keeping one ear out for the weather reports. There are storm warnings posted."

Donna had wandered around outdoors for a time in the middle of the morning, just to get a few breaths of fresh air, and she'd noticed that the clouds looked even more ominous than they had the previous day.

"Hugh said he's hoping to get the salvage operation into full swing by the middle of next week," Mabel added. "But the weather's a big factor. The biggest factor, I guess. Look, my dear, how about honoring us with your presence for dinner tonight. We'll go out somewhere, if you like."

Donna thought about the invitation, then said frankly, "To tell you the truth, Aunt Mabel, I'm bushed. I thought I'd settle for a can of soup tonight and go to bed early. May I have a rain check?"

"Of course you may," Mabel agreed promptly. Curiosity edged her voice. "It sounds to me like you're working again."

"I am."

"Then you're over that block of yours? Wonderful! Is the book going well?"

"Yes," Donna replied, feeling something of a fraud. But the book was going well. It didn't make any difference that it wasn't the same book to which her aunt was referring.

"I'm so glad," Mabel said. "I love your stories. I can't wait to read this one."

"It will take time," Donna warned, and Mabel laughed.

"I'll be patient," she promised. "I'm not so sure about Hugh. He's as much of a fan of yours as I am, in case you don't know it."

TOWARD DUSK it began to rain. It was a heavy rain, pelting down on the roof, and puddles began to form along the Nickersons' flagstone walk.

Donna had worked through the afternoon, and she was bone tired. Fatigue had left her with a dull headache, and as she took a couple of aspirin she thought of Hugh and the night he'd come over to the apartment in the Windcrest complaining of a headache. It seemed such a long time ago, but actually it was less than a month since she'd first met him. Incredible. In the space of less than a month her life had been changed irrevocably.

She showered and slipped on her white terry lounger. She decided to have a glass of sherry before she heated up her can of soup, but all the time she was moving around, her ears were attuned to the silent phone.

Why hadn't Hugh called her?

The sudden realization that he didn't know she had a phone swept over Donna, and she felt a complete fool.

Her fingers fumbled as she dialed the Windcrest. She told herself that chances were Hugh had gone out to dinner, but he answered his phone on the second ring.

Just hearing him say hello made her breathless. She paused long enough so that he said it again, and only then did she speak. "Hugh?"

She could picture the frown that would be creasing his forehead as he asked, "Is that you, Donna?"

"Yes," she answered, happiness giving her voice a light and frothy quality.

"Where are you calling from?"

"My apartment. I asked Mark this morning if I could have a phone put in and he worked the Nickerson brand of magic. Want my number?"

"Do I ever!"

She gave it to him, then said, "I talked to Aunt Mabel earlier. She told me you had supper with them last night."

"That's right. They took pity on my solitary state. I don't suppose there's a chance *you'd* take pity on my solitary state tonight, is there? I know this is last minute, but I haven't eaten yet. Have you?"

"No," she said. "I was going to heat up a can of soup. I just got out of the tub."

His question threw her off guard. "What are you wearing?"

"My terry lounger. The white one."

He groaned. "It's a damn good thing we don't have a video terminal on this phone line."

Donna felt as if his voice were actually caressing her. There was a seductiveness to his tone that washed over her, and she gripped the phone receiver as if it were a ballast, helping her to keep her balance.

"Look, Donna," Hugh said, "*could* I come over? What I thought was, maybe I could stop and pick up some pizza and a bottle of wine? How does that strike you?"

"It strikes me beautifully," Donna told him.

They opened the wine upon Hugh's arrival, but kept the pizza warm in the oven.

They needed no words tonight before moving toward each other. They became enveloped in each other's arms, eyes searching, lips clinging, latent feelings igniting to set their bodies afire.

Again it was raining, again the wind moaned, and nature's orchestration provided a perfect background for their passion. Donna was hungry for the strength and wonder of Hugh. She wanted to feel his hands all over her, and in turn she wanted her fingers familiar with every inch of him. They explored and tasted each other, and there seemed no limit to the nuances of feeling they could provoke.

It was late before they went out to the kitchen to get the pizza. They took it into the living room, making a spread on the coffee table, and Donna felt as if she were participating in a picnic planned for the gods.

Hugh's hair was rumpled, his shirt was wrinkled, and there was a faint stubble on his chin. But there was deep contentment in his gray eyes, and Donna's happiness matched his. She was living in the present tonight, and she didn't want to glance toward the future. Life was too wonderful just as it was.

At one point they heard a car door close. "That must be Mark or Althea, coming back from somewhere," Donna murmured, curled up against Hugh, her head on his shoulder.

He laughed. "It's lucky that you and your landlords aren't curious about each other."

"Live and let live," Donna said dreamily.

"A good philosophy, but few people seem able to practice it."

"Well, right now I can."

"I notice you said 'right now,'" he teased her. "Don't tell me that your curiosity bump isn't usually as big as most people's. You'd have to have a great curiosity in you, being a writer."

"What makes you say that?"

"Well," he replied thoughtfully, "it seems to me that it would take a certain amount of curiosity—or maybe you'd rather call it imagination—to figure out what makes people tick. And your characters are people, aren't they?"

"I hope so."

"Why don't you tell me about this book you're working on, Donna?" Hugh asked unexpectedly.

She drew back. She hadn't wanted his work or hers to infringe tonight.

"I don't like to talk about a book when it's in progress. It's just not good practice to discuss your work when it's ongoing. It's easy to say too much about your story line so that you actually lose your grip on it, or your interest in it. It's wise for a writer to keep up a little element of private suspense. It helps things continue to move. I think it was Hemingway who said he never stopped writing for the day at the end of a sequence or a chapter. He always started in on the next segment even if he only put down a couple of lines."

"Why would that be?"

"To get you into the story again," Donna said. "It's a procedure I follow myself, when I possibly can. Look, let's not talk about writing, all right?"

He smiled. "What would you rather do?"

"Can't you guess?"

HUGH SLIPPED AWAY at about the time dawn was breaking on the eastern horizon. Donna stirred as he rose from the bed, and she mumbled drowsily, "Hugh?"

"Shush, sweetheart," he whispered, bending to kiss her moist, warm lips. "I'll be in touch a little later.

Don't bother about getting ready for a run. It's still pouring out.''

Donna was conscious of the driving rain, but then she turned over and fell asleep again.

It was nearly nine when she awakened, and at first she was dismayed. She never slept this late, usually she was at work by eight o'clock at the latest. But right now she was in no hurry. She'd sent a proposal to her agent but so far had heard nothing back. She'd gone ahead with the book on her own. Once she was offered and accepted a contract for it there would be a deadline to contend with, but until then her time was her own.

Several times during the morning she went to the window to look out at the sea, dark gray and churning angrily, the tips of the waves frothing white.

She wished she would hear from Hugh. Twice she nearly dialed the motel, but she felt sure he wouldn't be in his room.

At noon she put on her slicker and boots and drove over to the shack. Mark was alone, and he greeted her as if he'd been craving company, which was unusual for him.

"What'll it be?" he asked her. "I can offer two specialties of the house. A succulent hamburger or an exotic hot dog."

"I'll take the hot dog, if you please, and maybe a side order of french fries," Donna said. "And coffee. Where's Althea?"

"She and Bruce drove up to Boston this morning," Mark told her with a scowl. "Bruce needed to check in with someone at the British consulate about something, and Althea went along for the ride. There wasn't much I could do to dissuade her. Business isn't exactly brisk today. You just missed Hugh, incidentally.''

Disappointment twisted, a hard painful knot, and Donna took a quick sip of the coffee.

"He stopped by with Brent and Jim and a couple of the others and they wolfed down a few hamburgers.''

"What about the crew?'' Donna asked. "Are you still feeding them?''

"You mean is Althea still feeding them?'' Mark corrected. "No, she makes brownies and stuff like that for them now and then, but mostly they're on their own. They have a cook on board and everything's functioning, like power and water. They can fend for themselves. The men have the loan of a van so they can go back and forth to town to shop. All the comforts of home, or almost.''

He paused. "Shall I load your hot dog with all the extra goodies, or do you want to do it yourself?''

"You can do it,'' Donna said. She hazarded a question. "Has Terry O'Connor written her story about you?''

He grinned. "It's due out in the Sunday paper. She sent a photographer over the last clear day and he took a whole bunch of pictures. Althea says we're going to be so swamped we'll never be able to handle the mob once the story comes out. We may have to press you back into service.''

"Yes, I feel I've let you down lately,'' Donna admitted. "I've gotten hooked on my work and I tend to lose track of time when I'm writing.''

"Look, that's what you're supposed to be doing,'' Mark said hastily. "We've managed. A couple of women from town have been working for us occasionally, it's been fine. You were here when we needed you the most," he reminded her.

"I think I'm the one who needed you the most," she countered. "Having your apartment is a godsend."

"I'd put it the other way. I like your being there, for Althea's sake."

"I don't see that much of Althea. She seldom comes over."

"She hasn't needed to yet," Mark said rather cryptically.

"What's that supposed to mean?"

"One of these days something's got to give with Althea and Bruce. If Hugh salvages the ship successfully, chances are that Bruce will sail off into the sunset with it. On the other hand, if the salvage effort fails, I suppose Bruce will fly into the sunset on a commercial jet headed for Scotland. What I'm saying is, it's like a time bomb, Donna. The bomb's bound to go off when whatever happens with Bruce happens, and that's when Althea's going to need you."

"You don't think there's a chance that she and Alex will work something out?" Donna suggested tentatively.

"How the hell could they?" Mark asked practically, and she could give him no good answer.

When she had finished lunch, Donna left Mark and headed back to the parking lot. She was about to get back into her car when she heard an engine throb behind her.

"Donna!"

She turned to see Hugh pulling up in a Jeep. He clambered down and came over to her, wearing the parka he'd been wearing the first day they met, the hood pulled up.

He was laughing. "Don't tell me you came over here to have lunch in this kind of weather?" he teased.

She grinned at him. "Guilty as charged."

"Mark's hamburgers are great, but are they that great?"

"I had a hot dog."

"And where are you off to now?"

"Back to work, I guess," she said. "What about you?"

"I should go back to work, too, but I don't want to. Look, there's a movie in Orleans I've been wanting to catch and they have rainy day matinees. How about it?"

She didn't hesitate. "You've sold me."

"Your vehicle or mine?"

"I've never ridden in a Jeep," she said. "Let's take yours. It *is* yours, isn't it?"

"The company's, yes."

He helped her up the steep step, then took his place behind the wheel. They lumbered out of the parking lot, and Hugh cut across town to the main road that led to Orleans.

"This movie's going to be familiar to you," Hugh warned her.

"Oh? Why should it be?"

"You wrote the story," he replied smugly.

"Are you taking me to see *A Thread Of Silver*?" she demanded. So far that was the only one of her books to be made into a movie.

"That's right. You don't mind, do you?"

"Hugh, I've seen it. And as you said, I wrote the story in the first place."

"I've seen it three times. This'll be the fourth, and I can't wait."

She shook her head. "You're impossible."

Hugh bought a big bucket of buttered popcorn for each of them, and as she settled into the folding leather seat next to him Donna felt like a schoolgirl playing hooky, a feeling she'd had on other occasions with Hugh.

"This is fun," she giggled, as the houselights dimmed. "I'm glad I let you talk me into it."

"It didn't take much talking," Hugh reminded her. He leaned down to whisper into her ear, "Anyway, you should follow your impulses more often."

It was an experience to watch her story come to life on the screen with Hugh at her side. To Donna's surprise, he became as immersed in the movie as if he'd never seen it before, and at one point she whispered to him, "You really are a mystery buff!"

"I told you so," he retorted, unruffled.

As the plot progressed, Donna began to remember working on the story, some of the problems she'd had with the plot and how she had resolved them.

The film had turned out well. She had been as satisfied with the final product as most authors usually are with a completed book. There were still things she'd change about the story if she had the opportunity to do so, she found herself musing, but that was the way it always was.

The woman in the story reminded her faintly of Althea—Flora, she corrected herself swiftly. She'd have to watch that. Flora should be a distinct personality from this heroine.

She began brooding about Flora, and she shifted restlessly. She never read her own books once they were in print, and seeing the movie version once would be enough in the future, she promised herself.

It gave her a sense of satisfaction, though, to see how much Hugh was enjoying her story, familiar though it was to him.

The wind was gusting as they came out of the theater, and the afternoon was dark. Rain still fell from the charcoal clouds, and Donna shivered.

"Damn it!" said Hugh. "There were gale warnings posted but I was hoping the pattern would change. It looks like we're in for something."

"Will this affect the *Portia*?" Donna asked.

He shook his head. "I don't think so. Just me." He smiled sheepishly. "That sounds pretty personal, doesn't it? What I mean is that it will affect our operation and hold up getting the barge with the derrick aboard it to the site. The barge is being towed up the coast by a tugboat, and the last report I had was that they were entering Cape Cod Canal this morning. Now it looks like the only thing we can do is to have them moor inside Provincetown Harbor until the weather clears. Just another thorn."

"You must be used to thorns by now," Donna said softly.

"I should be. So much hinges on the weather. And I think New England weather must be about the most unpredictable in the world." He shrugged philosophically. "Nothing I can do about it."

"Look, why don't you wait here under the marquee and I'll go get the Jeep."

"No," she said. "My clothes are rainproof. I'll go with you."

She didn't want to be separated from him for even a minute.

He grabbed her elbow and steered her across the rain-slicked street. When they reached the curb on the other side he paused to bend and whisper as close to her ear as her rain hood would permit, "Have I told you today that I love you?"

Donna's head swerved and she looked up into his eyes, oblivious to the rain, oblivious to everything but his nearness. She reached out to him, and their lips met. Their kiss was mixed with the rain and their own elixir.

"Oh, Hugh," she murmured, as he released her. "There's never been anyone like you. There never will be again."

He tried to smile, but there was a catch in his voice as he said, "I hope that's good."

CHAPTER TWELVE

IT WAS STILL RAINING the next morning. Donna needed to get out of the apartment for a while before starting work, so she drove uptown and bought a copy of the *Boston Globe*.

She stopped for a cup of coffee and an order of English muffins and thumbed through the paper, looking for any stories Terry O'Connor might have written about the *Portia*.

She didn't expect to see Hugh's face smiling up at her.

The photograph was an informal one, taken on the beach. He was wearing a Windbreaker, his hair was tousled, and he was squinting slightly in the bright sunlight—which meant that the photo was at least a few days old, Donna thought wryly.

The story, however, was up-to-date. Terry must have talked to Hugh the night before, because he was quoted as saying that the barge *Stardust* and an eighty-five-foot tugboat were going to stay in the sanctuary of Provincetown Harbor until the weather cleared.

MacDonough said that progress with the salvage operation has been delayed because of this latest shift in the weather, but he stated that he was not unduly concerned. The salvage company head, who is personally supervising the attempt to rescue the beached freighter, commented, "We're used to changing our game rules."

He stated that the delay was not likely to cause a serious hitch in his plans. "We intend to dredge a four-foot-deep trench to the waterside of the *Portia*, then we're going to move her on a high tide," MacDonough said confidently.

The 130-foot-high derrick aboard the *Stardust* will be used to haul the *Portia* off the shoreline, according to MacDonough.

Donna set the paper aside as she finished her coffee. Hugh's confidence radiated even in the quotes he'd given the reporter, yet she'd seen him at moments when he hadn't appeared nearly so sure of himself.

Yesterday afternoon, for instance. He had sounded like a small boy lost in the dark when he'd told her he hoped her saying no one else would ever be like him was "good."

Professionally he was very sure of himself, and with plenty of reason, Donna was certain. Personally he was as vulnerable as anyone else. She was sure of that, too, and this vulnerability endeared him to her all the more.

THE PHONE RANG as Donna was working on a flashback dealing with an episode in which Andrew, as a teenager, got into trouble and aroused his father's fury.

At first she hated the interruption, resenting the telephone's intrusion as she always did when she was writing.

Then, as it continued to ring, she realized that very few people knew her number. It could be Hugh, and it was.

"What do you do on yet another rainy day when the whole damned salvage operation's halted?" he moaned. "I hear there's a good German place over in the Cape Cod Mall. Want to try it out for lunch?"

The book lured her, but Hugh's offer won out.

"Yes."

He laughed. "I like women who speak in words of one syllable, especially when the answer goes my way. I'll pick you up in half an hour, okay?"

Donna managed to bring the scene she was working on to a quick—and temporary—conclusion. Then she switched off the computer, hastily brushed her hair and put on some makeup. There wasn't time to change, but the slacks and sweater she was wearing would do on a day like this.

"Don't talk to me about New England springs," Hugh said direly as he swung onto the mid-Cape highway. "I feel as if I'm in danger of contracting a terminal case of mildew. The men are getting cabin fever, too. A couple of them went up to Boston today just to do something, and Brent and Jim have been playing cribbage until they've worn the cards out."

"What about the *Stardust*?" Donna asked.

He glanced at her curiously. "How did you know the name of the barge?"

"How do most people know things? I read it in the paper."

"Terry's story? I missed the morning *Globe*," Hugh confessed. "Well, the *Stardust* is still in Province-town Harbor and so is the tug. The weather forecast is on the optimistic side, though. I checked with the

Coast Guard just before I drove over to pick you up. We may be able to get started in earnest in a couple more days."

"How long will it take?"

"How long will what take?"

"To get the *Portia* off the beach," she said patiently.

He laughed. "That's a good question. We may make it on the first try, if the tide and everything else cooperates. Sometimes it happens that way. But there have been so many snags in this operation I'm not making any bets. I'm only saying," he added firmly, "that no matter what you hear around town we *will* get her off. Frankly I'm getting pretty damned tired of the rumors. One of the selectmen actually called me last night to ask if it was true we were going to abandon the ship so that the town would have to take on the responsibility for her."

"What did you tell him?"

"I told him it was a nice thought but I couldn't afford it. Some other idiot has suggested she could be made into a parking garage. I understand it gets so crowded on Massasoit Beach sometimes they have to turn cars away?"

"Uncle Joe would know about that."

"I don't doubt it's true. Even so, can you think of a much more stupid idea?"

"People just like to talk, Hugh," she said mildly.

"Don't they though." There was a suppressed anger in his voice as he spoke. "People like to gossip, and as I hear it, there are rumors floating around about Alex and Althea."

"Oh, no," Donna protested.

"Oh, yes," Hugh said grimly. "If Mark's hearing what I've been hearing he must be foaming—to say nothing of what Alex will be doing if any of this gets back to him. Alex has a razor-edge temper."

So did Andrew. And Andrew, like Alex, had been implicated in a murder. In her mind Donna merged her fictional character with the real one and shivered.

"It's hard to keep secrets in a place like Devon," she said. "You should talk to Aunt Mabel about that. Uncle Joe was brought up in Brockton, but Aunt Mabel comes from a Cape Cod family as old as Mark and Althea's. She was born and brought up in Devon, she met Uncle Joe when he was working here one summer when he was in college. She can tell you all there is to know about local tongue wagging. And she'd be the first to say that one should consider the source."

"That isn't always easy to do," Hugh replied quietly. "If I start hearing rumors about us, Donna, I can make no promises about how I'll handle it. I don't have too long a fuse myself, especially when it comes to something that really matters to me. I don't want to hear anyone say *anything* about you."

"Not anything?" she teased, trying to inject a lighter tone into the conversation.

He smiled. "Maybe I am taking it too seriously, sweetheart," he admitted. "You mean so damned much to me, that's all. And I'd say that Alex feels the same way about Althea."

She hesitated only briefly. "Do you know Alex's wife, Hugh?"

"Heather? Yes, I've met her. I wouldn't say I know her, though. She'd be a hard person to get close to. She...well, she seems a very stiff-necked woman. She's about Alex's age, I suppose, but she appears older.

Her old mother lives with them, and she's a martinet. Alex hasn't had the kind of a household a man would yearn to go home to, and if there ever was any romance between Heather and himself in the first place I'd say it died long ago. But he has accepted his responsibility.

"There was a period, when Alex was deep in trouble, when I thought the marriage might come to an end," Hugh continued. "But people don't divorce as lightly in Scotland as they do here. Heather was bitter; she was of no help when Alex needed moral support the most, I'll tell you that. Alex was already going through hell, and she heaped on a few embers. Since then I think he's staying away from home as much as possible. But of course there are the two children. The boy must be into his teens, the girl is a year or two younger. The problem is that they're entirely under the influence of Heather and her mother, so Alex is a complete outsider to them. I would suspect that, if anything, they disapprove of him, or would if they were older."

"What a pity," Donna murmured.

"Yes, it is a pity," Hugh agreed, "because Alex is a man with a lot to offer. It's no wonder that sometimes he seems so driven. I know I said to you once that he, at least, had a wife and children to go back to. I wasn't facing the facts as they really are in Alex's life when I said that. I suppose what I mean is that I can't blame Alex if he has fallen in love with Althea. She's everything, absolutely everything, Heather has never been.

"Damn it," Hugh said roughly, staring moodily ahead at the highway. "Why do people have to be so unkind?"

It was a relief to get into the brightly lighted Cape Cod Mall, where the atmosphere dispelled the gloominess of the rainy day. The German restaurant brimmed with *gemutlichkeit*, and Hugh ordered imported beer and sauerbraten sandwiches for both of them.

He tried to get Donna to talk about her book, but she managed to evade him. Finally he asked, "Are you superstitious about discussing writing in progress, Donna?"

"Perhaps, a little bit," she admitted.

"You don't seem like a superstitious person."

"Oh, come on, Hugh," she teased. "If I spill salt I always throw some over my shoulder, and I never walk under ladders."

"What about black cats? Do you shudder if they cross your path?"

"I love black cats," she said, and he laughed.

"I've always liked cats myself. Dogs, too, for that matter. But I've never had a pet to call my own. My mother wasn't much for animals, though you'd think she might have been, living out in the country as she did." He grinned. "I was exposed to one cat for a while recently. An orange beauty by the name of Marmalade. She belongs to Charlie Evans, and one reason I was in his apartment was so that I could cat-sit."

"What did you do with her when you came to Devon?" Donna asked.

"Pawned her off on a beautiful blonde named Angela who happens to be Charlie's next-door neighbor," Hugh reported with a grin. "It was at Charlie's suggestion, I might add. Now Charlie's home again. I talked to him yesterday. It seems that Angela couldn't bear to let Marmalade go, so they're sharing her. Which means that they're having dinner together most nights and, I suspect, breakfast together quite a few mornings," Hugh concluded wickedly. "You'll have to meet Charlie. He's quite a character. I thought about calling him and asking him to join us here, but I was too selfish."

"Selfish?"

"I wanted you all to myself, Donna. Maybe I'll be more generous about sharing you once we get this ship off the beach."

DONNA HATED TO SEE the rain end. Hugh had warned that once the weather cleared he was going to have to get the real action going. As it was, it was more than a month since the *Portia* had taken up residence on Massasoit Beach, and Hugh told Donna the selectmen were claiming that having the ship around was costing the town a fortune.

She'd invited Hugh to have dinner with her, and they were drinking whiskey sours while the fish chowder she'd made simmered on the stove.

"They're having to pay overtime for the extra police on duty, the park department employees and a lot of the town personnel," Hugh admitted, "but I still can't buy their gripe. The town's been coining a mint with all the people who've come to see the ship. They've eaten here and slept here and bought truckloads of souvenirs. Some of that largess must filter back to the town coffer in a variety of ways, I would imagine."

"Rod Eldridge says having the *Portia* here has been the biggest bonanza that ever happened to Devon," Donna confided.

"He should know," Hugh said rather stiffly.

She nodded. "Rod's very active civically, and his position in the bank keeps him pretty much in the know about everything going on locally."

"I'm sure it does."

She laughed. "Hugh, Rod is a friend, nothing more."

"So you've told me."

"I'd have more grounds to complain about Terry O'Connor," she said lightly.

"You'd have no grounds to complain about Terry O'Connor, or anyone else I've met since I've known you," he corrected.

"No? You took her down to the ship site in your Jeep," she pointed out. "You've never done that with me."

He looked astounded. "I never thought you'd want to go."

"No? I'm as interested in your salvage operation as anyone could be," she told him, no longer teasing. "Your work fascinates me, I thought I'd made that fairly plain to you. I'd enjoy seeing any aspect of it, and I already told you that day we went to the movies that I'd never even been in a Jeep before."

"Come down to the ship with me in the morning," he offered. "I'd rather you didn't go aboard her, though. Alex might not object, but there's so much equipment on her right now it's bad enough having the people aboard who have to be there."

"You don't need to worry," Donna said with a smile. "I have no intention of negotiating that Jacob's ladder."

Hugh grinned. "It's not really that bad. It hugs the side of the ship, and it's just a series of rungs strung together. All you have to do is keep a tight grip, and whether you're ascending or descending it's wise not to look down."

Donna shuddered. "Enough said."

They'd had their dinner and were having coffee in the living room when a pounding sounded at the door. Donna opened it to admit both Althea and Alex.

Alex was white-faced and tight-lipped, and Althea looked as if she was about to burst into tears. "Donna," she said. "Hugh. We knew you were here, we saw your car."

"Please forgive us for interrupting like this," Alex added, and Donna knew this man would strain to be polite, no matter how difficult the circumstances.

"Come in, come in," she invited quickly.

"Yes, come in," Hugh echoed. "Donna and I were about to indulge in a nightcap. Will you join us?"

Alex nodded. "I doubt I've ever needed a drink more."

Donna remembered that Hugh had said there'd been rumors at one point that Alex had an alcohol problem, but she doubted it. She'd seen enough of him to think otherwise.

She felt a sudden, swift empathy for Alex Bruce. She was on his side. On both Alex's side and Andrew's side, she amended with a small inner smile. She could only pray they would both win out.

Hugh brought in brandy and a couple of different liqueurs. Althea asked for amaretto, and Alex chose the brandy.

Hugh had uncovered four reasonably small glasses in the kitchen, and he carefully meted liquid into each of them. Absently they drank a mutual toast, then Alex said tautly, his Scottish accent more pronounced than usual, "I don't know quite what the hell to do about this, Hugh. All sorts of nasty gossip has gotten back to Mark, and he's extremely angry. I can't say I blame him."

"Mark's being unreasonable," Althea put in. "I told him the next thing he knows the gossipmongers will be saying things about him and Terry O'Connor. He's been seeing quite a bit of her, a fact I'm sure hasn't gone unobserved. Everyone in Devon knows that Mark's been off women ever since he got out of the service."

"And what did Mark say to that?" Hugh asked.

"I wouldn't repeat it," Althea told him.

"Althea, you know you can't take everything you hear seriously," Donna put in. "Mark, of all people, ought to realize that."

"Maybe so, but he's *not* realizing it. He was ridiculous tonight. I'm surprised Alex didn't get up and...and slug him," she finished defiantly.

"It should have been the other way around, don't you think?" Alex asked tightly. "I'm the one in the wrong, Althea, and your brother is absolutely in the right. But that's not the point. The point is, how can we stop this? Do you or Hugh have any ideas, Donna?"

"Yes," Donna said. "I do. Just ignore it, that's all, Alex. As my Aunt Mabel says, consider the source. Don't pay any attention to what people say, and they'll get tired of saying it. I'm disappointed in Mark to think he didn't tell you that himself."

"This is too close to Mark for him to tell anyone anything," Hugh put in. "Donna's right, though. There's not a damned thing you and Althea can do about people talking about you, any more than there will be if they start talking about Donna and me."

He let this sink in, and Alex nodded thoughtfully. But then he said, "I have a bit more of a problem, Hugh. You know that."

"Yes, I know that. But the same course of action on your part still applies."

"And if we get beyond rumor?" Alex asked softly.

"I don't think anything's going to get beyond rumor," Hugh said firmly. "If it does, I'll be behind you, Alex. Good God, man, you should know that!"

"You've been behind me before," Alex admitted. "But for that I wouldn't even be here. And it might have been better for Althea if I weren't."

Althea covered his large, tanned hand with her small white one and said quickly, "Don't speak like that. If you hadn't come here, Alex, my life would never have been complete."

Her statement rang out in the room, brave and poignant, and Donna blinked away sudden tears. Her eyes found Hugh's, and they stared at each other. Though she wouldn't have phrased it just as Althea had, her feelings were the same. If she and Hugh had never met, her life could not possibly ever have been complete.

"Where is Mark?" she asked suddenly.

"I think he's gone uptown to see if any of the bars are still open," Althea replied. "It's so long since Mark's sought refuge in a bar he wouldn't know. Maybe this will be good for him. Between Alex and me and Terry and you, as well, Donna, Mark's been shaken out of his apathy, and it's a jolt he's needed for a long time. I can't be sorry about that. But," she added, her voice lowered, "I've never wanted to hurt him."

"Hell, you haven't hurt him," Hugh told her. "He's playing the protective older brother part, which is fine. But he's going to have to face a few facts. There are a number of things," he added, his expression grim, "that we're all going to have to take in stride."

MASSIVE WAS THE KEY WORD, Donna decided. Everything around her was massive. Sitting in the front seat of Hugh's company Jeep, she was closer to the *Portia* than she'd ever been before, and the vast bulk of the black-and-green ship astonished her.

The beach area immediately around her stirred with activity. Four-wheel-drive vehicles and pickup trucks with oversize wheels were parked on the sand at all sorts of odd angles. Men clustered in groups, turning occasionally to study the ship then going back into their huddles. The massive chains that curled out from the ship were oversize, and rubber hoses twisted across the sand like monster snakes. Huge rolls of cable were stacked as if a giant's child had been playing with them.

Hugh had left her briefly to consult with some of his men, and she'd assured him she didn't mind being alone, the scene captivated her. But now she saw Alex approaching the Jeep, and he came to stand by her window, smiling down at her.

"This is your first time down, isn't it?"

Donna nodded. She'd been relatively close to the *Portia* that memorable day when the ship had tossed helplessly, caught in the clutches of the raging sea, but since then she'd kept her distance. It was as if she'd felt instinctively that she had no real place there, that she'd be trespassing. Most of the time she'd headed in the opposite direction on her beach walks. On those occasions when she and Hugh had turned south on the beach, he'd halted at a midway point and they'd gone back toward the Snack Shack. She remembered his saying he'd soon be spending enough time at the shipwreck locale.

Alex said quietly, "I'd like to ask you aboard, Donna, but the ship's off limits to visitors just now for safety's sake." There was a sadness to the smile that twisted his beautifully shaped mouth. "Perhaps some other time, some other place, I'll be fortunate enough to be able to invite you and Hugh aboard for dinner with me."

Their gazes locked, and it was impossible for Donna not to be aware of how attractive Alex was. "I hope so, Alex," she said with feeling.

"I appreciate your support more than I can say, Donna," he told her, his Scottish accent seeming to give his words a special emphasis. He looked her right in the eye. "I was not guilty before, and I am not guilty of any kind of neglect or misconduct now, I assure you of that."

Donna knew by his words that Hugh must have told him he'd confided in her.

"This was truly an act of God," he said. "Under the circumstances, I am convinced there is nothing I or anyone else could have done to keep the *Portia* off this beach. The problem, of course, is my past. If it catches up with me, rumors will fly even faster than they have about Althea and myself. For Althea, especially, I hope that isn't going to happen."

"A lot depends whether or not Hugh gets the ship off the beach, doesn't it, Alex?"

He nodded. "Yes, it does. If Hugh's salvage efforts are successful, then this will go down merely as another incident in Cape Cod's colorful history. If the *Portia* can't be salvaged...well, there is certain to be more speculation. Conjectures will build, and rumors with them. So," he said heavily, "let's hope it doesn't come to that."

Donna was watching Hugh, who was at the center of a cluster of men, Brent Hancock and Jim Babson among them. He was wearing jeans and boots and a dark green Windbreaker. His hair was ruffled by the wind, which was blowing gently but steadily. He looked a part of the action, he clearly belonged there, a man destined to fight a primeval kind of battle. Hugh was capable of waging his own kind of war with the elements, of defying nature. Even the heaviest of odds would not daunt him.

In that way they were so different, Donna reflected. She'd never been a person to look for challenges. She'd refused more than one dare in her time, then had felt like a coward afterward, wishing she had displayed more courage.

She was at her best with a typewriter or a computer keyboard in front of her, conjuring up products of her imagination and bringing them to life on a printed page. She liked to think that in her book based on the *Portia* she would make her readers feel the cold, taste the salt and sense the danger. Yet all of that was so vicarious.

This was the real thing, she brooded, watching Hugh. If life was indeed a stage, Hugh was a person who would always be at the center of the action, while she, for the most part, would stay in the shadows, observing.

"I guess I'd best get back to the ship," Alex said quietly. "The *Stardust* was being towed around the hook of Provincetown, the last we heard. She'll be on the scene before too much longer and then the action should be starting. Hugh tells me he hopes to be prepared to make his first salvage attempt on the next lunar high tide. That's an especially high tide, and he wants all the water possible around when he starts moving the *Portia*.

"Wish us luck," he said softly.

CHAPTER THIRTEEN

THAT NIGHT Donna drove down the beach to the shipwreck site again with Hugh. The entire area was floodlighted, the *Portia* outlined dramatically against the black night. Donna felt, as she had in the beginning, that she was watching a movie being made. The huge ship, the lights, the figures in silhouette moving across the sand, and an atmosphere of tension and excitement lifted the scene out of the norm and gave it a total sense of unreality.

The rest of Hugh's crew had come into town that afternoon, following on the heels of the *Stardust*, now anchored just offshore. The barge and the towering derrick it carried were plainly visible in the glare of the floodlights.

"They off-loaded the front-end loader at Provincetown," Hugh explained. "She's the big baby that will be digging out the sand around the *Portia*, and I assure you she is indeed big."

He was sitting next to Donna in the front seat of the Jeep, his attention riveted on the activity before them. "The loader will be trucked along Route 6 through Orleans and then here sometime before dawn," he added. "She's a monster piece of machinery. I'm depending on her to gobble up that sand, then we'll be in business."

"What will you be using the derrick for?" Donna asked him.

"She's going to strike pay dirt for us. She's going to haul the *Portia* right off this shoreline—given a high tide and a reasonable amount of luck."

Was every piece of machinery in the salvage business female to Hugh, Donna wondered. Couldn't some of the equipment be a "he"?

She asked Hugh this and he chuckled. "Tradition," he said lightly.

Then, more seriously, he added, "Tomorrow we'll start dredging a trench to the seaward side of the ship." He went on, almost as if talking to himself. "If we can win the battle with the shifting sand around here, our problem will be at least halfway solved. Then all we'll need is the pull of the moon."

Donna was startled. "What?"

"We're waiting until the moon's nearly full," Hugh explained. "Remember, tides are lunar powered, and they're highest at the time of the full moon. We hope to make our initial attempt to get the *Portia* off by the first of the lunar high tides. If we don't succeed we'll still have some time to buy. The tides are expected to be above normal for several days this month, so if we can get the sand dug out, if we're ready, then we should have luck on our side."

There was enough light to see Hugh's grin. "A lot of 'ifs,' aren't there?"

"I don't know if I could live with them," Donna admitted.

"It's not a matter of choice, Donna. Have you heard the latest?"

"I'm not sure."

"Well, you know that there's a freighter permanently moored over in Cape Cod Bay, don't you? It was used for target practice by the Air National Guard for years."

"Yes. The *James Longstreet*. I remember seeing that big ship offshore the first time I ever came to the Cape. It never seemed to move. Finally I found out that it was a permanent part of the picture. Evidently it had done duty in World War II, but afterward the official decision was that this would be a good finale to its career."

"She, please, Donna," Hugh protested. "Her career."

"All right, her career."

"Well, they've been saying around town that it would be a good idea to let the *Portia* become a target-practice ship," Hugh reported. "I heard she'd be great for naval maneuvers. She could be shot at from the seaside."

He frowned.

"I guess my sense of humor is lacking at this point when it comes to that vessel. I'm getting enough subtle grief from the town fathers, and today the park department supervisor was complaining that they're about three weeks behind in getting ready for the summer season because of the ship. They've had to put all their manpower into keeping the snow fences up so the spectators won't tramp over the dunes and monitoring the crowds. There are park department employees on duty at night, as well as extra police, to be sure people don't sneak too close to the ship in the dark."

"For any reason?" Donna asked. "I can't imagine hordes trooping down to this scene at night. What harm would a few stragglers do?"

"There are sick people who might think it would be funny to do a sabotage job on the *Portia*," Hugh pointed out. "Maybe set her afire, even blow her up. Quite a disaster could be created, and no one wants to chance it, least of all me. From tomorrow on I'll be spending a major part of my time aboard her, Donna. I'll want to be right here. This is heavy-duty stuff and I don't want any of the men taking needless chances."

"What about you?" she asked, fighting back the feeling of depression on learning that Hugh was going to become even more involved in his work, which meant she'd be seeing much less of him.

"What about me?"

"I have an idea you've taken a few chances in your time. Maybe not needless ones, but I'll bet there have been moments when you've thrown caution to the winds."

"Only when I've had to," he said soberly. "There are no guarantees in this business, and yes, there are dangers. I'd be a fool to deny that. But I have no desire to risk my neck, Donna. And...well, maybe this sounds funny, but since I've known you my neck has become more valuable to me than it used to be. Look," he said, while his words were still sinking in with Donna, "I need to speak to Alex. Would you mind waiting here for a few minutes?"

"No," she said. "Of course not."

"I'll try not to be too long."

Donna watched him move across the beach, a feeling of love sweeping through her. She watched him pause when different men hailed him. Everyone seemed to know him, and she could sense an enthusiasm in their greetings even from this distance. It was easy to recognize that Hugh must be very popular with the men he worked with.

Despite what he'd said to her about not risking his neck, Donna was sure Hugh would never ask one of his men to do something he wouldn't do himself. That was admirable, but she also found it grounds for worry. She felt as if Hugh had a double-edged sword hanging over him: potential physical danger, plus the inherent perils that could stem from being so mentally fatigued that mind and body ceased cooperating. She was aware that Hugh's part in the salvage operation required a great deal of mental effort, far more mental effort than physical, and Donna knew only too well how exhausting mental exercise could be. After writing for hours at a time, she was often burned out when she went to bed, and as a result she slept poorly. It was different when she'd spend time out of doors, like the other day when she and Hugh had gone off to Provincetown together.

It was different when she had Hugh sleeping by her side, Donna admitted to herself. She felt a sense of sanctuary then, a security such as she'd never known before. With her head on Hugh's shoulder, she was lulled by love and the hope that maybe things could end "happily ever after" in real life.

Now she had to face the unhappy fact that Hugh wouldn't be spending many more nights with her until the *Portia* was freed. *If* the *Portia* was freed. And after that...?

Donna firmly shut her mind to the future.

Hugh apologized for having been gone so long when he got back to the Jeep. "There are so many damned things to think about," he complained as he shifted into gear and drove back across the dunes, away from the beach.

When they reached her apartment, he said, "I think I'd better say good night here, Donna. If I come in I'm not going to want to leave you, and I have to get back to the planning board. There are a few more wrinkles to iron out, and I need to handle them tonight."

He drew her into his arms. "Oh God, it gets harder and harder to leave you. I don't know how much more of this I can take."

She tried to keep her voice steady. "Any chance of a beach walk in the morning?" she asked. "It looks like the sun's going to be shining for a change."

"Yes," he said, "yes, I want to go walking with you. I may not get a chance to see you the rest of the day. And tomorrow night I'll be aboard the ship."

"Shall I bring along a thermos of coffee and some blueberry muffins?"

"Sure," he said, managing a lopsided grin. "We can have a breakfast picnic on the beach."

The grin faded, and he tugged her toward him, not kissing her but pulling her face against his. Donna felt the roughness of his skin, and the touch of him, the texture of him, had a strangely erotic effect. In so many ways Hugh was the sexiest man she had ever met, and it was impossible for her to be near him for very long without becoming aroused. Her body moved involuntarily, and she knew her movements struck a chord in him. He said hoarsely, "Donna, Donna, don't tempt me."

Her voice sounded very small. "I'm not trying to tempt you, Hugh," she told him, which was true. She couldn't help her own reactions.

"I can't leave you tonight," he told her. "I can't let you go. Donna, can I come in...for just a while?"

"You can come in for as long as you want."

There was an urgency to the way they made love that night. Once Hugh had left, Donna thought back on it and shivered. It was almost as if they'd both felt this might be their last time, as if they were determined to satiate themselves with emotions so powerful they would never be forgotten.

Theirs was a desire that seemed as endless as the tides. It was very hard to let him go. Very hard. The loneliness of her bed without him in it became so painful that Donna got up and made herself a cup of tea at three o'clock in the morning.

She walked to the window with her tea, sipping it as she stared out the window toward the ocean. Moonlight shimmered across the water, and for the first time in her life she wanted to blot out the moon. Perhaps if the moon could be made invisible there would be no lunar high tides. Then the *Portia* would have to stay on the beach for a long, long time, and Hugh wouldn't need to leave Devon.

Donna was startled by the faintest of knocks on her living-room door, and she opened it to find Althea on the threshold.

Althea was wearing a quilted robe over her nightgown, tied at the waist with a matching sash. It seemed to Donna that Althea's waistline had shrunk lately, and her face was haggard.

"I couldn't sleep and I saw your light," Althea said. "Do you mind if I stay with you for just a few minutes, Donna?"

"Of course not," Donna said quickly. "Can I make you a cup of tea?"

Althea shook her head. "No, thanks. I just want to be with you for a while."

So Mark had been right. Althea was going to need her. Donna only hoped she was up to fulfilling that need. Her own emotions were on shaky ground. She and Althea were facing the same problem. Inevitably the men they loved were going to leave them.

"Alex is going to be chained to that damned ship from now on," Althea said. "I know he'll see me every chance he gets, but the pace is picking up. You can sense it, can't you, even though I never know just what they're doing with all that stuff they've got around there."

Donna nodded. Tonight she'd been intensely aware of the pickup in tempo of the operation when she'd been on the beach with Hugh, even though, like Althea, little of what was going on made much sense to her.

"It'll be over so soon," Althea went on. "So soon. One way or the other. I just wish to God I knew how it was going to turn out. As far as Alex and I are concerned, it doesn't much matter. But it's the most important thing in the world when it comes to Alex's future. He's afraid that if the *Portia* isn't salvaged he'll never get another berth as captain on a merchant ship. Yes, I know about everything he's been through," she said, even though Donna had posed no questions. "Alex has had a rough life, I don't know anyone who's had a rougher one. It seems so...unfair."

"Life is often unfair, Althea," Donna pointed out gently.

"Yes, I know that. But the odds always seem to have been stacked against Alex and I'd give anything if something would go right for him. Hugh's a good friend to him," she added unexpectedly. "If anyone can help him, Hugh can."

"If Hugh can, he will," Donna said firmly.

"Yes, I think that, too." Althea looked up, her deep brown eyes darkly shadowed. "What's to become of you and Hugh?" she asked. "You love each other, don't you? I'm not wrong about that?"

"No, you're not wrong about that," Donna said, fighting for steadiness. "But I don't know what's to become of us." She smiled sadly. "It looks as if both you and I have fallen in love with men with whom we can have no future."

"What's to prevent you from having a future with Hugh?" Althea asked bluntly. "He's not married. At least, that's what Alex said."

"No, Hugh's not married and I doubt he ever will be," Donna said, and hearing the words spoken aloud gave them a harsh reality. "Hugh is dedicated to a career, and he's built a life in which there's no permanent place for a woman. He made that plain to me from the very beginning, so I knew what I was getting into."

Althea smiled faintly. "So did I. Alex told me the first time we had coffee together that he was married. But it's a marriage that was long over before he ever met me. His biggest regret is that he's so alienated from his children." She sighed and stood up. "Ah, well, I suppose I'd better try to get some sleep...and you had, too. Is the book still coming along well?"

"Yes, it is," Donna replied cautiously.

"I'm glad something's working out," Althea said ruefully, "because it looks as if you and I are destined to do some crying on each other's shoulders."

DONNA DECIDED early that morning that there was only one way to avoid crying on someone's shoulders, and that was to keep busy. Very busy.

She knew she looked almost as haggard as Althea. She made a thermos of coffee, packed a small basket with cups and blueberry muffins, then set off for the beach.

Hugh must have been watching from his window, because he loomed up almost immediately after Donna parked near the snack shop.

He took the breakfast picnic from her and they made their way through the sand and along the dunes until they found a small, protected spot in which they settled.

Donna had bought the muffins the afternoon before from a local bakery and they were almost as good as homemade. Eating her muffin, sipping her coffee, she let the salt breeze caress her face and forced her attention on the pleasure of the moment...with Hugh.

She glanced up to see him frowning at her. "You look like hell this morning, Donna."

"Thanks a lot," she said, trying to make a joke out of it.

"It's not funny," Hugh said roughly. "Do you feel all right?"

"I feel fine, Hugh. I didn't sleep very well, that's all."

"Have you been working too hard?"

She shook her head. "No." That was true enough. Although she'd been putting in a fair bit of time on her book she hadn't been overdoing it.

"It's me, isn't it?" he demanded abruptly.

Her lips tightened. "I don't even want to answer that. Look, it's a beautiful morning, the muffins are delicious, the coffee's terrific, if I do say so. Let's just relax and enjoy this, okay?''

"I've been finding it increasingly difficult to relax and enjoy things, Donna. Oh, there was a time not too far in the past when just being here with you would have been enough. But now I want more. Every time I'm with you lately, I begin to think about how much more I want."

"Hugh...look, you have a heavy day ahead of you, this isn't the time to get into our relationship," Donna told him, and hoped he wouldn't notice the edge of desperation in her voice. The fact was, she wasn't ready to get into a serious discussion with him about the problems between them.

Inadvertently she glanced down the beach to the *Portia*. There, in essence, lay the root of their problems, she thought wryly. There would always be another woman in Hugh's life, as, all along, he'd freely admitted. And when he'd salvaged one particular ship, there would be another one somewhere on a distant horizon.

For Hugh there would always be another ship. Donna couldn't imagine a human female who could offer a fraction as much competition.

"You're right," he said wearily. "It isn't the time to go into us. These next few days I've got to keep what wits I have left completely on the job." It was as if he was talking to himself, and he flashed her an apologetic grin. "Excuse me, sweetheart, I'm woolgathering."

Donna smiled. "It's allowed."

"I love you, do you know that?" Hugh asked her suddenly. He reached over and touched her hand in a singularly poignant gesture. "Sometimes I want to do that just to prove you're real," he said softly, and Donna felt a knot form in her throat and her eyes filled with tears.

She couldn't hold them back. She had no choice but to face Hugh with her eyes brimming.

"Drenched sapphires," he murmured, "and I'm responsible. The last thing I've ever wanted to do was to make you cry, Donna." He captured a tear on his finger. "Sweetheart, please. There's no way I can go off and leave you like this."

She brushed at her tears with a paper napkin and forced herself to smile at him. "When you tell me you love me I just go soft all over, that's all. Don't you know that most of the time when women cry it's from happiness, not sorrow?"

"Don't try to sell me that one."

She searched for words. "You've made me happier than anyone ever has, Hugh."

Emotion flared in his dark eyes, and she saw him swallow hard. "That goes for me, too," he said, almost under his breath. "Until I met you, I don't think I really believed there was such a thing as happiness."

IT WAS DIFFICULT for Donna to get back to her story that morning. Truth kept intruding upon fiction, and at moments she had difficulty separating the two.

She'd thought of having Andrew's wife die, conveniently, while he was overseas, so that he and Flora could come together at the end of the book, their problems resolved. But that seemed too easy a way to work out the situation and stretched credibility a shade too far.

No, Andrew and Flora would have to work out whatever was to be between them in the future, just as Alex and Althea were going to have to do.

That settled, Donna got up and paced around the apartment stretching her muscles. She knew that in her story she was also going to have to resolve the dilemma between Keith and Mary. But their romance seemed secondary. Keith was her protagonist, after all, yet she acknowledged that in a lot of the segments Andrew seemed to be stealing the show from him.

She couldn't have that. Keith had to remain dominant. But she was having a hard time defining Mary.

Maybe because Mary is really me, she admitted finally, *and it's difficult to dissect yourself and then put the pieces together to form a character.*

Donna toyed with character development for the balance of the morning, then, still dissatisfied, she decided to take a lunch break and drove over to the Snack Shack. She was hoping Hugh would decide to come up for a hamburger, but he didn't.

Once again the beach had turned into a carnival scene, and crowds were lined up waiting to be served. Donna slipped in the side door and managed to get Althea's attention long enough to ask if she and Mark wanted help.

"We could use a hand," Althea admitted, "but I hate to take you away from your work."

Donna was glad to be taken away from her work. She had some decisions to make about her story and she was wondering if she'd been premature in sending in a proposal. It was beginning to look as if she might have to change her plot line, and that was going to take rethinking, something she wasn't geared for this afternoon.

She welcomed the proximity of the shipwreck scene that working in the shack would give her. It wasn't so much being closer to the *Portia* as being where the action was.

All afternoon she listened to rumors about the salvage operation, most of them obviously uninformed ones. She heard people who were seeing the ship for the first time express their astonishment at the sight in a fascinating variety of ways, and she was further rewarded when, toward dusk, Hugh stopped by for coffee and french fries.

His eyes lit up when he saw her. For a moment the two of them stood staring at each other as if they were experiencing a small miracle. Serving him his order, Donna asked severely, "Is that all you've had to eat since breakfast?"

"No, ma'am," he said, giving her the full effect of his heart-tugging grin. "We had some tuna-fish sandwiches aboard ship, and the cook turned out some excellent canned tomato soup."

Mark was starting to close up the shack for the night, since the crowds were dwindling, so Donna moved over to the side of the counter to be alone with Hugh.

She snitched one of his french fries. "Will they be serving dinner aboard ship tonight?"

"Indeed so. I checked the menu, matter of fact. Corned-beef hash, stewed tomatoes, applesauce and chocolate pudding."

"You should be grateful for the canned foods industry," Donna told him.

"You shouldn't be such a cynic," he chided. "Speaking of food, what are you going to have for supper tonight?"

"I hadn't thought about it yet."

"See? You're the one who needs nutritional guidance, Ms Madison." He lowered his voice. "Seriously, I want to know that you'll be eating something hot and nourishing and getting a decent night's sleep. I worry about you."

"There's no need for you to worry, Hugh." She tried to smile but it didn't quite come off. "I'm a big girl."

"Why don't you take Althea up to the Chinese restaurant?" he suggested. "Alex isn't going to be able to get away, and my guess is that unless her brother spoon-feeds her, Althea's going to pass up dinner."

Donna nodded. "That's not a bad idea."

"Promise?"

"You do drive a hard bargain, don't you? All right, I'll try to teach Althea how to use chopsticks."

"I'm not sure that's such a good idea. You might both starve to death." There was a tenderness in his eyes as he looked at her that belied the teasing...and everything else except his love for her. Donna felt his love, and let herself bask in it.

As HE WALKED back down the beach to the ship, Hugh was wrestling with himself. It had taken every ounce of his willpower to leave Donna.

He knew it was vital to force everything out of his mind except the salvage operation for the next few days, but he'd never before found anything quite so difficult to do. He'd been able to devote himself with a rare single-mindedness to his profession all these years. Now the ship on his horizon was sharing him with another woman, and when it came to taking possession of his thoughts, Donna was winning out over the *Portia*.

He had never had to cope with such a problem before, and he wasn't pleased with the way he was handling it.

Standing in the circle of darkness outside the floodlit area, he surveyed the ship and the enormous front-end loader still at work under the lights, battling against nature as it devoured great clumps of sand.

The success of the excavating operation was essential to the next move. When a four-foot trench was dug along the seaward side of the freighter, the towering derrick on the barge offshore would be put into play. Cables had been strung from the derrick to the ship, and at the right moment, when the tide was high, they would swing the *Portia* around some forty-five degrees to seaward, until she was pointing straight toward Portugal. Then they'd pull her off the beach.

Hugh glanced at the sky. The moon was riding high, a serene silver. He had watched the moon in all her phases, shining upon oceans all over the world. Now he looked at her with new eyes, hoping she was his ally.

He needed all the help he could get.

CHAPTER FOURTEEN

TERRY O'CONNOR'S STORY about Mark appeared in the *Sunday Boston Globe* accompanied by a picture, three columns wide, that made Mark look like a prototype New Englander, and a surprisingly attractive one.

Donna was amused by Althea's comment, "I didn't know I had such a photogenic brother."

She hadn't had Hugh's opinion on the matter, because she hadn't seen him since the night he'd stopped by, late, at the Snack Shack.

The Monday *Globe* had another story about the *Portia* by Terry O'Connor, and as she read it Donna wished she knew half as much about what was happening in her own backyard as the Boston reporter evidently did.

She had fallen into the habit of going uptown and having breakfast and reading the paper while she ate. Hugh was too involved with the salvage operation to join her for beach walks any longer.

Huddled at a small corner table in the coffee shop, she became immersed in the story.

Yesterday the strong steel cables attached to elevated winches on the barge, *Stardust*, were taut. The barge is in position several hundred feet off Massasoit Beach in Devon, on Cape Cod. Two oceangoing tugs stood at readiness to help ease the *Portia*, which has been stranded on the beach since late March, past two sandbars and into the open water...if, that is, the initial salvage attempt by the Boston-based firm of Mac-Donough, Inc., is successful.

Another "if," Donna thought, pausing to take a bite of toast and a sip of coffee.

According to Hugh MacDonough, president of the salvage firm that has been commissioned to refloat the freighter, much depends upon the tides tonight.

"We're hoping to turn her bow toward the open water then to pull her away from the beach on our first try, and we're relying on the pull of the moon to help us," MacDonough said in an interview late yesterday afternoon.

Terry O'Connor had seen him more recently than she had, Donna thought, her silent words cresting over her, leaving a wash of sorrow.

"The tides are the highest of the month," MacDonough elaborated, "and we'll need a lot of water out there if this is to work. Our hope is that if we can get part of the ship to float, the rest will follow."

A giant front-end loader has been working around the clock, digging a deep trench through the massive sandbar that has been building up on the waterside of the *Portia*. Sand has been a continuing problem since the ship grounded in a severe northeaster. "We're dealing with tons of sand that has been displaced," MacDonough said, "and we've encountered a special problem in moving it. This is a constantly shifting, granular type of sand that is very hard to deal with."

The Massasoit Beach parking lot at this point resembles a giant construction camp, as does the beachfront in the area of the stricken ship. At night the operational scene is floodlit, and there's a grimness to the glaring site as men work around the clock trying to gain an upper hand on nature.

MacDonough is a veteran salvor...

At this point Donna put the paper aside. She knew all about Hugh MacDonough being a veteran salvor.

Her breakfast finished, Donna went back to her apartment and tried to concentrate on her book. But she was stalled, and the words wouldn't flow.

She had no fear that this was another case of writer's block. Her story was alive in her mind, the people real, she was in tune with the problems of her characters and she'd already made the plot changes she thought were necessary. She'd developed a basic antagonism that had always been between Andrew and his brother Keith, and in her story they had long been in love with the same woman, Flora.

Mary had been written out of the plot. It had been necessary surgery; there was no real place for her as the story stood.

That morning Donna sent Andrew, Keith and Flora on a temporary leave of absence as she accepted the fact that reality was intruding to the point where it was impossible to deal with fiction. Out there, beyond her windows, Hugh was moving toward the last stages of preparation before casting his bet on tonight's high tide.

And that's what it was, Donna thought, covering up her computer and stacking away the pages she'd printed out. Hugh's salvage attempt would be a gamble, no matter how much scientific knowledge and experience went into the preparations.

Man against nature. The phrase sprang to mind. It was one of the oldest of all battles, and this was the kind of war Hugh, in his work, constantly waged.

She could imagine that right now Hugh was as calm as steel, and the closer he and his men came to their moment of truth the more cool he would appear—on the outside. But she couldn't help but believe that he must be churning inside. So much depended upon his calculations.

She wondered how Alex was holding up. It was going to be a long and difficult night for Alex.

She gave up trying to stay away from the scene and slipped on a sweater and started out. Once she reached the beach she was glad she had a "reserved" place to park, because the public parking lot was full.

She stopped briefly at the Snack Shack to tell Althea and Mark she'd be back shortly to help them out. First she had to make a pilgrimage of her own down to the ship. She joined dozens of others who were trudging through the sand. The ship seemed to exert an almost hypnotic influence on the crowds who came to gape at her.

It was a long walk, and Donna's legs were aching by the time she got as close to the *Portia* as she could. For safety's sake an area had been roped off a distance from the ship, and special police were on hand to guarantee that the sightseers obeyed the rules.

Donna felt herself hemmed in by people, and she wished she could thrust her way past all of them. She wanted to get closer on the chance she might catch even a single glimpse of Hugh.

"They've been working day and night to get her ready, these past four days," she heard a man say, and she turned to see a familiar face. She didn't know the man's name but she did know he worked for the park department. It must be his day off, she guessed, yet he'd returned to the scene as if the ship had mesmerized him, too.

"Back-breaking work, and they've all gotten into it. Even MacDonough himself. He's no slouch," the man continued. "He's working with a nineteen-man crew, tons of equipment, but when you get to the bottom line it's the way he calls the signals that'll spell success or failure."

Donna was tempted to turn and say, "He can handle it."

She heard someone else say, "That supersize front-end loader's gobbling the sand in ten-cubic-yard gulps. But they still got a problem. The sand's built up not only on the seaward side but up ahead of the bow. Thousands of tons, the way I hear it. If you ask me, they're not going to be able to budge her."

No one's asking you, Donna retorted crossly, and wished she had the nerve to speak aloud.

It was almost impossible to identify any of the men working around the scene from this distance because they were all wearing the same kind of work clothes, many of them with their heads covered by parka hoods or wool caps. She thought, once, that she spied Brent

Hancock, and when she saw a figure descending the Jacob's ladder she was sure at first it was Alex, but a beam of sunlight touched the man's hair and his hair was much lighter than Alex's.

She knew that if she was to see Hugh, she would recognize him instantly. His silhouette was so familiar to her. The way he walked, the way he stood with his head thrust back when he looked at the ship, his every movement and gesture were unique to her. She could never mistake Hugh for anyone else.

After a time she decided there was no point in staying around any longer. Disappointed because what was going on seemed so remote from her and she wanted so much to be a part of it, she turned back.

At the shack she was immediately swept up into the rush of business, and for the rest of the afternoon she didn't have time to think about anything.

That evening once the business was closed, Donna and Althea slipped away and went out to dinner together again. They drove out of town to a small restaurant overlooking the bay in Dennis.

"I don't feel like talking to anyone tonight, so I don't want to run into anyone I know," Althea said frankly. "We're not likely to over there."

Donna could not have agreed more. Her aunt and uncle had asked her to have supper with them, and she had sidestepped the invitation.

She and Althea had a common interest just now, and there was no need for either of them to put up a front with the other. They sipped glasses of wine while they waited for their dinners, then Althea broke the silence. "Will I ever be glad when this night is over!" Then she added, "Mark's out with Terry O'Connor again. He's going to take her down to the ship later in our four-wheel drive.''

"Didn't he ask if you wanted to go along?''

"He didn't have to,'' Althea replied. "I told him I wanted to stay away. What about you, Donna? Do you want to be down there tonight?''

Donna thought for a moment, then said, "Not under the circumstances, no. It would be agony, watching and not knowing what was going on. If I could be at Hugh's side, that would be different. If I could do anything for him...''

Althea nodded. "That's the way I feel. I'd get in the way if I was there, and it wouldn't do Alex any good at all. In fact, he asked me to stay away. He's going to be on board the *Portia* when they try to pull her off. Somehow that terrifies me.''

"Nothing's likely to happen to the ship,'' Donna said quickly, and hoped she was right.

"I suppose not. I mean, I suppose there's no reason to think Alex might be hurt or anything. But even so...'' Althea paused. "Will Hugh be aboard her?''

"I don't know,'' Donna admitted. "He's been aboard her most of the time these past few days, as far as I know. But whether he'll need to be onshore or whether he'll stay aboard the ship when they actually try to move her, I don't know.''

She stared reflectively at her wineglass. "I've never thought about this all that much before, but has it ever occurred to you that all through history women have stood by and waited at times like this? It's only fairly recently that men have been called upon to wait for women in similar circumstances. Even today...well, I've never asked Hugh if there are any female salvors.''

"I'd say it's still pretty much a man's profession from what I've heard," Althea said, "but you never know. Women have proved their abilities in just about every field. I wonder what Alex is doing right now," she said, and Donna felt a twinge of empathy. She'd been wondering the same thing about Hugh.

Later that night, Donna stared out her window at the full moon. It seemed enormous to her as she gazed up at the silver circle silhouetted against a black sky.

That was going to be all to the good for Hugh—wasn't it?

Why did she feel so apprehensive, she asked herself. She felt so much in tune with Hugh, even though they were apart, and she was afraid for him.

This was the first time in her life that she had ever fully shared herself with another person, and it was scary.

MARK CAME KNOCKING at the door shortly after six the next morning.

Donna took one look at his face, and she knew what he was going to say.

"I heard the six o'clock news," he reported. "They didn't make it. She's still high and dry, Donna."

"Oh, God," Donna breathed.

"I thought maybe Hugh might have called you," Mark ventured. "Althea hasn't heard from Alex, either."

"What went wrong, do you know?"

"No, I don't. They gave a highly technical explanation. All I got out of it was that the plan didn't work, and they've gone back to the planning board and the calculators. Hugh must be in up to his neck," Mark said sympathetically.

She nodded. "Thanks for telling me, Mark."

"Yeah. I was sure you'd want to know."

She had wanted to know, of course, but the knowledge lay like a heavy lump within her.

She went into the living room, sank into an armchair and sat there for a time, trying to decide what to do next.

Finally she knew she couldn't stay away from Hugh any longer. At the least she had to hear his voice.

She dialed the Windcrest and asked to be connected to his room. The phone was ringing for the fourth time and she was about to hang up, having decided that he must still be on the ship, when he answered.

His voice was thick with sleep, and Donna realized she had awakened him. At once she was remorseful.

Her first words were, "I'm sorry, Hugh."

She was speaking about having awakened him, but he assumed she was referring to the *Portia*, and he said, "It's not the end of the world, sweetheart. We'll try again."

"I wasn't talking about the ship," she said quickly. "Oh, you must be exhausted!"

"I only got in half an hour or so ago," he admitted. "I guess I crashed out like a light."

"You're alone, Hugh?"

A thread of amusement laced through his tired voice. "Who did you think might be here with me, Donna?"

"I thought maybe Alex or someone might have come back with you."

"I'm alone, sweetheart."

"Could you...I mean would you...I mean...why don't you come out here?" Donna stammered.

"To your place?" He sounded genuinely surprised. "At this hour of the morning? What would Mark and Althea think?"

"Hugh," she pointed out, "there've been times when you've stayed all night."

"So there have been." He laughed softly. "I guess I've ruined your reputation, Donna."

"You don't sound very sorry about it."

"Maybe that's because I'd do the same thing all over again. Sweetheart…"

"Yes?"

"Do you really want me to come out there?"

Did she really want him! Her voice was trembling as she told him how much she wanted him. And it seemed forever until she heard his car in the driveway.

She opened the door without waiting for his knock.

He was unshaven, his eyes were red rimmed and bleary, and deep lines of fatigue creased his face, but no one had ever looked more wonderful to Donna.

She hugged him to her, clutching him as if she could not possibly bear to let him go again. After a time he released her and smiled down at her quizzically. "If this is the kind of reception I get when I've been a failure, why should I ever ask for success?"

They were standing just inside the kitchen door. Donna disentangled herself from him gently and asked, "Have you had anything to eat?"

"Is that the eternal mother in you speaking?" he teased. "No, I haven't had anything to eat. If my memory's serving me correctly—which it may not be—I skipped supper last night."

"Sit down at the table and I'll fix you something," Donna said, starting to bustle around, wanting to do something for him.

"If I'm to be given any choices, I'd like to start out with a large jolt of straight Scotch on the rocks."

"Coming right up," Donna said briskly., "How about ham and eggs and some biscuits as a follow-up?"

"Am I dreaming?" Hugh asked the room at large. "Nothing like this has ever happened before. Usually when my first salvage attempt doesn't come off I go hide in my room and lick my wounds."

"I can imagine," she said dryly.

"Nothing like this ever *has* happened to me before, Donna," he said, and she turned to look across at him, impelled by the seriousness in his voice. "You, I mean. You've put my life into such a new and special category. Do you have any idea how much you've come to mean to me?"

"If you persist in talking like that we're both going to get just one thing on our minds," Donna reprimanded. "And you're too tired for that."

He grinned. "Am I, now?"

"Yes, Hugh MacDonough, you are. Here's your Scotch. Now, don't gulp it all down in one big swallow."

He laughed and tilted the glass in a toast to her before taking a sip of the whiskey.

"That goes down well." He smiled, which only made the weariness in his face more eloquent to her. "Thank you for this, Donna. For asking me to come out here this morning, for...for having me around."

"I wanted you here," she said simply.

"When I got back to the Windcrest I nearly called you," he said, "but it was only five-thirty. I knew I'd blast you out of your sleep."

"I blasted you out of yours."

"Nothing better ever happened to me."

Donna heaped his plate with slices of crisply fried ham, eggs turned over lightly, and biscuits that had come from a package but were high and fluffy and looked delicious. She couldn't possibly have eaten anything herself, she was too tense, but she poured two cups of coffee and sat down opposite Hugh.

Hugh ate methodically, as if he needed the food for actual sustenance, and she didn't doubt that he did. He'd admitted that he tended to overlook meals when he was in the midst of a salvage job. Just at the time when he really needed to keep his energy up, she reflected.

When he'd finished Donna said, "Okay, now, into the bedroom with you."

He shook his head. "I've got to get back, Donna."

"Not now you don't," she said firmly. "You'd still be asleep if you were in the Windcrest, wouldn't you?"

"I suppose so."

"Very well. Tell me when you think you really need to get up and I'll come and wake you."

"Come and wake me?" He frowned. "Look, Donna, I'm not letting you give your bed up to me. And I've got to admit I wouldn't be of much use to you in it right now. You were right when you said I'm too tired."

Donna tugged at his sleeve. "You're too big for me to carry you, but I'll do something, if you don't move under your own power," she threatened. "Now come along, Hugh."

He followed her almost sheepishly and sat down heavily on the edge of her bed.

"Let me help you off with those boots," she suggested, and he shook his head.

"Hey, now, I can still do a couple of things for myself."

He stretched out without making any further protests, once he'd gotten the boots off. Donna pulled the covers up over him, tucking him in tenderly, as if he were a small child.

She bent to kiss his forehead, and he reached out to clasp her hand.

"I love you," Hugh said thickly, and a moment later was fast asleep.

HUGH HAD NOT TOLD DONNA precisely what time to wake him up, so she let him sleep. But as the morning wore on she began to be uneasy, because she was sure there would be people looking for him.

Finally at ten o'clock she awakened him gently. At first, when she told him what time it was, she was afraid he was going to be angry with her for not having roused him sooner. But he reached up to pull her down onto the bed next to him, encircling her in his powerful arms and kissing her with a gentleness that belied his strength.

"I have to get going," he said, "I guess you know that."

"Yes, of course I know it."

"Look, I doubt I'll be able to get back to you today."

"I know that, too," she told him.

"You must be the most understanding woman in the world," he said, his eyes never leaving her face. They were still red rimmed, but he looked far more rested.

"No," Donna corrected him. "I'm not. Lots of the time I'm not very understanding at all."

"You've been great with me," Hugh said softly.

₃ins to cost money. A lot of money." He shrugged.
We'll see."

Donna wished she could be half as philosophical as
Hugh. He had so much at stake, and he was so weary.
It seemed to her that he kept his cool about the situa-
tion remarkably well.

She slid back into bed after he left and dozed for a
time, but she had too much on her mind to sleep
deeply. When she got up she didn't even try to approach the computer. She decided to take refuge again
in working for Mark and Althea.

The failure of the initial salvage attempt had only
thrust the *Portia* all the more into the limelight, and
those people who had been pessimistic about the ship's
chances all along were even more so now.

Over and over again as she handed out hamburgers, hot dogs, french fries and onion rings, Donna
heard the refrain, "They're going to have to cut her in
chunks with blowtorches and truck her out of here.
That's the only way we'll ever see the last of her."

Even the optimists were swinging over to the side of
the pessimists. When Rod Eldridge stopped by for a
frappé shortly after the main lunch-hour rush had
subsided, he was glum about the ship's chances.

"Personally," he told Mark, "I think she, or what
will be left of her, is headed for the junk pile. Scrap
metal."

Donna winced. She could imagine how Hugh would
react to this, and she resented Rod's being so asser-
tive about something he didn't know all that much
about. She was sure Hugh was putting as much effort
into revamping his plans as a man could put into
anything.

There was no mistaking his relucta.
of her and slowly eased himself off the
and stretched. "Wish me luck tonight, D

"I will, darling. You know that."

She had brewed a fresh pot of coffee ir.
wanted some, and she waited in the kitchen w
used the bathroom. When he came back to her,
splashed his face with cold water until it was ru
and his eyes were clearer.

He accepted a cup of coffee and drank it black
Watching him, Donna ventured, "Do you think it will
work this time, Hugh?"

"It had better work," he said grimly. "I know what
the problem was last night. At least I think I do. Once
we attempted to put the pulley mechanism into operation I could see that we'd put too much faith in that
weight-dividing principle I told you about. We were
counting on the ratio of weight reduction for each
strand of cable going over a pulley. As it develops, the
Portia's an overweight lady. She weighs too much, especially under a pivot point near her center that's cru-
cial. What this means is getting back to the drawing
board and figuring out how we can deal with the
problem, and I don't have too many hours to come up
with an answer. The moon and the tides wait for no
man. In my business it doesn't take you long to learn
that nature's a hell of a lot bigger than any of us."

"But you are going to make a second attempt
tonight?"

"We hope to." He nodded. "We've still got some
lunar tides to work with, but I don't want to risk time
running out on us. That would mean the ship would
be stranded for another month, and at this point time

She voiced some of her thoughts to Terry O'Connor when the reporter stopped by for coffee shortly after Rod left.

Mark had gone uptown to lay in a few supplies, since the lunch crowd had almost depleted his stock, and Donna suspected that Terry planned to hang around until he returned.

"I've liked your stories," she ventured, as she poured a second cup of coffee for the reporter. "The one about Mark was excellent."

"I enjoyed doing it," Terry admitted. "I've enjoyed everything I've been working on down here, for that matter. Except that it wasn't much fun to write this morning's story. I was hoping Hugh would make it on the first try."

"After listening to people talk today, I wonder how much most of them really want him to make it at all," Donna said bitterly. "I've never heard so many prophets of gloom."

"Hugh will prove all of them wrong," Terry promised.

Donna wasn't about to tell Terry how fervently she hoped she was right. When Mark got back she slipped away from the Snack Shack, leaving Mark and the reporter by themselves for a while.

She was tired, very tired, but she knew she wasn't going to be able to get much rest until this night was over. Her heart was with Hugh in his struggle.

She was tempted to stop at the Windcrest to say hello to her aunt and uncle, but she really didn't want to be with anyone. Not even people she was as fond of as Joe and Mabel Brucker.

Right now she only wanted Hugh. She glanced at the motel units the salvage company crew were occupying and saw that although there was still a last swath of sunlight over the parking lot, the lights had already been turned on in the rooms.

She could picture Hugh at work and only wished there was a way she could share his burden with him.

CHAPTER FIFTEEN

THE MAN STANDING at Donna's kitchen door was a stranger.

He was tall and skinny, with hair so blond it was almost white, pale blue eyes and a beak of a nose.

"Ms Madison?"

"Yes." Donna nodded.

"I'm Charlie Evans," he said, and it took a moment for the name to register. This was Hugh's friend. The college classmate who had an apartment in Hyannis and owned a cat called Marmalade and had a beautiful next-door neighbor named Angela. The facts came tumbling one on top of the other.

Donna started to say something in the way of a greeting, then stopped, bewildered by his attitude. Charlie Evans's nervousness was obvious. His eyes shifted evasively, pinpointing a spot over her head to stare at.

Fear surged through Donna with tidal force.

"Hugh!"

Donna didn't realize she'd spoken Hugh's name aloud until Charlie Evans said quickly, "He's going to be all right, Ms Madison."

"Going to *be* all right?" she echoed.

He nodded. "I thought perhaps you'd heard about the accident. It was on the radio news."

"What accident?" Donna demanded, trying not to screech at him. "I seldom listen to the radio."

"It was a couple of hours ago," Charlie said. "Hugh had been working out some plans at the motel. He was going back aboard ship when he slipped on the Jacob's ladder—"

"Oh, God!" The cry was torn from her.

Charlie's blue eyes widened in alarm. He reached out and clutched her arm. "Are you okay?"

"Yes, yes, I'm fine. What happened to Hugh?"

"He was knocked out cold. The rescue squad took him over to the hospital in Hyannis. Alex Bruce and Brent Hancock went along with him. Brent knew Hugh and I are close friends. He called me and I went right over...."

Charlie paused, and Donna prodded, "Yes?"

"They've taken X rays and run a bunch of tests. Hugh's shoulder is wrenched and he has a slight concussion. They're pretty sure it's nothing more than that, but they want to keep him overnight for observation, and he's raising hell."

Charlie paused again. "Brent suggested I come out here and get you." He had released Donna's arm, but he looked as if he was standing ready to reach out and grab her again. She imagined she must be as white as a sheet. She'd always had the tendency to go deathly pale when anything happened to shock her, but her props seldom remained knocked out from under her. She had quick recuperative powers and already was feeling a surge of strength.

"What time is it?" she asked Charlie.

She'd been working and had lost all track of time. After heating up a can of chicken soup for her supper, she'd gone to the computer, this time viewing it as a safety valve. She couldn't spend the night pacing the floor, and she wasn't about to go down to the shipwreck site. As Althea had pointed out the night before, they would only be in the way. So finally she'd turned to the word processor, but she hadn't attempted to work on her book. Instead, she had immersed herself in writing a character sketch based on Hugh. At the moment it was therapy. Later it could be merged into the character of Keith.

There would be changes in the transition, of course. Keith was not Hugh, Keith was Keith. But Donna was convinced she would be able to understand her fictional creation better than she did now if she could gain a deeper knowledge of his real-life counterpart, so she had probed as she wrote, analyzing Hugh's character, his motivations, the reasons he was such a loner. She had taken him apart, but she'd done so with love. It wasn't her intention to be supercritical. She was simply trying for a deeper knowledge of the whole man...right to his core.

She had become fascinated with her project, and the hours had slipped by. Now, when Charlie Evans told her it was nearly midnight, she was astonished.

Her first thought was for the ship.

"What's going to happen to the *Portia*?" she asked fearfully.

"Nothing, for tonight," Charlie told her. "Brent phoned Jim Babson from the hospital and told him to shut everything off. When Hugh heard that, he went into orbit."

"I can imagine," Donna remarked dryly. Her mind was racing, but her emotions were beginning to outdistance it. It was impossible to be rational, knowing Hugh was hurt and in the hospital.

She tried to be logical about at least one thing. "Do you honestly think he'll want me there?"

Charlie grinned. "Hancock seems convinced you're the only person who may be able to talk some sense into him."

Donna was far from certain that Brent Hancock was right in his assumption. She wasn't sure she'd be able to deal with Hugh at all, let alone talk any sense into him. Chances were that once she saw him she'd be too upset. Even now her hands were shaking so badly it was all she could do to get her clothes on. She was glad she could leave the driving to Charlie Evans. If she had been called from the hospital and asked to come to Hyannis under her own power, she would have made it, but the attempt would have taken a toll. Her nerves seemed to have come alive, and she tapped her fingers noiselessly against the soft wool of her skirt, hoping Charlie Evans wouldn't notice.

When they arrived at the hospital, they found Hugh in a small private room. Fully dressed, he was sitting on the edge of the narrow bed and he looked furious. His left arm had been taped to his side to immobilize his injured shoulder, and one shirt sleeve hung empty. A bandage, held in place by adhesive, crossed his forehead diagonally, almost at the hairline. His skin had a gray tinge to it and he looked exhausted, but his eyes were blazing. Donna had never before sensed the latent power in him as fully as she did now. He was like a caged tiger, girding his strength to tear the bars apart and escape.

Standing on the threshold, she felt timid and out of place. She sagged briefly, and Charlie automatically reached out to grip her arm.

Hugh's eyes swept toward her and she wished she could sink through the floor. His gaze was scathing. But then he blinked and blinked again, as if he couldn't be sure of what he was seeing.

"Donna?" It was part question, until he became more sure of himself. Then he demanded roughly, "What the hell are you doing here?" But she sensed that some of the growl had gone out of the tiger.

She became aware of Alex Bruce sitting on a straight-backed chair at the side of the room, and Brent Hancock leaning against the wall, his arms folded.

Alex stood up and said, "I could do with a spot of coffee." He addressed the other man. "Do you think the cafeteria's open?"

They took the cue and moved with Alex toward the door, and it was all Donna could do not to cry out and beg them to stay. Even though some of the fire had died out of Hugh's eyes, he still looked formidable.

She heard the door close with a soft thud, and the silence in the small room became intense. Then Hugh said, "You never did like the Jacob's ladder, did you?"

Donna's mouth started to tremble. "N-no," she began, stammering, and she couldn't hold back any longer.

The tears came. She felt as weak as a rag, giving way, but she couldn't help herself. In part it was relief. Until she'd seen Hugh for herself she hadn't been sure what had happened to him. It seemed as if her heart had stopped beating the moment Charlie Evans had told her Hugh had been hurt, and it was only now beginning to resume its pace.

"Sweetheart—" Hugh's voice was low and rough "—stop that, will you? I can't take it when you cry."

He held his free arm out to her. "Come here."

Donna held back. "I shouldn't. I might hurt you."

He laughed. "It would be an icy day in hell before you'd ever hurt me. That's one thing in this crazy life

I've grown sure about. Will you come over here, or do you want me to try to make it across that shiny floor to you?''

She knew he meant it, and she didn't want him moving, so she went to him and let him fold his right arm around her. She heard his pulse throbbing with a deep and even beat, and that reassured her as nothing else could have. She looked up and met Hugh's eyes. The anger had faded entirely, and there was only a fine haze of pain left, mixed with a great deal of tenderness.

Hugh pulled Donna's head onto his good shoulder, his lips brushing her hair, then nuzzling her forehead. His voice was so low she had to strain to hear it as he said, ''This is a hell of a thing to happen, and it's my own fault. A big, clumsy ox like me should know enough to be more careful.''

''How did it happen, Hugh?''

''I was too damned tired, bleary eyed,'' he confessed. ''Even with my new reading glasses my notes were beginning to melt together. But I figured out what had to be done, Donna. I started back to the ship, and I was in too much of a hurry. I forgot that when I start to go up something there's a lot of me to follow behind. I slipped, that's all. I feel like Humpty Dumpty,'' he finished wryly. ''My head's like a cracked eggshell. A hollow cracked eggshell.''

She glanced at him anxiously. ''Why aren't you in bed?''

''Because I'm getting the hell out of this place.''

''Hugh, that's ridiculous,'' she protested.

''The doctor who attended me when they took me to the emergency room will be stopping by before he goes off duty. I intend to get a release from him. If he won't give it to me, I'll walk out.''

She shook her head. "How can you be so stubborn? And so foolish?" she wailed.

He managed a grin. "I guess I was born that way." The grin widened. "You're calling me a stubborn fool, Ms Madison?"

"Yes," Donna said defiantly. "Yes, I'm calling you a stubborn fool."

Surprisingly his eyes misted. "Oh God, Donna," he said simply. "I love you so. When I saw you standing in that doorway I thought I really had whanged my head. I wasn't seeing too clearly and I thought I must be hallucinating. But you know what?"

"What?"

"I caught the scent of you. That perfume you use...it's elusive, not quite spice, not quite flowers. It wafted across to me, and I knew you were for real. I knew I hadn't bashed my head up to the point that my mind was playing tricks on me."

His arm tightened around her. "You're very real," he said with satisfaction. "I like the feel of you and the substance of you, though you could do with a few more pounds."

She drew back. "You're trying to divert me," she accused. "Hugh, I want you to stay here tonight."

He started to shake his head but then stopped, wincing. "No way. I've got to get back to Devon, Donna. The moon isn't going to be on our side forever. My damn carelessness has cost us, and I've got to make up for that. We're going to have to get the *Portia* off that beach tomorrow night and I need to be there."

"You won't be anywhere if you fall flat on your face again," Donna informed him. "Except in a room like this, in a bed like this, and in a lot worse condition than you're in now."

"I'll make a bargain," Hugh said suddenly.

"What kind of bargain?" She was suspicious of any offers from him.

"Let me come home with you."

"What?"

"You can fuss over me." He smiled sheepishly. "I wouldn't mind in the least having you fuss over me for the next eighteen hours or so."

"Why eighteen hours, Hugh?"

"I'm still able to read the dial on my wristwatch," he told her. "Eighteen hours from now, I'll be on board the *Portia.*"

Donna stared at him in dismay. What could one do with a man like this? His spirit was made of steel as strong as the hulls of the ships he salvaged.

He moved slightly, and she saw him wince again. "Damn it," she exploded, "your head hurts and your shoulder hurts and I don't know where else you hurt, but this is absurd!"

"Would it be too much trouble to put me up at your place?" he asked her, ignoring her outburst. "All I want to do is sleep, Donna, and I can do that a lot better if I know you're near me. I won't interfere with your work."

"I wasn't thinking about my work."

"Anyway, I'll be quiet, I'll behave myself." He added wryly, "With this shoulder I won't be able to do anything else for a couple of days, as far as *we're* concerned."

Donna felt herself coloring, as if the hospital walls had ears. "You're impossible, Hugh."

"Yes," he agreed calmly. "I've been told that before."

"I can imagine you have been...more than once." Donna couldn't help but wonder who else might have told him he was impossible, and she fought to suppress a rising jealousy. Hugh had never made a secret of the fact that there had been women in his life, and she was realistic enough to accept the fact. Still, there were moments when she wished she knew more about his past, and other moments when she was happy she didn't.

"Look," she said, "stay put and behave yourself just for tonight, will you?"

"Let's see what the doctor says," Hugh temporized.

To Donna's private consternation, the physician who had attended Hugh in the emergency room was willing to sign him out of the hospital. There was a proviso, though. Hugh had to give the young doctor his word that he would stay quiet for the next twenty-four hours and report back immediately if his headache worsened or any new symptoms developed.

"We'll see to that, doctor," Brent Hancock promised, when Hugh remained silent, and Alex concurred.

Brent and Alex had followed the rescue squad to the hospital in one of the company Jeeps. Charlie Evans was elected to be the chauffeur on the return trip to Devon since he had a comfortable car to ride in. They put Hugh in the passenger seat, where he could stretch his long legs out, leaving Donna to sit in back and stare at his big, shaggy head.

It was a beautiful head. She studied its shape as the miles passed, and it was all she could do to keep herself from sliding forward and enmeshing her fingers in his thick hair.

Hugh was exhausted, and there was no conversation in the car. Once Charlie glanced back over his shoulder to say, in a low voice, "I think he's dozed off," and Donna felt a pang of alarm. She'd heard that you were supposed to keep anyone suffering from a concussion awake, and she'd considered pacing the floor with Hugh until she was sure it would be safe to let him sleep. But the doctor had placed no such restrictions, and if there had been a danger point, it must have passed, she reasoned.

At the house it was a struggle to get Hugh out of the car and even more of one to get him undressed and into Donna's bed. Drowsy from the medication he'd been given, he was almost a deadweight. Donna knew that if Charlie hadn't been around, the love of her life would have had to go to sleep in the work clothes he'd been wearing when he slipped off the ladder.

Once Hugh was settled she offered Charlie coffee and cake. Charlie accepted a cup of coffee, declined the cake, and left with the promise that he'd check with Donna in the morning to see if there was anything he could do.

The lights had been out in the Nickersons' house as they drove up, otherwise Donna would have slipped across to tell Mark and Althea what had happened. But there would be time enough for that in the morning. Right now it was more important to get some rest herself. She had the suspicion that handling Hugh the next day was going to be like dealing with a captured bear.

She was wrong initially. The first two times she peeked in on him he was still asleep. Though his face was grizzled and he needed a shave, he looked surprisingly young, almost cherubic.

The third time she discovered that his eyes were open, and when he saw her he blinked much as he had in the hospital the previous night. Then he said, "So...this isn't a dream."

"No," she told him, sitting down on the side of the bed and taking his hand in hers. "This is reality."

His eyes swept over her. "I didn't know reality could be so beautiful."

"Flatterer."

"You *are* beautiful, Donna," he said solemnly. "But sometimes when I look into your eyes I feel I'm going to drown. They're so deep, so blue. Where did you sleep last night?"

The question came so quickly she was taken aback by it. Hugh had a way of changing subjects so abruptly that it took her off-balance.

"I slept on the couch," she told him.

"What was wrong with the other half of this bed?" he demanded.

"Darling, I wasn't about to crowd in on you."

"Having you next to me wouldn't be crowding in, in my opinion," he said stubbornly.

"You needed space last night. You were exhausted and you were hurting. How does your head feel?"

"Like I got the worst end of a barroom fight," he admitted. "And before you ask, my shoulder's as sore as hell. But I'll live, sweetheart."

"The doctor gave me some medication for you," she said, about to go and get it.

"Skip the pills. I'm not trying to be Spartan, I just don't want to fog up my senses with any drugs today. I can take the pain, and I need to be as alert as possible."

"Hugh—" she tried to sound firm "—you are not going anywhere today, and you are not doing anything."

"I can think, can't I?" he glowered.

"Yes, I suppose I can't stop you doing that. But I wish you'd just...take it easy. Mentally and physically."

"I'll take it easy as long as I can, Donna. Has Brent been over?"

"No. Were you expecting him to come over?"

"I thought he might feel inspired to bring me some clean clothes. It's okay, though. We can take care of that later. Right now I'll catch a shower, then I can put on what I was wearing last night. Would you happen to have a razor that can handle a man's beard?"

Donna had a small, pink, feminine electric razor. The thought of Hugh using it brought a smile to her lips. "I don't think so."

"Well, Brent can bring mine over. I must look like I've been lost in the woods for a month."

She saw him wince as he sat up in bed and she said swiftly, "Take it easy, will you? Look, Hugh, I don't think you should take a shower. Why don't you just sponge off a little bit and get back into bed? I'll bring your breakfast in here."

"The hell you will!" he growled. "I'd have to have two broken legs before I'd eat my breakfast in bed."

Donna sighed. She'd been right in the first place. She was dealing with a captured bear, all right.

She fixed waffles and sausages for Hugh's breakfast, after consulting him about his preferences, and was surprised at the way he was able to wolf the food down. She'd had a piece of toast while he was still sleeping, and she had no appetite for anything else. She was still too worried about him, despite his outward ruggedness.

He was preoccupied enough to let her get by with only sipping a cup of coffee while he ate, and she knew that his thoughts were with the ship. It was going to be a monumental task to divert Hugh from the *Portia* today, and she wasn't sure she could handle it.

Charlie Evans called while Hugh was still eating his breakfast, and Hugh insisted on getting up and talking to him on the phone.

"I don't know how Charlie got in the act last night," he commented, returning to the table.

"Brent knew how close a friend of yours he is, and he called him up."

"How did Charlie happen to go out and get you?"

She hesitated. "Brent seemed to think it would be a good idea," she said finally.

Hugh grinned. "The hell he did! I guess I'll have to give old Brent points for more intuition than I thought he had."

Hugh's grin soon faded, though, and Donna suspected that his head and shoulder were both aching.

While he was in the bathroom, Donna tried to reach either Brent or Jim Babson at the Windcrest, but neither of them was in. On a chance that she might not have left for the Snack Shack, Donna walked across the breezeway to the Nickerson house and found Althea in the kitchen doing the breakfast dishes.

Neither of the Nickersons had heard of Hugh's accident, and Althea was appalled. Anything that happened in connection with the *Portia* carried an extra weight for Althea, Donna realized, because she associated it with Alex.

Mark had already left for work. "I suppose he knows all about Hugh's accident by now," Althea said.

There was little doubt of that, Donna thought. Everything that happened concerning the ship was fodder for the town gristmill, and this would make the second in the week's catastrophes. Calamities came in threes, Donna could hear people saying, so what would be next?

She tried to turn her back on superstition as she asked Althea if she thought Mark would mind lending Hugh his razor.

Hugh was pleased to get the razor but disgruntled that it had not been possible so far to reach either Brent or Jim. He admitted he'd tried to reach them at the Windcrest himself while Donna was over at the Nickersons'.

Donna came to a decision. She didn't want him working on plans connected with the ship today; he needed to rest. Yet the enforced idleness was going to do him no good when he so obviously was brooding about his work.

"Look," she offered, "I can go over to the Windcrest and get anything you want, including some clean clothes."

"I hate to put you out like that, Donna," he said. "You should be writing."

"No, I shouldn't be. This is my day to play nursemaid." When he heard that he glowered at her, then laughed.

She set out with a list of the things Hugh had requested. Because she wanted to be sure she didn't forget anything, it took her longer than she'd thought it would to check all the items off the list.

Then she stopped by briefly to tell her aunt and uncle that Hugh, despite anything they might have heard, was very much alive at her place and raging to get into his act again.

There was no milk at the apartment and they could do with some rolls for lunch, so she stopped in a convenience store for a few things on her way back to the apartment. In all, she estimated she'd been gone more than an hour. As she parked outside her apartment, worry inevitably nagged at her. She only hoped Hugh hadn't decided to take off and trot down the beach to the *Portia* under his own power.

He hadn't. He was sitting in an armchair in the living room, reading. It was the first time Donna had seen him wearing his new glasses, and they were very attractive.

At first, Donna wasn't aware for a moment what he was reading. Then, to her consternation, she saw he was holding a sheaf of the computer paper she used to print out her first drafts on.

She'd been so upset the night before when Charlie had come to the house that she hadn't thought about putting her work under cover, as she'd been doing of late. She'd left the manuscript of her book in progress on a corner of her worktable, and the printout of the character sketch she'd been working on—dealing with Hugh—right next to the computer.

She felt sick when she realized it was the character sketch he'd been reading, and remembered the things she'd written.

She wouldn't have wanted him to see this, not without an explanation first of what it was she'd been trying to accomplish. But in all honesty she wasn't sure how she could have explained to a nonwriter what she'd been attempting.

Basically she'd been searching for an understanding of the man now sitting in front of her, looking at her levelly over the rims of his glasses, his eyes the color of dark charcoal. There were still so many gaps in her knowledge of him, and she yearned so desperately to know every facet of his nature.

She swallowed hard and forced herself to meet his eyes. "So this is what you think of me?" he said coldly.

Donna shook her head in protest. "No, no. You shouldn't have read that, Hugh."

She was still holding the tote bag of things she'd brought for him, having dropped off the groceries in the kitchen. She balanced the bag from one hand to the other, then set it down on the nearest chair. Its weight was suddenly unbearable, and she felt as if all her strength was seeping out of her.

"You've never met anyone like me before, have you, Donna?" Hugh asked curiously.

What was this leading to?

"No," she said. "No, I haven't. But I think you know that. I've made it plain enough that you're unique to me."

"Unique?" He toyed with the word, flooding it with bitterness. "Unique? Is that what you call it?"

He thrust the papers aside with a gesture that unmasked his fury. "Damn you," he said, his voice tight. "Damn you, Donna! You're the only woman in my life I've ever felt this way about. I've never loved a woman as I love you. And all this time you've been making a damned guinea pig out of me!"

CHAPTER SIXTEEN

DONNA WAS HORRIFIED. She moved toward Hugh, her eyes eloquent, her outstretched hands raised in a gesture of supplication. She had gone as white as she had when Charlie Evans had told her that Hugh had been hurt. But Hugh didn't appear to notice. He was looking at her as if he'd never seen her before.

"Hugh," she pleaded. "Please..." She choked on her words, and hot tears filled her eyes.

He frowned. "Don't cry, Donna," he commanded sharply. His words were rebuke. He couldn't stand seeing her cry, he'd told her that more than once. But she'd thought the other times that he'd been touched by seeing her respond to him emotionally, just as she was touched when he responded to her. Now Hugh was acting as if her tears were an act put on for his benefit.

Donna felt sick. Could he have lost his faith in her so quickly?

He thrust his glasses into his shirt pocket and stood up. The bandage on his head showed stark white against his ruddy skin, and the shadows under his eyes were dark by contrast. Donna suspected he was still in pain, though she was sure he'd deny it if she asked him. She was sure he would also refuse to take any of the medication the doctor had left for him.

He was a stubborn man, stubborn and unyielding. As he stared across the room, avoiding her eyes, she realized she was seeing a new side of his nature, and she wasn't sure she liked it. Hugh could be difficult, he was used to having his own way, and he had a tendency to balk at times. But he was also warm and generous, loyal and caring, and much harder on himself than he was on others. She had hurt him. It surprised her to see how much she'd hurt him by writing about him.

Donna became aware of her own blind spots. At times she could be so preoccupied with her own work that it never occurred to her that what she did could affect others. She could be unyielding in her own way, as stubborn as Hugh, and just as easily hurt. She'd already recognized that they were two very different people, yet there were basic similarities between them for all of that. And most important, love had formed a tremendous bond between them.

Hugh was moving toward the door, and Donna knew she couldn't possibly stop him if he wanted to go. Even in a weakened condition he was a lot stronger than she was.

Nevertheless, she moved toward the door herself, ready to block it with her body if necessary.

Her voice was thin. "Where are you going, Hugh?"

"For a walk," he said tersely.

"Please," she began, then she stopped, forcing herself to draw a deep breath and marshal her inner reserves.

She could match this man, damn it. She was no moral weakling. She sounded far cooler than she felt, though, as she said, "If you leave here I'll call the rescue squad and ask them to go after you."

He glared at her. "Are you insane, Donna?"

"No. I'm not going to have you striding out of here in a huff just because you've leapt to a lot of wrong conclusions.'' She had reached the door ahead of him and felt the urge to spread-eagle herself across its smooth wood surface. Instead she stood taut, her chin tilted at a defiant angle. ''Have some common sense, Hugh. I know nothing I can do will keep you from climbing back aboard the *Portia* tonight. But until then, try what the doctor ordered, will you? Go stretch out on the bed and get some rest while I fix lunch.''

She forced herself to speak assertively, which was no mean feat in the face of the storm emanating from Hugh's cloud-gray eyes. It was all she could do not to flinch visibly, to say nothing of breaking down in tears again. She yearned to sneak off to a corner where she could be alone and let the flood come. She wanted to weep until there were no more tears left in her, just an aching, bruised heart.

''There's no need for you to fix my lunch,'' Hugh said roughly.

''There's every need,'' she contradicted him. ''You may think you're larger than life but you're as human as the rest of us. Maybe a little bigger, maybe a little stronger, but you still ache and bleed like the rest of us, Hugh.'' She drew another breath. ''Go lie down,'' she said wearily.

He didn't answer her. At that point Donna was concentrating her gaze on the oval braided rug in the center of the living-room floor because she didn't think she could bear to see the dislike on his face for another minute. But when he asked quietly, ''Why did you write that thing about me?'' she had to look up at him.

''It would be difficult to explain.''

''You think I'd be too thickheaded to understand, is that it?''

"Perhaps," she replied honestly. "I don't know. Your reaction has...staggered me. It's out of all proportion."

"Is it, Donna?" he asked softly. "Suppose our positions were reversed and you came across something like that that I'd written about you?"

"You had no right to rummage among my papers in the first place, Hugh."

"Rummage among your papers? What are you accusing me of now? Snooping? Hell, Donna, I didn't realize that what you write is sacred. I saw the pages lying there and I wanted to see what you were doing. You've been reticent about talking about your work, but I thought that was because you were shy. It seems I've misread you," he finished, his voice laced with irony.

"My work's a very private thing to me, Hugh. It's something that comes out of me and more often than not even I don't understand where my ideas and words and people stem from."

"You knew where I 'stemmed from,'" he pointed out.

"Yes, I did."

"What were you trying to accomplish?"

She sighed. "I was trying to understand you," she said, and met his blazing skepticism with another tilt of her chin.

"You didn't understand me? I had the feeling you and I were getting to know each other pretty well."

"We were. This...went beyond that. I was putting my thoughts about you down on paper, trying to see beyond the obvious, trying to—" She shook her head sadly. "There's no use trying to spell it out."

"Because I would be too dense to know what you're talking about?"

"What makes you think I would ever accuse you of being dense, Hugh?"

"Well," he said, "you're the creative personality. I'm not. You have the edge on me there, at least when it comes to fantasizing. I still can't understand why you'd want to fantasize about me, and I admit I don't like what I read. You make me come on like a selfish bastard with tunnel vision where his work is concerned. You paint me as a loner who'd never want to share his life with anyone else. You make me sound so damned smug and sure of myself and complacent and self-righteous. If that's what I saw in the mirror every time I shaved I couldn't live with myself," he concluded, suppressed violence in his voice.

"Now, damn it, will you get away from that door?" he suggested in a calmer tone. "It's not going to kill me to go out and get a breath of fresh air."

She moved away, edging toward the kitchen, not wanting to watch him leave. If he was going to insist on making his way a mile down the road to the Windcrest, or even all the way down the beach to the *Portia*, he'd have to take the consequences.

Donna sank down at the kitchen table and buried her head in her hands. But she held back the tears. Hugh might not come back, but if he did come back she was going to be dry eyed.

AN OLD WOODEN CLOCK hung on the kitchen wall, and Donna had never noticed its ticking before. Now the sound beat against her eardrums, and she felt as if the passing minutes were knocking holes into her head.

She'd developed a throbbing headache, one that probably rivaled Hugh's at the moment. She pressed her hands to her temples and felt the tautness there.

Her neck muscles were stiff, and the ligaments pulled tight.

She hadn't looked at the clock when she'd heard the door close after Hugh, so she didn't know how long he'd been gone. She was tempted to call the Snack Shack and ask Mark to keep an eye out for him, or to try to rouse her uncle for the same thing, but Hugh, she knew bitterly, wouldn't thank her for her solicitude.

She had to do something. She had bought chowder stock when she'd stopped for milk, and now she blended it with the milk and butter and added a liberal sprinkling of pepper and a dash of salt. She put big, puffy rolls in the oven to warm and set the table with a single place...for Hugh.

While she went into the bathroom to get a couple of aspirin, she left the chowder simmering on the stove. When she returned to the kitchen, Hugh was standing at the stove stirring the contents of the pot.

Without turning toward her he asked, "May I join you?"

"The place at the table is for you," she told him.

"You're not eating?"

"No, thank you," she said politely, and thought unhappily that they were acting like strangers.

"You need some food," he said, and before she could stop him he took another soup bowl out of the cupboard and placed it next to the one she'd put on the side of the stove. "Where are the spoons?"

"Hugh, please..." She swallowed hard. "I...I couldn't."

"I didn't go far," he said abruptly, by way of answer. "I've been sitting on the top of the steps...thinking. I owe you an apology, Donna."

"No," she said. "No, you don't owe me anything."

"On the contrary, I do owe you an apology, and I really am sorry. I overreacted, I admit it. I didn't take what you'd done into proper context."

Donna's knees felt rubbery, and she sat down on one of the kitchen chairs. "I don't know what you mean."

"I realise I've thought of you only as a woman, not a writer."

"I still don't know what you mean."

"As a writer, I guess it's your business to take people apart. I'm sure you look at the people around you differently than most of us do. I guess that's what I was thinking about when I said that yours is a creative personality and mine isn't. We see things differently, Donna, and it could hardly be otherwise. The people in my life mean a great deal to me. The people I work with, the people to whom I'm close. I don't dissect them," he finished deliberately.

Donna stared at him dully. For a moment, when he had said he'd overreacted to her profile about him, she'd had a glimmer of hope. Now it faded. Hugh's statement sounded fine enough on the surface, but his opinion of what she'd done hadn't changed in the slightest. In fact his evident attempt to understand the so-called creative mind made her feel all the more helpless. He was putting her into the last kind of category she wanted to be in. She was a writer, yes. As a novelist she was intensely interested in people. She was quick to cut away the superficial and dig deep in trying to know people, she admitted that. But she'd never thought of it as a dissection. It was an ugly word, an ugly concept.

"Come and eat your chowder," he said, and she stared at him in disbelief. There was no way food could settle in her stomach when she felt as she did now.

"No," she said. "No. I told you. I can't."

She walked out of the kitchen and the apartment seemed to be closing in on her. She'd loved its smallness, its coziness, but now the living room seemed like a little box, and the only other place to escape to was the bedroom or the bathroom. Hugh was in the kitchen, and she didn't want to go near him. She didn't dare go near him. She felt sick all over.

She huddled in a corner of the couch and wondered if it would be better if he knew everything about what she'd been trying to do. If she hadn't been trying to define Keith's character to herself, she wouldn't ever have started in on her analysis of Hugh. Her desire to explore Hugh as a person had followed that. It had not come first.

Would that make sense to Hugh? And how would he feel about her writing a book based on Alex Bruce and the *Portia* and himself, even though in her book she was dealing entirely with fiction and was using the ship and the people around her only as background?

She had the sinking feeling that Hugh would dislike the thought of her basing a novel on Alex and the *Portia* even more than he'd disliked her character portrait of him. He'd asked a number of times how her work was progressing, once it was plain she'd gotten over her lingering case of writer's block. She'd been less than honest in her response to him. She hadn't wanted anyone to know what she was working on, and this had become a kind of superstition. She'd felt so dried up creatively for so long that the fresh flow of words and ideas had been something to be guarded jealously, until she was sure her talent was back to stay.

But long before now she'd known she was going to see the *Portia* book to its conclusion. Her enthusiasm for the book had only mounted as she worked on it. The story compelled her, her characters compelled her, and though Alex Bruce had been the pattern for Andrew, Andrew was now Andrew, Keith was Keith and Flora was Flora. They all stood alone.

During the past week she'd received an enthusiastic letter from her agent about the proposal, and there was every reason to think her publisher would be equally pleased and would offer a contract.

She knew she should have shared her good news with Hugh. She should have faced up to his possible reaction and made every effort to make him understand why she was so excited about doing the book, and made him see that her story no longer had anything to do with Alex or Althea or himself. It had grown up. It, too, now stood alone.

Donna started when she heard Hugh's voice. She looked up to see him standing in the living-room doorway, and he looked so tired, so constrained, that it tore at her heart. She wanted to rush over to him, to throw her arms around him and try to comfort him. But she was sure that right now he'd only hold her off.

"May I use your phone?" he asked, and the formality of his tone hurt.

"Of course."

She watched him dial, and his fingers seemed to be trembling slightly. Then she realized he was being put through to a special number, evidently a field telephone at the shipwreck site.

She heard him say tersely, "This is MacDonough. I want to get over there. Send a Jeep out to the Nickerson house for me, will you?"

She watched his face darken as he listened to the response at the other end of the line, and then he said roughly, "Regardless of what Hancock says, I'm okay. No problems. Look, would you rather I walked?"

She saw him start to slam down the receiver, then he caught her watching him and he lowered it gently onto its cradle. His eyes met hers, and there was raw pain in their depths, but he'd never sounded so polite as he did when he said, "The chowder was delicious, Donna. Thank you for making it. Thank you for everything."

The house was full of Hugh after he left. The imprint of his head still dented Donna's pillow, and the towel thrust over the shower curtain in the bathroom smelled of the shaving soap he'd used, borrowed from Mark. She'd never identified the scent with Mark, had never even noticed it before, but Donna knew that from now on it would remind her of Hugh.

He'd washed out his chowder bowl and had turned it upside down to dry by the kitchen sink, the spoon he'd used shiny clean next to it. She'd forgotten to tell him she'd put rolls in the oven to warm. She turned the oven off, knew the rolls would never be eaten, and decided to crumble them later and throw the crumbs out on the beach for the sea gulls.

There was an impression in the chair cushion where Hugh had been sitting, and he'd gotten the pages in her sketch all out of order. As she tried to straighten them her hands shook, but the pages eluded her grasp and scattered across the rug.

It was the last straw. The tears came and Donna's eyes were still red rimmed when Althea arrived late in the afternoon with a casserole in one hand and a square cake pan in the other.

"I was going to make lasagna anyway, and I made some extra for you and Hugh," Althea said. "I baked an extra applesauce cake, too. If you like, I can bring over some vanilla ice cream later, to put on top." She looked around. "Where is Hugh? Sleeping? I wanted to say hello to him but I can come back later."

Donna looked at the food in Althea's hands and nearly started to cry all over again. She wasn't sure she could speak steadily, but she tried. "He's gone back to the ship."

"You can't mean it."

"I do mean it."

Althea looked at Donna dubiously, then took the food out to the kitchen. On her way back she paused to switch on a table lamp.

"It's getting dark in here," she complained, then peered across at Donna. "What's happened?"

Donna sank back on the couch. "It's a long, long story, and right now I'm not up to telling it."

Althea sat down in the chair Hugh had been sitting in when he'd read the character sketch. Donna wondered if she would erase the impression he'd made on the seat cushion, then decided that was impossible. For her the impression would always be there.

"I had to get away from the shack," Althea said bleakly. "Mark understood. He got a couple of people in to help him. The pace is picking up down there—you can feel it. Men keep coming up from the ship just to take a break. You could cut the tension in the air. Or maybe I should say the excitement. I guess it's a combination of both."

She paused. "Brent Hancock stopped by this morning and said he was glad Hugh was out here with you. He was counting on you to keep him here. That's why I was so certain Hugh would be around."

"No one could keep Hugh here tonight," Donna said flatly. "I presume that's what Brent was referring to. He doesn't want Hugh aboard when they try to take the *Portia* off again?"

Althea nodded. "That's about it. Brent said Hugh's done all the homework, now it's up to the rest of them to carry out the lesson. He seemed pretty sure they could do it, too. He seems certain they're on the right course this time.

"I suppose it isn't that Hugh doesn't trust Brent and the others," she went on. "I guess he's just the kind of man who has to be at the center of the action himself."

How right Althea was! Yes, Hugh had to be at the center of the action. He was as dedicated to his career as anyone she'd ever seen. Perhaps that was what had nettled him so when he'd read her character sketch of him. She'd delved into that facet of him. She'd pictured him as a man to whom a ship would forever come first, and a woman second. Had that stung Hugh?

Damn it, he had it coming, Donna thought angrily. Hugh had only reinforced her belief in her own supposition, and she'd never felt so miserable.

Althea refused to take the food she'd brought back home with her, even though Donna tried to prevail upon her to do so. At the moment, food was wasted on her. It would be, she knew, until the fate of the *Portia* was decided.

She was beginning to think that the ship's fate and her own were entwined. But that was ridiculous. She was confusing Hugh's destiny with hers, the past twenty-four hours had taught her that their lives were not meant to run parallel courses.

She couldn't stay in the apartment that night. It was cool for late April, almost cold. The full moon always brought colder weather, the local people said. Donna slipped on a wool jacket before going out to her car, and even then she was shivering, though she knew part of that was from nerves.

As she slid behind the wheel, she glanced at the Nickersons' house. A yellow light was burning over the front door but the house itself was in darkness. Unless Althea was huddled somewhere inside, yielding to her private sorrows, it meant that both the Nickersons must be out.

Donna drove toward the beach and became one in a series of cars doing the same thing. To her surprise she found the Snack Shack still open for business, and shivering customers were lined up to buy coffee and hot chocolate.

She slipped in the side door and didn't even ask Mark if he needed her. She simply said, "Let me help," and he nodded.

Donna shrugged into an apron, and only then became aware that Althea was working, too. Pale and tight-lipped, she was brewing fresh coffee and making pots of hot chocolate, intent on keeping busy.

Right now that was the only way to go, Donna decided grimly.

It was good to work, and there was plenty to do. A steady stream of customers continued to call for hot beverages. Many of the people carried their coffee or hot chocolate with them, sipping from the paper containers as they trudged down onto the beach to get as close to the shipwreck scene as they could.

After a time Mark said to Donna and Althea, "Look, if you two want to go down there you can take my four-wheel drive. You know the cops, they'd let you through."

Althea shook her head. "I'd rather stay here."

"How about you, Donna?" Mark asked. "You know how to operate my four-wheel drive, don't you?"

"Frankly, no," she said, "and tonight's not the time to take a chance with it. Anyway, I'd rather stick around, Mark."

He nodded. "Well, I'm going to stay open as long as people need something hot to drink." He looked up at the moon. "She's full enough, but the sea's calm as a millpond. I don't know whether that's going to be a help or a hindrance."

Mark was restless. Everyone was restless. As the night inched forward, tension mounted in Donna until she thought she would snap.

She wished that one of the men from Hugh's salvage company would stop by the shop, but none of them did. The reason was obvious. They were down on the beach, fighting to get water under the *Portia*, fighting to get her off the shifting sand.

What would happen if they succeeded? Hugh and Alex would almost certainly both be going with the ship. They were aboard her right now, Donna had no doubt of that. If she sailed, they would sail with her.

She had been forcing herself not to think of the future, but now it intruded like a tidal wave, sweeping everything else aside.

She had wanted Hugh to succeed. She knew what it meant to him. Yet in a direct way his success would spell her failure—if she hadn't failed with him already. He'd been a polite stranger as he'd left her house today, and there'd been a wall of ice between them. She shivered when she thought about it.

If Hugh sailed with the ship, he would not come back.

IT WAS NEARLY MIDNIGHT when Terry O'Connor stopped by. "I'm going down again, Mark. Want to come along?"

Mark looked questioningly at his sister and Donna. "Think you can handle things here?"

"Go ahead," Althea said tonelessly.

She had been moving like a zombie the past hour as people started to filter back from the beach, all of them with their own stories to tell.

Some of them swore they'd seen water all around the ship, yet others discounted this. Some said the ship had moved around and at one point her bow was pointing out to sea. Others disclaimed this.

So much for eyewitnesses, Donna thought grimly.

She yearned to know the truth, but when Mark and Terry came back to tell her she wished she hadn't heard it.

"Another setback," Mark said, pouring a cup of coffee for Terry and one for himself.

Althea was white-faced. Even her lips seemed to have lost their color.

"What this time?" she asked.

"It looked like they were making progress," Mark reported. "They were trying to bolster the pulling power by using the two tugboats as well as the derrick, and I'd swear she'd started to move around when one of the cables attached to the derrick snapped. You could hear the damned thing go. It let loose with a crack that whistled clear into space. The *Stardust* started heaving. Lucky it was so calm, not that I suppose anything that sturdy could ever capsize."

"I talked to Hugh MacDonough," Terry put in. "He says the problem with the cable was bad enough, but the tide tonight was against them, as well. It was a flat tide, he said. He'd hoped the surge in the surf would help lift the ship but—" Terry spread her hands wide "—no dice. I honestly think, though, that Mark's right. She did move a little. I saw it."

"What did Hugh say?" It was Althea who asked the question. Donna couldn't bring herself to speak his name.

"Well, he said she made a little progress. He says her bow's maybe thirty feet closer to pointing out to sea than it was. But the thing is, she *has* moved. Hugh's always said that the first task was to turn her so the bow would point straight seaward, which meant a full swing from the broadside position she's been in all this time. I think they were on their way tonight, despite the bad luck with the cable. In my opinion, tomorrow night should do the trick."

"Is that what you're going to put in your story for the paper?" Mark asked, raising a skeptical eyebrow as if he was sure Terry wouldn't pin herself down in print to such an opinion.

She laughed. "You're right, Mark. That would be sticking my head out, and I've learned to protect my neck. But strictly between us, I'm betting on Mac-Donough and his trusty men. Hugh's said all along that they've got to swing her around five hundred feet. If they move her thirty, that's a start. If nothing else happens tomorrow night..."

Hugh, Donna recalled, had always said that his business was full of "ifs."

CHAPTER SEVENTEEN

THE FOCUS of a whole town was on the *Portia* the following day. The stricken ship was no longer simply an attraction that had brought thousands of sightseers to Devon for the past few weeks. It had turned into a local concern.

The fact that two salvage attempts had been made and both had failed emphasized the ship's plight. On that late-April day, when the willows were greening and the tulips were blooming and winter seemed over at last, no one was thinking much about spring. The ship had become larger than life to the town, yet all too real.

No one talked about anything but the *Portia*, Donna discovered. She stood in the checkout line at the pharmacy waiting for the girl at the counter to finish telling the customer in front of her that her father had said at breakfast that the ship was going to be dismantled, probably before the day was out.

"They've given up on her," the girl, a pretty brunette, said sadly. "It's too bad."

While her customer commiserated, Donna shifted her weight impatiently from one foot to the other. She'd come to the pharmacy to get a fresh supply of aspirin. She'd never been a pill taker, but another in a series of tension headaches had descended upon her in full force that morning.

She'd lingered to browse, picking up a few birthday cards to stash away for the future, splurging on a luxury vial of bubble bath and buying a couple of magazines. There were some interesting paperbacks on the stands, but she knew her concentration was too limited just now to sustain reading a book.

Finally she was able to pay for her purchases. She started toward the door and found herself staring directly at Hugh. He'd shaved that morning and was clear-eyed, but telltale shadows of fatigue still brushed his face, and the fresh white bandage across his forehead brought back too vividly everything that had happened since Donna had gone to him in the hospital the night before last.

He drew her aside. "Do you have time for a cup of coffee?"

She hadn't expected such an invitation. The way he'd left her the day before brought a memory tinged with frost, and she looked up at him questioningly.

He said gently, "I'd like to have a cup of coffee with you, Donna, if you have the time to spare."

She nearly laughed. She had the time to spare. He was the one who didn't have time.

She nodded. "All right."

His glance was quizzical, but he made no comment. "Hold on just a minute then, will you? I'm after some aspirin."

At least in some ways they were running parallel courses, thought Donna.

Hugh managed to get through the checkout line much faster than she had—probably the Mac-Donough charisma, she conceded. Even old ladies made way for him, since he had only one item to purchase.

"Anywhere special you want to go?" he asked.

"The coffee shop next door's all right."

The shop wasn't crowded, and Hugh steered Donna to a corner table that offered reasonable privacy. "I think everyone's at the beach," he remarked.

"I haven't been down yet myself."

"I imagine Mark will be able to use an extra pair of hands today, if you have it in mind to work for him," Hugh told her. "If they've been clocking the daily visitors, today should set a banner record. Bigger than the weekends, I'd say. There are more local people down there than I've ever seen around before. I get the strange feeling they've come either to preside at the *Portia*'s funeral or to say goodbye to her."

"And which is to be?" she asked him.

She hadn't meant to pose such a question at all, and once she had she wished she could have taken back her words.

"We should get her off on tonight's high tide," Hugh said, and though he spoke without hesitation, Donna had the feeling he wasn't as sure of himself as he sounded.

As if to underlie this, he added, "With a little bit of luck."

A silence fell between them, and it was not a comfortable silence. Donna was wondering whether or not Hugh would have gotten in touch with her again if they hadn't happened to bump into each other accidentally. But this was a question she wasn't about to ask him.

He said suddenly, as if the words were being forced from him, "I've missed you so damned much. I need to talk to you about so many things. This is the wrong time for us, Donna. It's a miracle we've done as well as we have."

She watched him stir sugar into his coffee, then lace it with cream. There was an economy to his movements. Hugh did things purposefully and made few wasted gestures.

He said few superfluous things, too. She was only really beginning to appreciate that. He was not a man of few words and was too fluid a conversationalist to ever be termed taciturn, but what he said counted.

She was still staring at his hands when she became aware that he was studying her. She didn't want to look him in the eye, but he'd always been able to compel her in this way, and he did so now.

"Want to know something funny?" he asked.

She couldn't think of anything in the world that would seem very funny just now. "What?"

He reached into his pocket and pulled something out, then showed it to her, his palm outstretched. She found herself looking at the wampum tie tack she'd bought for him in Provincetown and she frowned, puzzled.

"Would you believe this? I've carried it with me ever since you gave it to me, except the other night. I'd taken a shower and switched shirts before I went over to the ship, and I left the tie tack in the other shirt pocket. I won't make that mistake again."

"Hugh," she protested, "you're not that superstitious."

"No, I'm not at all superstitious. It isn't that. This is a part of you, symbolically, so I never want to be without it again, that's all."

Donna tried to fathom just what he was saying to her, but she couldn't be sure. She didn't know whether Hugh meant it was the only thing he'd be taking away from Devon that would represent her if he left, or...

She gave up. She'd slept too poorly and was far too befuddled to make much sense out of anything.

They finished their coffee and walked into the parking lot together. Hugh glanced skyward, watching the tree branches bending in a rising wind. "I like the looks of that breeze. Right now that's all to the good, as far as we're concerned."

He opened the door of Donna's car for her. She slipped behind the wheel not knowing what to say to him, not knowing what to do next. She felt tongue-tied and inept and such a failure.

She hadn't intended to bring the subject up, but she couldn't hold back any longer. "Hugh," she began with difficulty, "about the book...I'm sorry."

She realized at once that he didn't know what she was talking about. "What book?"

"That sketch you found—I don't deny I was writing about you, but it was going to be converted into something else," she tried to explain.

"Another language?"

"No, not another language. I was trying to capture something of you so that I could mold some of...of your character into a character in my book," she said lamely.

He stared at her. "Are you saying you're putting me in a book, Donna?" he demanded. "I thought what I saw was supposed to be just a character sketch...not the real thing."

Donna sighed wearily. "I'm not putting *you* in a book. A novelist never puts an exact person into a book. At least I don't. Characters are components of truth and fiction. A character in a book is usually made up of more than one individual. It's hard to explain."

"So in this case I was slated to become some kind of montage?"

"No, no, not that, either," Donna protested. "Look, I'm sorry, I shouldn't have gotten into this. I know you have to get back to the ship."

"Fifteen minutes more or less won't make that much difference to the *Portia*," he told her, "but it might with you and me." Before she knew what he intended doing, he crossed around to the other side of her car and slid into the front seat opposite her. He leaned back against the door folding his arms, his head tilted at an angle as he surveyed her. "Okay. Tell me."

"It goes back a while," Donna said feebly.

"Then begin at the beginning."

"When I came up here I took advantage of the opportunity to have the Bruckers' apartment because I needed a change of pace so desperately," she began, wishing she could make him understand what it had been like for her—the magnitude of her frustration, the reality of the fear she might never be able to write again.

"I was so...empty. I'd been trying for longer than I like to think about to get the book I was supposed to write on paper, and nothing would come. It was as if I'd...dried up."

She managed a slight smile. "It's not an uncommon affliction with writers. I understand it happens to most of us at one time or another, but it's awful. I was afraid I'd lost it."

He nodded. "I can imagine you were."

"I came up here sure that it would be different. I was certain that once I got out and started walking on the beach and breathing all that good salt air the cobwebs would be vaporized right out of my mind and the words would start flowing. But it didn't happen that way. You remember, when I first met you I told you about some of this.''

He nodded again. "Yes, you did.''

"Well, the *Portia* was the biggest thing that had happened around here in years. It affected me just as it affected everyone else in town. But with me the effect began to be different. I started thinking about the ship, and especially I started thinking about Alex Bruce.''

"Alex?'' Hugh seemed surprised.

"Yes. He came on as such a mystery figure at first. Dark, rather saturnine and very handsome. I began to think about different things in connection with him and the ship, and a vague sort of story started to form in my mind. I began to make notes about it.''

"Yes?'' he encouraged.

"Well, it just evolved,'' Donna said. "And you loomed up more and more in my plot.''

"In your plot, or in your life?'' he asked gently.

"Both.''

"So you wrote me into the book?''

"You simply became a part of the book. Some of the things that had really happened dovetailed with what I'd been thinking about, and I began to merge people and ideas.''

"Did you write Althea into the book?''

"She became a part of it, too.''

"So would you say this is truth you're dealing with, rather than fiction?'' he asked, eyeing her keenly.

"No, no,'' she protested, "not at all. My story's complete fiction, Hugh.''

"What about you? Are you in it, too?''

"No,'' she said. "I was in the beginning, but I soon realized I had no part in the plot. So I just wrote myself out.''

He repeated the words thoughtfully. "You just wrote yourself out."

He reached out his hand and tilted her chin between his fingers, forcing her to look at him. "And where did that leave me, Donna?"

"You—no, not you—*Keith*—goes off at the end of the story to salvage another ship," she said unhappily. "Andrew and Flora come together again. Keith and Andrew are brothers in my story and they've always been in love with the same woman. Flora and Keith nearly married, but in the end Flora goes back to Andrew."

"And Keith goes off into the sunset by himself?" said Hugh, a strange note in his voice.

"Yes...yes, but that's essentially what Keith wants, Hugh."

"Does he?"

"Hugh, this is a *story*," she insisted.

"I know that. But I don't seem able to avoid feeling that you've settled my fate for me. As for Alex and Althea, have you by chance settled their fates for them, too?"

"How could I do that?" she implored, hating the direction the conversation was taking. "I have no influence over any of you. And as for Alex and Althea, Althea knows that Alex will be leaving here. I think she's conditioned herself to the fact that he'll be going back to his wife in Scotland. It's going to be hard for her, but she'll accept it and survive."

"Is that fact or fiction, Donna?" Hugh asked, a dangerous glint in his eyes. "Will Althea 'survive,' as you put it, all that easily? That negates any depth of feeling she may have for Alex, don't you think? And *is* Alex going back to his wife in Scotland? Are you so sure of all your facts, Donna? What about Mark?" he persisted. "Will he revert to being a woman hater, or will he continue to see the lovely reporter from the *Boston Globe*?"

Donna flinched at the caustic note in Hugh's voice but replied bravely, "I've never made a specialty of crystal-ball gazing, Hugh."

"Haven't you? Hearing you, I'd think the contrary. I also have the strong feeling that in some areas of your life you're not able to separate truth from fiction, Donna. At least not yet."

Hugh was a big man, but he could move quickly. Using his right arm he pulled her toward him. He couldn't help twisting slightly as he moved and she saw him wince, but that didn't stop him, and he claimed her mouth with his.

As he released her, he let out a deep breath. Then, his voice laced with a thick anger he couldn't hide, he said, "Think about it, Donna. Next time around, how about trying for the truth?"

DONNA DIDN'T HAVE TIME to think about much of anything for the balance of the day—and that was the way she wanted it.

She knew she had just one chance of hanging on to her sanity until she learned what the *Portia*'s fate was going to be, and that was to keep busy. Fortunately the shack had never been quite such a beehive of activity. There was no time to think. No time to do anything but fill orders for the curious, tired, cold, hungry and thirsty people who kept descending in swarms, even after darkness fell.

Mark and Althea knew a lot of people, and Donna was thankful for that as the hours moved on. Every now and then someone from the police department or the rescue squad or a park or highway department employee on overtime hours, would stop by for coffee and bring a report with some authenticity to it. The ship had been turned so that her bow was pointing seaward, and though that represented a giant step forward, the salvors had a long way to go.

The *Portia* was still anything but free of the sand that had held her in its clutches so tenaciously, and there was no guarantee that she ever would be. That message was reiterated so often Donna began to wonder if people were merely being pessimistic or if the odds really were that great against the *Portia*'s ever leaving Massasoit Beach.

Then just after midnight, Terry O'Connor appeared at the Snack Shack to say exultantly, "She just may make it."

Mark looked from Althea to Donna then back to Althea again. "That does it," he said quietly. "Put up the Closed sign, Althea. I'm shutting up shop and turning off the lights. Come on."

At his words, neither woman hung back. The two of them huddled together in the rear seat of Mark's four-wheel drive, and Terry sat next to Mark up front. Fortunately Mark had gone to high school with the police officer on duty at the final checkpoint, and they were passed through with no problem.

Mark slid his vehicle into position aslant a dune overlooking the shipwreck site, careful even in this tense moment to park carefully so he wouldn't damage the fragile vegetation in the area. Below them was an eerie scene, dominated by the play of lights and shadows created by the glaring floodlights. The great green-and-black ship had been moved around so that her bow now did point straight toward Portugal, yet she still seemed wedged into the sand, rooted to the beach as ever.

"I wish we had a walkie-talkie," Mark said. "We could listen in to what they're saying." He nodded toward the men clustered at the water's edge. "They must be talking back and forth with the crew on the barge and... My God," he exclaimed, awestruck. "Look at her! She's heading out!"

Donna leaned forward. At first she thought Mark was mistaken, but then she saw the great ship begin to slip forward slowly, slowly, as if she were being tugged by an invisible hand.

"The *Stardust* has begun to winch her," Mark said, his voice almost a whisper but still vibrating with excitement.

"I'm not sure I believe this," Terry breathed. "Mark, I've got to get to a phone."

"Not right now, you don't," Mark said. "Sit tight, Terry, no one else is going to get this story ahead of you. Look at her!"

The ship was moving by inches, but she was moving. Then she began to slide forward, covering feet rather than inches, and Donna couldn't sit still any longer. Heedless of Mark and Terry and Althea, she wrenched the door at her side open, nearly tumbling out onto the sand. Then she began racing for lower ground, sliding down the balance of the dune and running across the beach, her feet given wings.

She was almost at the water's edge when she stopped. She stood, her breath coming fast, staring at the ship, which was moving more and more rapidly. She heard a man standing nearby say, "Boy, she's flying!" and her turbulent feelings echoed the admiration in his voice. She, too, was cheering for the *Portia*, everything else forgotten.

Someone yelled, "She's floating free!" and a great exultation welled up inside Donna.

"Hugh, oh Hugh, my darling," she murmured to the man aboard the ship, though he couldn't possibly hear her. "You've done it!"

A voice at her elbow asked, "Are you okay, Donna?"

She thought for a moment it was Mark, but it turned out to be Jim Babson looking down at her solicitously.

"Yes, I'm okay," she told him, her voice trembling. "It's unbelievable."

There was triumph in his laugh, but he said quietly, "No, it isn't, really. Hugh would be the first to tell you that. All along it was just a question of having a job to do and doing it. It's seldom we get a ship off without some setbacks. This one looked touch and go for a while, but I don't think Hugh ever doubted she'd be out there again, riding high."

The *Portia* was beyond the breaker line in deep water, though not all that far offshore, and she was indeed riding high.

She'd traveled past the floodlit area and was visible only because of her own lights. Donna's eyes were glued to the ship, and she didn't know whether she first saw or simply sensed its lack of motion.

"What's happened?" she cried out apprehensively.

"She'll ride at anchor for the night," Jim Babson explained easily. "The Coast Guard will be inspecting her in the morning to decide whether or not she's safe for towing. My guess is that we'll get the green light."

"And what will you do then?" Donna asked.

He gazed down at her curiously, as if he expected she would already have known this.

"We plan to take her to a shipyard in Connecticut and put her in dry dock," Babson said. "What happens next will depend on what they discover there. If she's fit for future sea duty, the company will sell her. If not, she'll be scrapped. Either way," he added assuringly, "Hugh will come out ahead, you can bet on that."

"Good."

She wanted to ask him if there was a chance Hugh would be coming ashore tonight, or if he'd stay with the ship. All sorts of questions brimmed, but the man at her side couldn't give her the answer to most of them. Only Hugh could do that.

She said good-night to Jim Babson and turned back to join Mark, Althea and Terry. Her pulse was still thudding, and emotion choked her. She wanted—she needed—so desperately to be with Hugh.

She found Mark and Althea alone in the car. Althea was still sitting in the back seat, and Mark reached over to open the front door for Donna.

She climbed in and must have looked her question, because Mark said roughly, "Terry got a ride back to a phone booth with one of the cops. She wanted to call in her story to be sure it makes the morning edition."

He was frowning, and it was Althea who reminded him, "It's her job, Mark. Don't take it so personally."

He managed a wry smile. "Yeah, that's right." He shifted into gear, and they slowly moved off the dune. After a moment he added with a hint of humor in his voice, "I'll catch up with Terry later."

Donna wished the same could be said about Althea and Alex...and about Hugh and herself.

CHAPTER EIGHTEEN

DONNA DROVE down to the beach the next morning at the break of dawn. Gold streaks spiraled skyward on the eastern horizon, but the sun had not yet started its climb above water that stretched serenely as far as the eye could see.

There were no waves to ruffle the sea, and only a faint breeze touched Donna's cheeks, leaving a feather-light caress.

Hugh's four forty-foot trucks stood at the end of the parking lot. Beyond them, at the edge of the asphalt, the enormous front-end loader was silhouetted against the awakening sky. Four mammoth anchors, yards of massive chains and the rest of the paraphernalia used by the salvors lay around in calculated disarray.

Donna felt strange as she walked past the snack shop. Mark had gone back and closed up the shutters after they'd returned from the beach, and the shack had an abandoned air. It might be abandoned for a time, after today. With no *Portia* to draw them, tourists would not be coming to Devon again for a while.

As she cleared the dunes to stand on the open beach, her eyes misted. The ship floated offshore, surrounded by water. Finally Donna accepted that what she'd seen last night had been reality after all. Over the intervening hours it had been easy to imagine they'd all been dreaming. She'd half expected to see the ship still broadside to the beach, mired in the sand.

But the ship was free. Looking at the green-and-black freighter, Donna envied the other woman in Hugh's life.

And you're the winner, she told the *Portia* silently. *It was you who took first place in his affections. I'm a very poor second.*

Watching the ship, Donna wondered if Hugh was still asleep behind one of the portholes in the crew's quarters, or if he and Alex and the others were already up, making ready for the Coast Guard's inspection.

She turned away and walked back to her car slowly, her head bowed. Her joy over Hugh's success was untarnished, but she felt so very alone. Everything that happened with the vessel from now on would be offstage as far as she was concerned. The ship would be going out of her life, and Hugh with it.

She'd hear from him, she felt sure of that. He wouldn't be so callous as to put her out of his life without another word. But distance would have its own enchantment for Hugh, because that's where his work would be. It was impossible not to feel that she'd lost him.

It was too early for anything to be open in town, but Donna didn't want to go back to her apartment. She drove across to the bay side of the Cape, but the vista there only reminded her of the night she and Hugh had stopped at the beach in Orleans and waded in the frigid water like a couple of silly kids.

It seemed impossible that they'd managed to be so carefree with the *Portia*'s potential fate always hanging over their heads.

At six o'clock Donna drove back into town and bought a copy of the *Boston Globe*. She still didn't want to go back to her apartment, nor did she want to go into the coffee shop to eat. There was a chance she might run into someone she knew, and right now she needed to be alone.

She bought a container of coffee and a cruller and drove to a small town landing overlooking a freshwater pond. A lone fisherman sat on the shoreline casting for trout, but neither he nor Donna was about to invade each other's privacy.

She opened the paper and saw that Terry O'Connor had made the front page with her story about the *Portia*. The success of Hugh's salvage mission was the main news story of the day, and Terry's account was accompanied by a dramatic night photo of the floodlighted ship with its bow pointed seaward.

Terry had gotten all the facts, Donna noted as she read, and some of them had come from Hugh. Somehow the reporter had made contact with Hugh once the ship had started moving. Donna could only assume that the media had been given a way to contact him aboard the ship, probably via a special phone hookup.

Terry had had access to him and she hadn't. It wasn't jealousy that Donna felt, but a deep, unsettling bleakness.

It was shortly after midnight today when the 520-foot freighter *Portia* moved slowly into the North Atlantic, and the salvors who had failed in two previous attempts to free the stricken vessel from Massasoit Beach in Devon, on Cape Cod, began to celebrate their own Fourth of July in April.

Earlier in the week the salvage operation appeared beset by catastrophe, first when attempts to move the giant ship failed, then when Hugh MacDonough, president of the salvage firm of MacDonough, Inc., of Boston, suffered a fall from the forty-four-foot Jacob's ladder that had provided the only means of boarding the freighter during its month-long stay on the Cape Cod beach.

Terry went on to detail the story of the northeaster, which had sent the vessel to its potential doom in the first place. She had embroidered in her report details about the carnival atmosphere that had prevailed in Devon in recent weeks, the mixed blessings of a springtime boom in the town, and the equally mixed feelings of the local residents when it had finally become apparent that Hugh MacDonough stood to win his bet with nature.

Donna skimmed on.

The *Portia* is now the property of the salvors who dragged her off the beach. Reports indicate that they stand to make a hefty profit on the ship, no matter what direction fate may now lead her.

MacDonough, reached aboard the vessel as she rode at anchor of Massasoit Beach, refused to say how much money his company will be deriving from the salvage operation. But according to available statistics, most successful salvage stories come with multimillion dollar endings. Salvors customarily receive not only the vessel in question, but an undisclosed sum of money from its insurer.

MacDonough acknowledged that if his attempts to pull the ship off the beach had failed, and he had had to resort to the last-ditch method of cutting the ship apart in order to remove her, his company would have lost money on the venture.

"But I never seriously thought that would happen," he said this morning. MacDonough added that the job was primarily a pulling and tugging operation all along, "and that's what did it in the long run. Essentially it was the steady pulling that got her off, the steady hauling and refleeting of the pulling blocks. We started in shortly after midnight, determined to get her into the water this time," MacDonough said. "We first pumped seawater into her hull to lower the bow and lift the stern, then we were ready to go."

Terry concluded her story by saying that the ship would be inspected by the Coast Guard that morning and, if pronounced sufficiently seaworthy, would then be towed to Connecticut, where she'd be put into dry dock.

Hugh MacDonough had stated that initially the ship "looked good." MacDonough reported that although it would be impossible to give an accurate assessment of any damage that might have been done to the *Portia* until she was in dry dock, thus far the ship was drawing no water. This bodes well for her future.

Donna folded the paper and put it next to her on the car seat. She hadn't touched her coffee or the cruller, and she had no appetite for either. She tossed the closed coffee container into a trash can and broke up the cruller and scattered it at the edge of the pond to tempt any wandering sea gulls.

When she drove back to her apartment, Althea intercepted her. "Mark wondered if you could possibly come over to the Snack Shack and help us out this morning," she said apologetically.

Donna had expected Althea to be wiped out. It stood to reason that the previous night must have taken a terrific emotional toll on her, but she was sure that if a mirror was held up in front of the two of them, Althea would look better than she did.

It's that staunch, old New England character, Donna decided. Althea was loaded with it. She had her stiff upper lip in place.

"Donna," Althea continued, before she could answer the Nickerson request for help, "we'll manage if you don't feel you can make it. I know you have your work to do. It's just that Mark thinks we'll be swamped today, until the ship moves out."

Donna nodded. "You probably will be. I'll be glad to help out, Althea. Just give me a minute to change my clothes."

She'd started out that morning in faded jeans and a sweat shirt, and although working at the Snack Shack didn't require much better in the way of attire, she wanted to put on something a bit less worn and weather-beaten.

She and Althea drove over to the shop together. It was not quite seven-thirty but the parking lot was already partially filled, and people were streaming down the path to get a final glimpse of the ship.

As they made coffee and prepared for the first rush, Althea asked, "Have you heard from Hugh?"

The question surprised Donna. How did Althea think she could have heard from Hugh? "No," she said. Then curiosity prompted her to add, "Have you heard from Alex?"

Althea nodded. "He called me from the ship this morning. I thought maybe Hugh had managed to call you. Probably," she added graciously, "he's been so tied up with all the last-minute details he wasn't able to."

Donna avoided answering her by taking an order from the first of the day's customers.

A couple of the local women who had been helping the Nickersons occasionally appeared midmorning to ask if they were needed, and Mark said, "Stick around." He added to Althea, "Why don't you and Donna take a break and walk down the beach to see what's going on?"

"I'd just as soon stay here," Donna said quickly, which was true, but as the morning wore on she began to feel a slow, steady pressure weighing her down. It soon turned into a restlessness so intense it was all she could do to contain it. Finally she knew she had to go out on the beach to see for herself what was happening.

She went alone. She walked to the break in the dunes then stepped out onto the open beach, and a great lump rose in her throat as she looked toward the *Portia*. The ship was leaving Massasoit Beach like a queen, with two oceangoing tugs as her escorts. She rode high and proud, and there was something unbelievably poignant about watching her.

Donna blinked back tears, and the ache in her throat grew to such proportions she couldn't swallow.

"Good luck, *Portia*," she whispered softly. "You came first with Hugh from the very beginning, but I still wish you well."

BY EARLY AFTERNOON the freighter had disappeared over the horizon. At first her gantries were still visible, but then her superstructure faded from sight, and the clusters of people watching from the beach saw only the open sea.

Cars began to leave the parking lot, then Hugh's trucks started to move out, laden with equipment. By the time Mark closed shop for the day there was nothing left to prove that the ship had ever been there except a rack of postcards and a few T-shirts that hadn't sold.

As he cleared up paper cups and napkins and put away the condiment containers, Mark commented, "I think this will be our swan song, ladies."

Besides Mark only Althea and Donna were left at the snack shop. The women who had come to help earlier had long since gone home.

"I think I'll close up tomorrow unless we have an unexpected rush of business," he said. "My guess is that things will be dull for another few weeks now that the ship's gone. We're only at the end of April, remember. Our regular season doesn't start for another month. I'm thinking that I might even take a trip for a couple of weeks. That would still give me time to fix up this place like I was starting to do when the ship beached."

Althea looked at him curiously. "Are you going anyplace special, Mark?"

"Well, yeah," he said reluctantly. "Terry's got an assignment that's going to take her to Maine, and then she plans to take a week's vacation. I thought I might tag along to Maine just for the change of scene. Then maybe we'll fly down to Bermuda for a week, or someplace where it'll be a little warmer.''

Althea's face was a study, but she didn't say anything. It was only when she and Donna were driving home later that she remarked, ''I can't get over Mark.''

''I'm glad Terry happened,'' Donna said sincerely. She managed a smile. ''Mark needed to find out that women can be people.''

''I think he already found that out with you,'' Althea told her unexpectedly. ''He thought you were tied up with Rod Eldridge, that's all. He didn't think he'd have a chance.''

''I was never tied up with Rod,'' Donna said. Nor would she ever be now. Rod was friendly enough when they met, but Donna suspected their dating days were over, and she felt almost relieved.

''Mark has never had that kind of personal interest in me anyway,'' she went on. ''Oh, I think he likes me, Althea. But I don't think he's ever thought of me as a woman. I think he's always considered me a fellow sufferer.''

''What a way to put it, Donna,'' her friend protested.

''It's true. I was a fellow sufferer, though I'd gotten over George long before I came to Devon.''

That, too, was true. George Farrish had long been out of her thoughts and out of her life, a part of her past she had no wish to revive.

Althea asked suddenly, ''Are you just going to let Hugh walk out of your life, Donna?''

The question startled Donna, and she bit her lip as she considered it. ''What else would you suggest I do?

It doesn't seem to me that I've been given an alternative any more than you have with Alex."

"I *was* given an alternative with Alex," Althea told her. "Maybe you remember…a while back Alex and I drove up to Boston one afternoon because he had business at the British consulate."

Donna nodded. "Yes, I remember. Mark was upset about it."

"I know. When we set out that day, I didn't know what Alex's business involved," Althea admitted. "But before we got to Boston he told me he planned to investigate possible grounds for divorce in Scotland. That's when he offered me an alternative. He told me he'd never petitioned for a divorce from Heather because there had been no particular reason to. And he said he still wouldn't now, unless I'd agree to marry him if he was successful."

Donna stared at Althea, astonished. "What happened?"

Althea's voice was steady. "I told Alex I'd go with him wherever he wanted me to go or wait for him here forever, whether or not he got a divorce. I hadn't thought they recognized divorce in Scotland but it seems they do.

"Alex spoke to people at the British consulate, and he discovered that the grounds are stiff. As far as he could learn there aren't many though we still hope there may be some loopholes. The grounds include adultery, desertion, cruelty, incurable insanity and presumed death." Althea rattled them off one by one. "Grim, aren't they?"

"Very grim," Donna agreed.

"As I say, we still hope there may be a loophole. Alex will find out about that when he gets back to Glasgow, but he's going to get a divorce, no matter what he has to do. He plans to try for a serious talk with Heather. If she will be cooperative it will make matters easier, especially where the children are concerned. He's going to try to do his best for them. But no matter what, Alex and I have made our choice, Donna. It won't be easy, but we're going to spend as much of the rest our lives together as we can."

She added softly, "Don't give up on Hugh too easily. It's your happiness that's at stake."

HUGH WAS NOT going to give her the same choice Alex had given Althea. Donna realized that increasingly as the day the *Portia* sailed away from Devon turned into night, and night rendezvoused with morning.

By then she knew the time had come for her to move on. In six more weeks she'd have to move anyway, so that the apartment would be vacated for the Nickersons' summer tenants. There was no point in marking time for the next month and a half.

She was sure her aunt and uncle and Mark and Althea would all put up arguments when she announced she was going to leave, so she decided to get her things in readiness, then make her announcement at the very last minute.

She didn't want to have to explain her actions. She felt in her heart that the moment had come when she needed to get away from Devon as much as she'd needed to come there in the first place, if she was ever to be a whole person again.

Hugh had set the pace for both of them. There was no way she could have called him to offer her congratulations on his successful salvage operation, but he could have called her. He could call her now, if he wanted to, but Donna had a strong feeling that her phone was not about to ring, and she was right.

She turned on the TV morning news, something she almost never did, and suddenly a picture of the *Portia* moving under the Cape Cod Canal bridge filled the screen.

It was a close-up shot, and Donna found herself scanning the decks anxiously, hoping to catch even a glimpse of Hugh. Some of the crewmen were leaning over the deck rails waving happily, their faces creased with wide grins. But neither Alex nor Hugh was in evidence.

She turned away from the television set, a renewed sense of hopelessness nagging at her. After a while she drove into town again and bought the *Globe*, promising herself this was the last time she was going to do it.

That was another good reason for leaving, she told herself. As long as she stayed in Devon she'd be seeking word of the ship, primarily to learn what Hugh was doing. Back in her apartment in New York, all of this would fade into memory.

She thought of her book. No, there was no chance of the *Portia*'s saga fading into memory until she finished the book. But when she was in her own place again she could settle down to business without further interruptions of any nature.

Once again, Donna took coffee and a doughnut to the beach with the morning edition of the paper, and once again she bypassed the food in favor of reading.

Terry O'Connor explained that the Coast Guard had declared the ship seaworthy enough to proceed to dry-dock in Connecticut with the aid of the tugboats. But it had been decided that risks would be minimized if she traveled around the hook of the Cape at Provincetown then via Cape Cod Bay to the Canal—

the course Alex Bruce had plotted for her in the first place.

By now, according to the newspaper account, the ship was probably arriving in Connecticut. Soon her fate would be decided. Donna was pulling for the freighter. She wanted to think that the *Portia* would be plying the high seas again. When she had last glimpsed the ship, the freighter had appeared to have plenty of life in her.

Later that morning Donna began to pack her things. She stopped at the supermarket to pick up a few cartons, and they were all she needed to stow the possessions she'd brought with her to Devon. They'd been few, and she'd accumulated little more—except for the small cranberry glass pitcher Hugh had bought her in Provincetown...and a badly dented heart.

There wasn't much she could do about the heart, but she packed the little pitcher carefully. Some day, she promised herself, she'd be able to look at it without starting to ache.

By lunchtime Donna could have left town, except for her computer and the printer. She needed help to move both. It wasn't that they were so heavy, but they were awkward, and she was always afraid she'd drop one or the other. She fought back the memory of Hugh helping her move the computer and the printer into the apartment in the first place.

She wasn't ready, even now, to tell Mark and Althea she was leaving—to say nothing of the Bruckers. She'd been avoiding her Uncle Joe and Aunt Mabel, and this was something she'd have to come to terms with before she left. The Bruckers didn't deserve that kind of treatment from her.

Donna decided her only course was to take things a step at the time. First she'd go over to the Windcrest and explain to her aunt and uncle that she felt she'd be better able to finish her book back in New York. Before nightfall she'd confront both Mark and Althea and tell them the same thing.

She'd leave Devon first thing in the morning.

THE BEACH PARKING LOT was almost empty. The Snack Shack was closed, the shutters in place, and it looked so forlorn.

Donna drove down to the end of the lot, where there was a spot from which it had been possible to catch a glimpse of the *Portia*. As she parked she found herself actually craning in the effort to see the ship.

Come on, she chided herself.

She drove back up to the Windcrest, but there was no answer at the Bruckers' apartment. Frustrated, she sought out Cynthia Doane in the office and was told that her aunt and uncle had gone over to Hyannis for the afternoon.

"They said they'd be back by five," Mrs. Doane added.

Donna glanced at her watch. It was not quite three, and there was no way she could hang around that long.

"I'll catch them later," she promised.

As she walked back to her car she wondered what to do next. She had to keep busy, but she'd just about finished packing and there was very little left to do.

She thought about going over to Hyannis and taking in a movie at the mall, but that had been a disappointment the last time she'd tried it alone, and besides, it wouldn't be fair to the movie. In the state she was in, even an Academy Award winning story wouldn't appeal.

But the beach appealed. She looked out at the path that led past the shack and something tugged at her. Once more, just once more, she had to walk out there and scan the shore for a ship long since gone to another port.

The sun was behind Donna as she walked, commencing its descent toward the western horizon. She trudged through the heavy sand, still plowed into ruts by thousands of footprints. She cleared the opening in the dunes then stopped, her eyes automatically roaming south toward the stretch of beach where, until yesterday, the huge green-and-black ship had dominated the skyline.

Just behind her, a man said, "I thought I might find you here."

Donna swerved. It would have been easy to think she was hallucinating, yet no one had ever been more real than Hugh was right now. Still, she stared at him disbelievingly. "How did you get here?" she asked, barely able to manage a whisper.

"I drove from Connecticut," he said, his eyes never leaving her face.

"And the ship?"

"The *Portia*'s fine," he answered impatiently. "What about you?"

"Me?" She didn't know what to say to this.

"Donna." Hugh's voice was strained. "If you hadn't been here, I don't know what I would have done. I tried your apartment. I have to confess that I peeked in your windows. It looked like you've been packing...."

"I have been packing," she said.

"So, you're going to leave." There was an odd note of pain in his voice, and she glanced up at him in surprise.

"Yes, I'm going to leave." What else had he expected?

He answered the unspoken question. "I thought you might wait for me."

Her voice was ragged. "Why would I have waited for you, Hugh?"

It was a clear day, made cloudy by his gray eyes. "I thought we had a fair bit of unfinished business between us."

She couldn't hedge. "It seems to me you pretty well finished it."

"Are you speaking of *me*, Donna?" he asked her. "Or are you confusing me with the mythical Keith?"

Anger surged. "I'm speaking of you, damn it," she snapped.

"So it really was me, not Keith, who was to sail away into the sunset? Come on, Donna, don't think I'm going to follow your plot line, because I'm not about to!"

He stood so close to her she could feel his breath on her face, a big, wonderful man. She loved him so intensely it was all she could do not to fling herself into his arms and capitulate to whatever terms he was prepared to offer. But something deep within her caused her to hold back.

"What's so wrong with my plot line, Hugh?" she asked tightly.

"Everything. Everything, damn it. I'm not willing to fade off into the sunset, Donna, unless you force me to."

He went on, as if the words were being torn from him. "I've been doing a hell of a lot of thinking, for longer than you may realize. And I hate to say it, but I suddenly came to realize that Alex Bruce has been a bigger man in this than I have. He's had the guts to offer himself to the woman he loves, problems and all. I, on the other hand, have lacked the courage.

"Maybe," Hugh continued slowly, "it's because I couldn't believe that I'd met someone after all these years with whom I might actually be able to share my crazy life. Someone who...for the first time in that whole crazy life...has taught me what love really means."

A wry smile creased his face. "You may have something to say about this," he said softly, "but I'm not willing to let you go."

Donna closed her eyes tightly, wanting to believe what she was hearing, yet not quite daring to do so.

"We may have some rough seas ahead," Hugh admitted. "You and I are both rugged individuals, Donna, and we're different. Very different." His smile widened to a grin. "Maybe that's what I find so attractive about you," he drawled infuriatingly. "I'd hate like hell to marry someone like me."

Donna felt a tentative finger touch her chin. Hugh tilted her face upward toward his. His voice was barely a whisper, but it was an urgent whisper. "Say something," he pleaded.

"What do you want me to say?" Her voice, too, was soft.

"Donna, please!" Hugh dropped his hand from her chin to reach out and shake her gently but firmly. "Ouch!" he complained. "My blasted shoulder still hurts."

Donna frowned at him. "What else can you expect?" she demanded acidly. "You haven't done a thing the doctor ordered."

Hugh's mouth twisted, and she saw hope flare in his eyes. "Are you always going to nag me?"

"Yes," she said. "Yes, I'm always going to nag you."

Hugh had been holding his breath, but now he expelled it. "Can I count on that, Donna?"

THEY WALKED SLOWLY up the beach together, then cut through the path past the snack shop. "I'll probably have to go to Connecticut tomorrow and stay there till we find out what's to be done next," Hugh said.

"Will Alex be in real trouble because of this?"

Hugh frowned. "What do you mean?"

"Will he blamed for what happened to the *Portia*?"

Hugh shook his head. "No. The record shows that the ship's misfortune was due to a mixture of nature's forces and neglect in upkeep on the part of the owners. Alex is home free this time around." He hesitated. "Is there any chance you might be able to come along to Connecticut with me tomorrow?"

His surface casualness didn't fool Donna, but in response she matched it.

"I think I might be able to manage that."

"If there was a shipwreck in Madagascar, or maybe in Patagonia, or in some other remote corner of the world, would there be a chance of your coming with me?" he asked mischievously. "I never thought I'd ask any woman that. But in your case, you'd be able to pick up some terrific plot material."

Donna pretended to consider the possibility. "You have a point. A writer can always use a change of scene and some fresh ideas."

Hugh's smile was wicked. "Come make your life with me, my love, and I'll give you plenty of fresh ideas."

They had reached the middle of the parking lot and came to a mutual stop. Hugh looked down at Donna, serious now, the question burning in his eyes. She kept him wondering about her answer for only a moment, then she could tease him no longer.

"You'll never get rid of me," she promised him, her voice shaky.

Hugh enfolded her in his arms, ignoring his aching shoulder, and she became consumed by his kiss. But even in this most wonderful moment she sent a silent message to the *Portia*.

You're a great lady, she told her rival. *But I'm afraid you came in second after all.*

Discover the new and unique

Harlequin Gothic and Regency Romance Specials!

Gothic Romance

DOUBLE
MASQUERADE
Dulcie Hollyock

LEGACY OF
RAVEN'S RISE
Helen B. Hicks

THE FOURTH
LETTER
Alison Quinn

Regency Romance

TO CATCH
AN EARL
Rosina Pyatt

TRAITOR'S
HEIR
Jasmine Cresswell

MAN ABOUT
TOWN
Toni Marsh Bruyere

A new and exciting world of romance reading

*Harlequin Gothic and Regency
Romance Specials!*

Available in September wherever paperback books
are sold, or through Harlequin Reader Service:

Harlequin Reader Service
In the U.S.
P.O. Box 52040
Phoenix, AZ 85072-9988

In Canada
P.O. Box 2800, Postal Station A
5170 Yonge Street
Willowdale, Ontario M2N 6J3

CR-C-1

You're invited to accept 4 books and a surprise gift Free!

Acceptance Card

Mail to: **Harlequin Reader Service**®

In the U.S.
2504 West Southern Ave.
Tempe, AZ 85282

In Canada
P.O. Box 2800, Postal Station A
5170 Yonge Street
Willowdale, Ontario M2N 6J3

YES! Please send me 4 free Harlequin Superromance® novels and my free surprise gift. Then send me 4 brand new novels every month as they come off the presses. Bill me at the low price of $2.50 each—a 10% saving off the retail price. There are no shipping, handling or other hidden costs. There is no minimum number of books I must purchase. I can always return a shipment and cancel at any time. Even if I never buy another book from Harlequin, the 4 free novels and the surprise gift are mine to keep forever.

134 BPS-BPGE

Name	(PLEASE PRINT)	
Address		Apt. No.
City	State/Prov.	Zip/Postal Code

What readers say about
HARLEQUIN SUPERROMANCE™

"Bravo! Your SUPERROMANCE [is]... super!"
R.V.,* Montgomery, Illinois

"I am impatiently awaiting
the next SUPERROMANCE."
J.D., Sandusky, Ohio

"Delightful... great."
C.B., Fort Wayne, Indiana

"Terrific love stories. Just
keep them coming!"
M.G., Toronto, Ontario